PLEASE IGNORE
VERA DIETZ

PLEASE IGNORE
VERA DIETZ

by A.S.King

EMBER

Text copyright © 2010 by A.S. King
Cover art copyright © 2012 by Dana Edmunds/Getty Images

All rights reserved. Published in the United States by Ember, an imprint of Random House Children's Books, a division of Random House, Inc., New York. Originally published in hardcover in the United States by Alfred A. Knopf, an imprint of Random House Children's Books, New York, in 2010.

Ember and the colophon are trademarks of Random House, Inc.

Visit us on the Web! www.randomhouse.com/teens

Educators and librarians, for a variety of teaching tools, visit us at www.randomhouse.com/teachers

The Library of Congress has cataloged the hardcover edition of this work as follows:
King, A. S. (Amy Sarig)
Please ignore Vera Dietz / by A.S. King. — 1st ed.
p. cm.
Summary: When her best friend, whom she secretly loves, betrays her and then dies under mysterious circumstances, high school senior Vera Dietz struggles with secrets that could clear his name.
ISBN 978-0-375-86586-2 (trade) — ISBN 978-0-375-96586-9 (lib. bdg.) — ISBN 978-0-375-89617-0 (ebook)
[1. Best friends—Fiction. 2. Friendship—Fiction. 3. Secrets—Fiction. 4. Death—Fiction.] I. Title.
PZ7.K5693Pl 2010
[Fic]—dc22
2010012730

ISBN 978-0-375-86564-0 (pbk.)

RL: 9.1

Printed in the United States of America

10 9 8 7 6

First Ember Edition 2012

Random House Children's Books supports the First Amendment and celebrates the right to read.

**For my parents, who taught me about
flow charts . . . and everything else.**

What is your original face, before your
mother and father were born?
—Zen koan

PROLOGUE

Before I died, I hid my secrets in the Master Oak.
This book is about my best friend, Vera Dietz, who eventually
found them.

—Charlie Kahn
(the pickle on Vera's Big Mac)

To say my friend died is one thing.
To say my friend screwed me over and then died five months
later is another.

—Vera Dietz
(high school senior and pizza delivery technician)

PART ONE

THE FUNERAL

The pastor is saying something about how Charlie was a free spirit. He was and he wasn't. He was free because on the inside he was tied up in knots. He lived hard because inside he was dying. Charlie made inner conflict look delicious.

The pastor is saying something about Charlie's vivacious and intense personality. I picture Charlie inside the white coffin, McDonald's napkin in one hand, felt-tipped pen in the other, scribbling, "Tell that guy to kiss my white vivacious ass. He never met me." I picture him crumpling the note and eating it. I picture him reaching for his Zippo lighter and setting it alight, right there in the box. I see the congregation, teary-eyed, suddenly distracted by the rising smoke seeping through the seams.

Is it okay to hate a dead kid? Even if I loved him once? Even if he was my best friend? Is it okay to hate him for being dead?

• • •

Dad doesn't want me to see the burying part, but I make him walk to the cemetery with me, and he holds my hand for the first time since I was twelve. The pastor says something about how we return to the earth the way we came from the earth and I feel the grass under my feet grab my ankles and pull me down. I picture Charlie in his coffin, nodding, certain that the Great Hunter meant for everything to unfold as it has. I picture him laughing in there as the winch lowers him into the hole. I hear him saying, "Hey, Veer—it's not every day you get lowered into a hole by a guy with a wart on his nose, right?" I look at the guy manning the winch. I look at the grass gripping my feet. I hear a handful of dirt hit the hollow-sounding coffin, and I bury my face in Dad's side and cry quietly. I still can't really believe Charlie is dead.

The reception is divided into four factions. First, you have Charlie's family. Mr. and Mrs. Kahn and their parents (Charlie's grandparents), and Charlie's aunts and uncles and seven cousins. Old friends of the family and close neighbors are included here, too, so that's where Dad and I end up. Dad, still awkward at social events without Mom, asks me forty-seven times between the church and the banquet hall if I'm okay. But really, he's worse off than I am. Especially when talking to the Kahns. They know we know their secrets because we live next door. And they know we know they know.

"I'm so sorry," Dad says.

"Thanks, Ken," Mrs. Kahn answers. It's hot outside—first day of September—and Mrs. Kahn is wearing long sleeves.

They both look at me and I open my mouth to say something, but nothing comes out. I am so mixed up about what I should be feeling, I throw myself into Mrs. Kahn's arms and sob for a few seconds. Then I compose myself and wipe my wet cheeks with the back of my hands. Dad gives me a tissue from his blazer pocket.

"Sorry," I say.

"It's fine, Vera. You were his best friend. This must be awful hard on you," Mrs. Kahn says.

She has no idea how hard. I haven't been Charlie's best friend since April, when he totally screwed me over and started hanging out full-time with Jenny Flick and the Detentionhead losers. Let me tell you—if you think your best friend dying is a bitch, try your best friend dying after he screws you over. It's a bitch like no other.

To the right of the family corner, there's the community corner. A mix of neighbors, teachers, and kids that had a study hall or two with him. A few kids from his fifth-grade Little League baseball team. Our childhood babysitter, who Charlie had an endless crush on, is here with her new husband.

Beyond the community corner is the official-people area. Everyone there is in a black suit of some sort. The pastor is talking with the school principal, Charlie's family doctor, and two guys I never saw before. After the initial reception stuff is over, one of the pastor's helpers asks Mrs. Kahn if she needs anything. Mr. Kahn steps in and answers for her, sternly, and the helper then informs people that the buffet is open. It's a slow process, but eventually, people find their way to the food.

"You want anything?" Dad asks.

I shake my head.

"You sure?"

I nod yes. He gets a plate and slops on some salad and cottage cheese.

Across the room is the Detentionhead crowd—Charlie's new best friends. They stay close to the door and go out in groups to smoke. The stoop is littered with butts, even though there's one of those hourglass-shaped smokeless ashtrays there. For a while they were blocking the door, until the banquet hall manager asked them to move. So they did, and now they're circled around Jenny Flick as if she's Charlie's hopeless widow rather than the reason he's dead.

An hour later, Dad and I are driving home and he asks, "Do you know anything about what happened Sunday night?"

"Nope." A lie. I do.

"Because if you do, you need to say something."

"Yeah. I would if I did, but I don't." A lie. I do. I wouldn't if I could. I haven't. I won't. I can't yet.

I take a shower when I get home because I can't think of anything else to do. I put on my pajamas, even though it's only seven-thirty, and I sit down in the den with Dad, who is reading the newspaper. But I can't sit still, so I walk to the kitchen and slide the glass door open and close it behind me once I'm on the deck. There are a bunch of catbirds in the yard, squawking the way they do at dusk. I look into the woods, toward Charlie's house, and walk back inside again.

"You going to be okay with school tomorrow?" Dad asks.

"No," I say. "But I guess it's the best thing to do, you know?"

"Probably true," he says. But he wasn't there last Monday, in the parking lot, when Jenny and the Detentionheads, all dressed in black, gathered around her car and smoked. He wasn't there when she wailed. She wailed so loud, I hated her more than I already hated her. Charlie's own mother wasn't wailing that much.

"Yeah. It's the first week. It's all review anyway."

"You know, you could pick up a few more hours at work. That would probably keep your mind off things."

I think the number one thing to remember about my dad is that no matter the ailment, he will suggest working as a possible cure.

THREE AND A HALF MONTHS LATER—
A THURSDAY IN DECEMBER

I turned eighteen in October and I went from pizza maker to pizza deliverer. I also went from twenty hours a week to forty, on top of my schoolwork. Though the only classes worth studying for are Modern Social Thought and Vocabulary. MST is easy homework—every day we discuss a different newspaper article. Vocab is ten words a week (with bonus points for additional words students find in their everyday reading), using each in a sentence.

Here's me using *parsimonious* in a sentence.

My parsimonious father doesn't understand that a senior in high school shouldn't have a full-time job. He doesn't listen when I explain that working as a pizza delivery girl from four until midnight every school night isn't very good for my grades. Instead, my parsimonious father launches into a ten-minute-long lecture about how working for a living is hard and kids today don't get it because they're given allowances they don't earn.

Seemingly, this is character-building.

Apparently, most kids would be thankful.

Allegedly, I'm the only kid in my school who isn't "spoiled by our culture of entitlement."

This was supposed to keep my mind off Charlie dying— which hasn't worked so far. It's only made it worse. The more I work, the more he follows me. The more he follows me, the more he nags me to clear his name. The more he nags me, the more I hate him for leaving me with this mess. Or for leaving me, period.

I'm at the traffic light outside school and I slip the red Pagoda Pizza shirt over my head. I don't care if it messes up my hair, because I need to look a mix of crazy, disheveled, and apathetic to maintain the balancing act of getting good tips and not getting robbed. I reach under my seat and feel around for the cold glass, and when I find it, I slide it between my legs and twist the metal cap off. Two gulps of vodka later, my eyes are watering and my throat automatically grumbles "Ahhhhh" to get rid of the burning. Don't judge. I'm not getting drunk. I'm coping.

I pop three pieces of Winterfresh gum into my mouth, slip the bottle back under my seat, and turn left into the Pagoda Pizza delivery parking lot.

My boss at Pagoda is a really cool biker lady with crooked yellow teeth, named Marie. We have two other managers. Nathan (Nate) is a six-foot-five black guy with square 1980s glasses, and Steve is in his forties, drives a Porsche, and lives with his mom. One of the other drivers told me that he's loaded and he only works here for fun, but I don't believe what the other drivers say. Most of the time, they're stoned. They tell me, when we're mopping the floor or washing the dishes after closing, that when they're high, they can't look at Marie because her teeth freak them out.

Marie is running the store tonight, and when I get in, she smiles at me, like a bagful of broken, sun-aged piano keys, and hands me my change envelope and my Pagoda Phone for the night. Nate is cashing out his day-shift receipts on the computer behind the stainless-steel toppings island. "Yo, Vera! What's shakin'?"

"Hey, Nate."

"Anyone ever tell you that you look fine in that uniform?" he asks. He asks this at least twice a week. It's his idea of endearing small talk.

"Only you," I say.

"It's like you were destined to be a pizza delivery technician," he adds, then slams the cash drawer shut and struts into the back room with me, where he slaps a deposit bag onto the old desk in the office and removes his hokey MC Hammer leather coat from the hook on the back of the door.

"Destiny's bullshit," I answer. I should know. I've spent my whole life avoiding mine.

YOU'RE WONDERING WHERE MY MOTHER IS

My mother left us when I was twelve. She found a man who was not as parsimonious as my father and they moved to Las Vegas, Nevada, which is two thousand five hundred miles away. She doesn't visit. She doesn't call. She sends me a card on my birthday with fifty dollars in it, which my father nags me about until I finally go to the bank and deposit it. And so, for all six years she's been gone, I have $337 to show for having a mother.

Dad says that thirty-seven bucks is good interest. He doesn't see the irony in that. He doesn't see the word *interest* as anything not connected to money because he's an accountant and to him, everything is a number.

I think $37 and no mother and no visits or phone calls is shitty interest.

She had me when she was seventeen. I guess I should feel lucky that she stuck around the twelve lousy years she did. I guess I should feel lucky she didn't give me up for adoption or abort me at the clinic behind the bowling alley that no one thinks we know about.

She and Dad grew up together, next-door neighbors. Just like Charlie and me. "I followed my heart," he claims. Some good that did him. Now he's stuck with me and three bookcases full of self-help Zen bullshit, has no friends, and maintains an amazing ability to blow off anything that's remotely important.

When I turned thirteen, Dad told me the truth about Mom.

"I'm sure this will never come up, but in case it does, I want you to know the truth."

Make a note. When a conversation starts out like this, brace yourself.

"When you were just a little baby, your mother took a job over at Joe's."

Of course, this meant nothing to me. I was thirteen. I had no clue that Joe's was a bring-your-own-beer strip joint where women danced around half naked getting dollar bills stuffed into their panties.

"What's Joe's?"

With no shame or recognition of how badly I could take this, my father said, "A strip club."

I knew what *that* was.

"Mom was a—a stripper?"

He nodded.

"And people *know* this?"

"Just people who were around back then—whoever knew her." He struggled a bit then, seeing how disgusted I was. "It was only for a few months, Vera. She wanted her freedom back after dropping out of school, getting kicked out of her house, and having—uh—a baby so young. I was still drinking then. She wanted something that she never got back," he said. The words came out garbled and stuttery. "She—she—uh—wanted something she never found until she ran off with Marty, I guess."

Marty had been Mom and Dad's podiatrist.

Dad and I used to sit in the waiting room and play twenty questions during Mom's longer-than-normal appointments for verrucas.

Dad still hits an AA meeting when he needs to. He says it's a curse—alcoholism. Says I should never even try the stuff because the curse runs in our family. "My father was a drunk, and so was his father."

Well, if it's as easy as catching my future from a blood relative, then I guess I'm due to be a drunk, pregnant, dropout stripper any day now.

THURSDAY—FOUR TO CLOSE

Around 5:15 the dinner rush starts. Nothing we can't handle. It begins with phone #2 ringing while Marie is taking an order on phone #1. Soon after, while Jill's taking an order on #2, #3 rings. Running the store becomes a blur until about seven.

There are three drivers working, and we manage to time ourselves so that only one of us is in the shop at a time. Marie organizes the runs and has the next one waiting for us when we come in, and is able to remember which order gets Coke, which order gets Sprite, and which order gets a tub of coleslaw. For two hours, I am a driving, knocking, smiling, change-making machine. I am a natural at this. My Pagoda Phone never rings, because I never forget anything. Customers like me and give me tips, which I stuff into a crumpled, waxy Dunkin' Donuts bag I keep on the floor behind my seat.

On my way home from my last run, Charlie makes me eject Dad's Sam Cooke CD and turn on the radio. He makes me put on Hard Rock 102.4, where they're playing a song I hate by AC/DC, but I listen to it anyway.

I take a left into the McDonald's and line up for the drive-thru. I'm addicted to the new wraps they have on their good-for-you menu, with the grapes in them, but I always get a chocolate shake, so it's not like I'm trying to be healthy or anything.

"Go to the first window."

She's waiting there with her hand out. Doesn't she know that people need a minute to get their money ready? She rolls her eyes as I dig through my Dunkin' Donuts bag for five singles. She doesn't say thank you.

"Go to the second window."

Rather than go back to Pagoda Pizza to eat, I circle the parking lot and find a darkened spot between floodlights. I leave the car running for the heater. It's cold tonight. Second week of December and I've been using my ice scraper every morning this week. As I eat, a grape keeps jumping from my wrap onto my lap, where I've laid out a few napkins. I pick it up and pop it into my mouth, but it jumps out again, as if it's being controlled by a string and not just fumbled by my slippery fingers.

"Cut it out, Charlie," I laugh.

I pluck the grape from my lap, grip it tightly, and place it in my mouth.

I eat half the wrap and feel full, so I roll it in its wrapper and stuff it back in the bag, and I collect the napkins from my lap and stuff them in, too. There are four leftover napkins on the passenger's seat, and I press the button to open the glove compartment, where there are at least a hundred napkins, and I layer in four more and close it.

Then I open it again, retrieve one, and grab a fine-point Sharpie marker from my purse. In the dim glow of McDonald's parking lot floodlights, I write *I miss you, Charlie* on the corner, then fold it up and put it in my pocket. I imagine him watching me do this. I half feel his disappointment that I didn't burn it or eat it or any of the other things he would do with his scribblings.

I circle around the back of the building toward the drive-up trash receptacle and see how many bags missed the mark, how many spills are down the front of it, how many drivers just left their crap there to blow away in the wind rather than open their door and try again. I drive up to it, toss in the bag, and then drive out onto the main strip, toward Pagoda Pizza. A block away, I retrieve the napkin from my pocket, rip off my message, and place it on my tongue. It sticks. I reach under my seat and grab the bottle. I take a gulp, breathe the heat out of my throat, and chase it with a big mouthful of chocolate shake.

Before I leave the car, I pull out my Vocab list for the week. Tomorrow is Friday—test day. This is one of the reasons I love Vocab class. Every week is the same. There are no deviations from the class schedule. List on Monday, sentences due Wednesday, test on Friday. Every student knows what to expect. I wish Mrs. Buchman ran the world so life would be as easy.

THURSDAY—FOUR TO CLOSE

It's past nine. We're down to the closing crew—two drivers, a pizza maker/prep cook, and Marie.

"Vera—are you doing the town run?"

I look around. I'm the only driver in. "I guess so."

"Can you wait a second and drop this one off on your way?"

It's Fred's Bar, on the last corner before the bridge into town. I check the times on the other orders and do the math. Thirty minutes isn't as long as you think. It takes about fifteen minutes to make the pizza, so I only have fifteen minutes to get it to the door. Stopping at Fred's Bar will kill my whole town run.

"I'll be late for the Cotton Street place."

Marie whips the Fred's Bar pizza out of the oven early (the crust isn't quite brown), slaps it into a box, and cuts it into triangular slices. "The Cotton Street people can kiss my ass if they have a problem," she says.

I pack the three town orders in separate hot bags, grab a six-pack of Coke and a six-pack of Sprite, and load up the car.

On my way out, James returns from his last run. I have a crush on James, but he's twenty-three, so I shouldn't. But I'm lonely since Charlie died, and James has that familiar smoker smell. And he's cute and he likes to listen to the same kind of music as me. He calls it *eclectic*, which is better than what the assholes at school call it.

I drive down the empty, sloped parking lot to the main strip and take the left into town. When I get to Fred's Bar, I pull over, two tires on the curb, and stick my flashers on. I grab the red-and-black-checkered hot bag with their order and open the door to the smoky, dingy dive and Tammy Wynette singing "Stand by Your Man." I probably deliver to Fred's three nights a week, and two of those nights, Tammy Wynette is playing, and no matter how much good music I play afterward, the song sticks in my head.

But the real reasons I hate going into Fred's Bar are: The regulars stare and give me the creeps. Ninety percent of the time, they forget to tip me. There are pinball machines in the back and it reminds me too much of the bar where very bad things happened to Jodie Foster's character in *The Accused*.

I drive over the bridge into town. The whitest town on Earth—or, more accurately, once the whitest town on Earth until the Mexicans moved in. Once you get through the crowded old suburbs where the large Victorian homes sit on the hill and past the rows of cupola-topped row houses, it's an ugly town—a mishmash of 1940s asphalt shingles, multi-colored bricks, and gray concrete. There's too much litter, and too many people look angry. Dad says it wasn't always like this. He says it's not the Mexicans' fault that the city council would rather spend the city's money on new arts initiatives and a big, flashy baseball stadium than more police on the streets. So now, while there's wine, cheese, and doubleheaders downtown, poverty has taken over and crime is at an all-time high uptown. I lock my doors. It's bad enough that my middle-class car (with the PRACTICE RANDOM ACTS OF KINDNESS bumper sticker) draws attention, let alone the suction-cup Pagoda Pizza flag on the roof.

I get to the railroad tracks and when I slow down to clear them, a drugged-up woman comes out of the shadows and pulls her sequined boob tube down, and I look at the road and keep driving. I try not to think of my mother and make a mental note to stop taking Jefferson Street into town.

The Cotton Street order is a minute late, but they don't seem to notice or care. The guy doesn't even look at me, and gives me a twenty and mumbles, "Keep the change," which translates into a two-dollar-and-four-cent tip for me. Rare for a town run. Two more stops on my way back to the store— one family with hyperactive children who pocket a dollar of my tip, and one old man who ordered a large hot Italian sandwich and pays in exact change. He smiles at me and cocks his head upon realizing I'm a girl.

"Be careful," he says.

I drive back the long way, over the mountain on the dangerous S curves, toward the enormous, glowing, gaudy pagoda that watches over our town. Most people think the pagoda is a cute tourist attraction and a quirky addition to our otherwise boring little nowhere city. I think it's a monstrosity. But then, I grew up just down the road from it, and I know the story behind it. As I climb the hill and shift down, the motor roars with effort. I finally reach the top, pass the red neon eyesore, and coast down Overlook Road, past my house.

The light in the den is on and I can see the morphing glow of the television. Dad is probably ignoring whatever muted movie is on Channel 17 while skimming the day's paper. He never turns the sound on when he doesn't have to. I asked him once why he doesn't just turn the TV off.

"Something about it makes me feel like I'm not alone," he said.

I bet there are millions of people who'd agree with him, too. Not me. I'd rather feel something for real than pretend it's not what it is. (Which Zen guy said, "If you want to drown, do not torture yourself with shallow water"?)

A BRIEF WORD FROM
KEN DIETZ (VERA'S DAD)

My mother did the best she could by herself. Didn't stop me from becoming an alcoholic. Didn't stop me from dropping out of high school and knocking up the seventeen-year-old girl next door. Didn't stop me from wondering what life would have been like with a father, either. I think losing a parent robs confidence from a kid. With Vera, I'm trying to find ways to teach her how to grow her own self-esteem. I'm not sure if it's working, but it's all I have. Because my father left when I was three, I have no idea what a father is supposed to do, so I'm winging it.

One day, when I was a kid, I found a videotape of *The Midnight Special* TV show from 1973 at the bottom of my mother's underwear drawer. That was back when she used to work as a secretary at the local plumbing contractor's office. I read the label on the front. It said CALEB SR., which was what she called my dad on account of my oldest brother being Caleb Jr. I popped it into the VCR and watched it. Billy Preston played a few numbers, and behind him was my dad, a long-haired skinny white hippie playing his horn. Aside from a few pictures in worn envelopes, this was all I would ever have of him because when he left, he didn't leave a phone number or an address. I watched that tape until it finally wore through. I bought every Billy Preston album there was, and grew my hair long.

Vera doesn't know how lucky she is to have had the most important years of her life with her mother.

About two months before ~~Cindy~~ Sindy found out she was pregnant with Vera, we went up to the pagoda and climbed out onto the rocks perched high above the city. We'd been dating on and off since junior high, but had only just started to take it to the next level, in the back of my crappy Ford Tempo. ~~Cindy~~ Sindy was a year younger than me, so I was eighteen at the time and she was seventeen.

"Do you know the story of this place?" I said.

"I think you mean, do I care?" she said, folding her homework sheet into a paper airplane.

"You live in this town and you don't know the pagoda story?"

"Nope."

"Do you want me to tell you?"

"Nope," she said, snapping her gum.

She launched the airplane and it caught a current and circled down toward the town, like a promise of something good. We watched it together until we couldn't see it any-more. I held my hand out for a piece of homework. She gave one to me and started folding the next one. We flew home-work airplanes for two hours, daydreaming about who would find them and where they'd land and wondering if anyone would see them in flight, like we were seeing them. Free. Dar-ing and swooping with the currents—the way we felt as teenagers in love.

Then Vera came.

The beginning was hard, but we got through it. Once I quit drinking and started making decent money at the little accounting firm I'd interned with, we bought the house on Overlook Road. ~~Cindy~~ Sindy said it was sacred because it was so close to the pagoda, even though she never cared enough to hear its sordid (and *very* not-sacred) history, and I liked it because it was secluded and far away from the trashy suburb we'd both grown up in. The three of us climbed trees and planted gardens together. ~~Cindy~~ Sindy raised a brood of chickens one year and sold the organic eggs at the local farm-ers' market. We taught Vera about nature and ecology. We took walks, hiked, and stayed healthy.

Then, when Vera was twelve, ~~Cindy~~ Sindy left me. She never called or wrote or cared again—just like my dad.

When Vera turned sixteen, four years after ~~Cindy~~ Sindy left, I brought her up to the pagoda and flew paper airplanes with her. I asked her if she wanted to know the story of how the pagoda was built, and she said yes. So I told her, and it was like everything was right in my life again. I watched the planes soar down toward the city, and I felt redeemed and whole. I remember thinking, *Kenny Dietz, you have finally grown up, son.*

I estimate that I spent over $2,300 on self-help books, workshops, and videos to make myself into the man ~~Cindy~~ Sindy wanted me to be. But all it really took was seeing Vera all grown up—nearly the same age as her mother when we sat in the very same spot, doing the very same thing.

She asked me about her grandfather, and I showed her *The Midnight Special* Billy Preston video on YouTube, and she thinks I look like him. I don't think I do, because I got my mother's brown hair, but she claims I have my father's eyes. Either way, I became an alcoholic like he was, the same as his father was, which my mother told my brothers and me about five years too late. That's why I'm telling Vera everything about me and ~~Cindy~~ Sindy *now*. I'm giving her a chance to evade her destiny. The trick is remembering that change is as easy as you make it. The trick is remembering that you are the boss of you.

KEN DIETZ'S AVOIDING YOUR DESTINY FLOW CHART

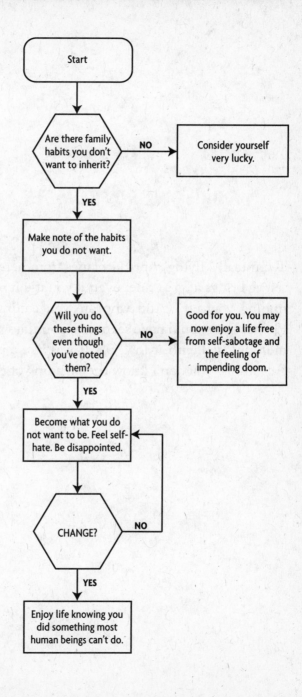

A BRIEF WORD FROM THE PAGODA

Technically, flying paper airplanes from here is littering. Littering brings a $300 fine, even if you use it as a metaphor for finding yourself. (And who are you calling a monstrosity? Please. You should have seen this mountain when the quarrymen finished with it in 1905. It was like a pile of shale shit. Seriously—you don't know the meaning of *eyesore*.)

THURSDAY—FOUR TO CLOSE

When I get back to the store, it's nearly ten and Jill, the resident stuck-up-ex-cheerleader-turned-food-service-worker, is in the back, doing prep work. She's made a big vat of dough and is weighing it, shaping it into balls, and plopping it into trays that will go into the freezer for tomorrow's pies.

Marie's in the office finishing the part-time drivers' cash-out receipts, smoking a long menthol cigarette, and listening to a hard rock radio station. "Free Bird" comes on and she turns it up. James is on the back steps, folding pizza boxes. I see he's working on large ones, so I haul up a flat-packed stack of small boxes, grab the utility knife, cut away the plastic binding, and get comfortable next to James, with the stack to my left. Sometimes, when the part-time drivers are here and there are no runs to take, we have contests. I can fold a box in four seconds. My fastest time yet was thirteen in one minute. James has me beat by one, with fourteen.

But we don't rush now.

Jill passes us to go to the bathroom and gives a raised eyebrow, as if to say that we're sitting too close, and James, for kicks, waits for the toilet-flush sound and slides right into my hip and puts his strong arm around me. When Jill walks out, he gives me a kiss on my cheek and makes a loud heavy-breathing sound and Jill rolls her eyes and throws her hands up. James doesn't know that his breath in my ear is the nicest thing I've ever felt in my life, and when I blush, he's too busy rocking out to the end of "Free Bird" to notice.

It's a bland Thursday night and the phones are quiet. There are no sports on TV. We'll be lucky to make one pizza between now and midnight, when we officially close. We finish folding our fifty boxes apiece and start on closing duties.

"You want cooler or dishes?" James asks, taking a broom handle to the stack of ready boxes to straighten the tower we've made.

I hate both. "I can't face the dishes again tonight."

So I move to the front of the store and start stocking the cooler with six-packs and occasionally catch a glimpse of myself in the huge plate-glass windows that make up the front wall. I'm there for about ten minutes before the door opens and a thousand Charlies come in.

They're wearing his favorite Sonic Youth T-shirt with the hole in the front left shoulder. They're wearing his favorite oil-stained Levi's 501's with the frayed bottoms. They don't say anything. They just glide in, surround me, and then inflate themselves to fill the space completely and breathe my air right out of my lungs. I am suffocating.

I look at the nearest one and see through his translucent skin. I say, "You aren't Charlie."

I say, "Charlie is dead."

He smiles at me. I see four eyes behind his Charlie mask. Eight eyes. I see sixteen eyes. Thirty-two. He is an alien. From outer space. He is a trick-or-treater. He is an embryo. He is a dream.

"Did you say something?" Jill asks, poking her head around the corner from where she's making a big vat of sauce.

I look over at her, and they are gone.

THE FIRST NIGHT IT HAPPENED

The first night it happened, I followed them into the strip mall parking lot. They were all stuffed into a silver-gray Honda—all thousand of them. This was back in November. Charlie had only been dead two months then.

One minute I was sitting on the side of a country road, taking shots of Smirnoff and counting my tips before I went back to the store to close, the next minute I was in the middle of a science fiction movie, complete with a jet-powered Honda Civic and a thousand translucent zombielike beings who looked like Charlie.

When I followed them to the mall, they stopped outside Zimmerman's Pet Store and all thousand of them got out, holding hands and two-dimensional, like cutout accordion dolls. They climbed into the front window with the black Labrador puppies and beckoned with flat, paperlike fingers.

They are trying to get me to come to terms with what happened there. They are trying to get me to clear Charlie's name, but I'm just not ready to do that yet.

HISTORY—AGE ELEVEN

The first time Charlie Kahn tried to make me smoke a cigarette, I was eleven years old. I combated him with health class facts and my father's numbers.

"Did you know a pack-a-day smoker spends one thousand, five hundred dollars a year on cigarettes? Holy shit, Charlie, that's like the price of a car!"

He inhaled, and then exhaled through his nose. He never coughed. Smoking was probably good for him. It was the only time he'd actually sit still for five minutes.

"What's fifteen hundred bucks? People spend that in a month on shit they don't even need. Like lawn ornaments. Who the fuck needs lawn ornaments?"

We'd just walked past the Ungers' house on our way to the blue trail. The Ungers were my neighbors on the other side, though their house was at least a hundred yards away from mine on Overlook Road, which put it close to two hundred yards from Charlie's house. (The order, starting at the hairpin curve, was the pagoda, the Ungers, us, the Kahns, and then the Millers way down the hill, on the other side of the road, and then the lake.) The Ungers had a boat in the driveway that they used twice every summer and two Cadillacs. The Ungers had three faux-Grecian birdbaths and a garish assortment of rose-and-blue-tinted lawn balls. They had lawn jockeys (the black kind) and three cement deer—a doe and two fawns. They had gnomes.

Charlie and I liked to hide the gnomes. Or just move them around. One time, Charlie got two of them and laid them down on top of each other. "Gnome sex!" he said, which embarrassed me completely, but still, I laughed.

"Well, smoking's bad for you," I said. "And you know it."

Charlie put out his cigarette on the road and the two of us headed toward the blue trail—a three-mile-round hiking path on the city's land between the pagoda and the lake, where people walked their dogs (but didn't clean up after them) and brought their families on weekends. Just as we got to the trail, a car crept up Overlook Road. It slowed, and then stopped.

"Hey, kids! What're you doin'?"

"None of your business," Charlie said, scowling.

"Want ten dollars?"

"For what?" Charlie moved in front of me on instinct.

"I—uh—take pictures for the newspaper."

"And?"

The guy was too weird to be for real. His car was too skanky—a white boxy Chrysler that hadn't been washed in months.

Charlie stared at him.

"Pretty blond pigtails," the guy said, shifting his head around to see me behind Charlie.

"Fuck off," Charlie said. "You fucking pervert."

"Hey, come on now, kid, I wa—"

"Vera! Run!"

I ran. Up the blue trail to the first fork in the path. I took the right, which was the circle back to the small parking area on Overlook Road, right across the street from our houses. I didn't look back until I heard fast footsteps behind me. Then I heard the car take off.

Charlie was jumping, he was so full of adrenaline. "Holy shit. That guy was a *real* pervert."

"You think?" I asked, checking each shoe sole for dog shit.

"He offered me twenty after you left."

"Ew," I said. "I think we should tell my parents." I knew his wouldn't believe us or care. There was a reason Charlie was such a bright blazing sun. He came from endless cold, black space. "Did you get his license plate number?"

"No. Let's go to the tree," he said, reaching into his pocket for another cigarette. "We can think about it then."

"But what if he comes after us?"

"Let him try and climb the Master Oak. The spirit of the Great Hunter will protect us."

HISTORY—AGE SEVEN

The first time Charlie Kahn told me about the spirit of the Great Hunter, we were seven. We were in Mrs. Grogan's first-grade class, counting to one hundred.

He leaned in and whispered, "The spirit of the Great Hunter loves the number seventy-two."

"Why?" I whispered back.

"I don't know. Maybe that's when he died."

"You mean 1972?"

"No, like how old he was."

"Oh," I said, naturally embarrassed, even though being wrong with Charlie was something I was used to by then.

As far as Charlie was concerned, the Great Hunter was an Indian spirit who lived in our woods. He drank from the lake. He watched the stars from the ridge. He protected hikers and hunters and tree-climbing little urchins like us, and he created the most sacred tree of all, the Master Oak, for us to grow up in.

"How do you know?" I asked.

"My dad told me." Charlie adored his dad, like any seven-year-old son adores his father. Mr. Kahn loved to take him deer-spotting in mid-autumn, let him shoot a BB gun at targets behind the house, and told him stories about the Great Hunter.

Later that morning, we had library time. The librarian gave us a picture to color. It was March. The picture was of some sort of leprechaun wedding. There were a bunch of forest animals on the fringes, throwing shamrocks at the happy couple.

"Do you think we'll get married one day?" I said.

"To each other?" Charlie asked.

"No, silly. I mean to other people." (But really, I'd meant to each other.)

He was cutting out the leprechaun even though that wasn't the point of the project.

"I don't want to get married," he answered, separating the bride from the groom. "Too much yelling."

I nodded as if I agreed, but my parents meditated and did yoga together, and didn't yell.

"Anyway"—he crumpled the paper with the hole from the groom and the image of the bride and tossed it, basketball-style, into the dull gray wastebasket ten feet away—"the Great Hunter rides solo."

Secretly, I mourned this.

FRIDAY—FOUR TO CLOSE

Today was a Vocab test and I drew a complete blank on the word *swivet*. So here's me using *swivet* in a sentence.

The thousand Charlies have me in such a swivet, I forgot to study for my Vocab test. I will not follow them into Zimmerman's Pet Store no matter how many times they try to drag me there. I will avoid the Pagoda Mall for the rest of my life if I have to.

When I get to Pagoda Pizza after school, Marie is standing in the front with Greg, the owner, a BMW-driving yuppie who talks down to women, and she is nodding her head as he tells her crap she already knows.

"You need to have the employees stock the cooler whenever it gets half empty so there's always cold soda," he says. "And make sure when they cut the six-packs into fours and twos that they don't puncture the cans with the knife."

Marie has to pretend she's interested even though she

knows much more than he does about how to run his store. This is Greg's first time running a business, I bet. Any other business owner would be more concerned with the employees cutting them*selves*, not the stupid cans.

I walk into the back, where James and two part-time Pothead drivers are folding boxes and Frisbee-tossing them to the top of the stack, trying to land them without teetering the whole thing down on top of us.

"Greg's here, man. You might want to stop fucking around," I say.

"Greg's an asshole," Tommy Pothead says.

"Yeah—Greg can suck my dick," Dylan Pothead says.

"Hey." James slaps Dylan lightly on the forehead. "Don't talk to Veer that way, man."

"Sorry, Vera." Dylan makes a mocking bow. "I meant Greg can place his delicate BMW-driving mouth around the throbbing head of my member."

James shrugs.

"Whatever," I say. I turn to James. "What am I? Your little sister?"

James grabs me, tucks me under his arm, and gives me a gentle noogie. He smells like Marlboros and soap.

I squeeze onto the back steps after getting my change envelope (a ten, a five, four ones, and a dollar in change) and Pagoda Phone from the office, and fold boxes until the store phones begin to ring. Then I work up front because I have the ability to talk to customers and enter their orders into the computer, and the Potheads don't. I send James on the first run—a five-stop cockroach-part-of-town circle—and then I set myself up for a trip through pastel suburbia. This time of year, it's twice as fun because everyone has their Christmas lights up and is participating in the Who-Can-Flaunt-the-Tackiest-Collection-of-Obnoxious-Holiday-Bullshit Contest. This may prove me as parsimonious as my father, but who spends that much money on corny inflatable light-up Santa Clauses and spinning, singing reindeer? Who thought it was a good idea to mold plastic Nativity scenes that light up at night? Seriously. There are still children starving in Africa, right? There are still children starving right here in this shitty little town.

I take as many suburbia runs as I can. Part of it is for better tips. Part of it is for safety, too. I can't send James or the Potheads on every town run, but I can't ignore the fact that I'm a girl. I never thought about this until I had a delivery on Maple Street during my first week delivering. I was about five minutes early, but the guy who answered the door said I was late. I knew I wasn't. The sticker on the box said 7:32, and it was 7:55. I was seven minutes early. But he argued with me at the door, and when I told him to call my manager, he somehow got me to come in and walked me all the way through the skinny row house to the kitchen in the back, where I put the pizza down on so many skittering roaches, the box made a crackling noise. He got agitated then, when I reminded him to call my boss, and I realized I was so stupid to have ended up in this guy's kitchen. Luckily, he wasn't a crazy rapist. Luckily, he was just a poor guy who wanted free pizza.

Though most people don't even look at their pizza delivery person and most people never even figure out I'm a girl—especially in my steel-tipped boots with the Pagoda

Pizza baseball cap down over my eyes—I still prefer suburbia. I guess it feels familiar or something. I know the roads. I know people who live there.

I forget, until I drive by the high school on my way back from the burbs, where a thousand spinning, singing Santas live, that there's a football game tonight. We're playing Wilson, an old rival. The last Wilson versus Mount Pitts football game I went to, I was fourteen and Dad and I took Charlie with us. When we dropped him off after the game, I saw Mrs. Kahn was crying and seemed really shaken.

As we drove out of Charlie's drive, I said, "Dad? Do you think Mrs. Kahn is okay?"

Dad said, "She's fine, Vera."

"But she didn't look fine, did she?"

"Just ignore it," Dad said.

When he said that, I felt myself deflate a little. I'd spent the better part of my life hearing my father say "Just ignore it" about the loud arguments I'd hear coming through the woods from Charlie's house.

In summer, the trees cushioned us. I couldn't see Charlie's house and I couldn't hear Mr. Kahn yelling. In winter, I could hear every word, depending on the direction the wind blew. I could hear every slap and every shove. I could hear him call her "stupid bitch" and could hear her bones rattle when he shook her. If I looked out at night, I could see the tiny orange ember at the end of Charlie's cigarette getting brighter when he inhaled.

"Ignore it," my father would say, while my mother fidgeted in her favorite love seat.

"But can't we call someone to help her?"

"She doesn't want to be helped," my mother would say.

"She'll have to help herself," my father would correct. "It's one of those things, Vera."

Dylan Pothead is smoking a joint in the parking lot when I get back. He holds it toward me, soggy end up.

"No thanks, man."

"Suit yourself."

"Is it slow?"

"Dunno. You tell me," he says, giggling.

There's another reason I like James. He doesn't smoke pot. Says it makes him paranoid.

When I go in, it's Friday night chaos. There are three different stacks of orders and the oven is packed with more.

"Where are the rest of the drivers?" Marie asks, wiping sweat from her forehead with the back of her wrist.

"Dylan's outside," I say.

She looks up and squints out the plate glass. She knocks and startles him to attention, and he arrives in the store, still exhaling pot smoke.

"Get your lazy stoner ass over here and pick this up."

She throws the hot bags to him, inserts the pizzas, shows him where they're going on the map on the wall, and just as he's forgetting the two six-packs of Coke, she runs over and balances them on top of the pizzas and opens the door for him.

We watch him burn rubber as he takes off down the parking lot.

"That kid is a total idiot," she says.

Marie says the basic requirement for employment these

days is a heartbeat, which is why she doesn't fire him. Even though he doesn't mop the floor right when he closes, he still gets the same money I do, and I mop right. When he does the dishes, there's dry food stuck on them in the morning that someone has to chip off with a table knife, but he's still on the schedule, week after week.

It seems the older people get, the more shit they ignore. Or, like Dad, they pay attention to stuff that distracts them from the more important things that they're ignoring. While he's busy clipping coupons, for instance, and telling me that a full-time job will teach me about the real world, Dad is overlooking that the guy on Maple Street could have killed me and chopped me up and distributed my body, piece by piece, along the side of the highway. He's overlooking every story on the news about drivers being robbed at gunpoint, or getting carjacked.

It's one thing if he wants to ignore it. I guess that's fine. I mean, I ignore plenty of stuff, like school spirit days and the dirty looks I get from the Detentionheads while I try to slink through the halls unnoticed. But there's something about telling other people what to ignore that just doesn't work for me. Especially things we shouldn't be ignoring.

Kid bullying you at school? Ignore him. Girl passing rumors? Ignore her. Eighth-grade teacher pinch your friend's ass? Ignore it. Sexist geometry teacher says girls shouldn't go to college because they will only ever pop out babies and get fat? Ignore him. Hear that a girl in your class is being abused by her stepfather and had to go to the clinic? Hear she's bringing her mother's pills to school and selling them to pay for it? Ignore. Ignore. Ignore. Mind your own business. Don't make waves. Fly under the radar. *It's just one of those things, Vera.*

I'm sorry, but I don't get it. If we're supposed to ignore everything that's wrong with our lives, then I can't see how we'll ever make things right.

It's ten-thirty and we're nearly down to closing crew. Dylan wants to leave early to go to a party, so he has Marie cash him out while I take my dinner break sitting on the cold stainless-steel counter in the prep kitchen, next to the sink.

"You working New Year's Eve?" Marie asks, counting out his commission.

"You kidding?" he says, shaking his head. "Count me out, man."

"We could really use extra drivers. I'll pay double commission."

Dylan isn't even listening.

"I'll do it," I say. Because what else do I have to do on New Year's Eve now that Charlie is gone?

HISTORY—AGE THIRTEEN

The first New Year's Eve I can remember making it to midnight was when I was eleven. It was snowing and my mom was still there, and when the ball came down in Times Square, I ran outside, barefoot in the snow, and I yelled "HAPPY NEW YEAR!" Charlie answered, "HAPPY NEW YEAR!" and it was so quiet from the insulating snowfall that it sounded like he was standing right next to me, even though he lived a hundred yards down the road and a skeletal woodland separated us.

The next year, Mom said that we had to celebrate New Year's Eve as a family. She made homemade eggnog and put out a bunch of leftover holiday (we couldn't say "Christmas" anymore, because Mom and Dad "leaned toward the Buddha") cookies on a tray. We didn't know it yet, but this would be her last New Year's Eve with us. It wasn't any different than the previous ones. She looked into space a lot, didn't say much, and kissed my father when midnight came, as if she were punching a time card.

Things changed when I was thirteen. That year, Sherry Heller invited Charlie and me to her basement New Year's Eve party so we could all watch her make out with her big-nosed boyfriend from Midland Catholic. He was a football player. He even put his hand up her shirt while the rest of us—the ten or so who showed up—watched from the mold-stained outdoor furniture that had been brought out of storage for the party.

"Want to try that?" Charlie asked.

"No," I answered, knowing he was kidding.

"How about you?" he asked, winking at Marina Yoder.

She considered him. "Nah. I've got a cold."

I studied him. Other girls didn't like him because he wasn't groomed. But I liked that. He bought his clothes old—frayed, holey, faded. He liked oversized hooded sweatshirts with tattered cuffs—the more tattered, the better. If he had a string hanging from the seam of a ripped-up flannel shirt, he'd leave it there. Where normal people would want to cut it off, Charlie would want it to dip in his soup and let the liquid drip down his elbow.

He wasn't a slob, but his hair was greasy sometimes, and if it was, it was because he wanted it to be. I don't think there was one time I ever saw him with combed hair. It suited him messy, sweeping over his thick eyebrows, and made him look mischievous and interesting.

Mrs. Kahn gave up trying to make Charlie "look decent" in the fourth grade. I remember the day clearly. It was picture day. November sometime. I wore a pair of green corduroys and a nice blouse with embroidery around the collar. Charlie wore a gray sweatshirt with an oily stain on the sleeve, and his mother argued with him the whole way to the bus stop.

She was holding a crisp-ironed white button-down church shirt and a comb. He finally turned to her, grabbed the shirt, threw it to the side of the road, thick with decomposing leaf mold, and ground it in with his foot.

Before she could react, he snatched the comb and flung it far into the trees, and said, "Just go home. Who cares about stupid school pictures?" And she went home, like a trained monkey, after a lifetime of Mr. Kahn treating her like a trained monkey.

The night of Sherry Heller's New Year's Eve party, I still had that fourth-grade picture in my wallet. His hair finger-combed over his left eye, and the edge of the oily stain on the sweatshirt barely visible in the bottom right corner.

After another twenty minutes of Sherry and her boyfriend making out, Charlie nudged me and looked at the door. We walked the mile home together and celebrated the new year in the middle of the tree-lined road, full moon lighting the way, Charlie sucking on a Marlboro and me spinning around like a ballroom dancer on crack because I drank too much Coke.

"Veer?"

"Yeah?"

"I say we never go to a fucking New Year's Eve party again."

"You're on," I said, still spinning.

"It's always a letdown."

"Not for Sherry's boyfriend, I bet."

"Yeah, I bet they're doing it on the glide-o-lounger right now, squeaking up a storm."

"Ew." I thought about my mother, pregnant at seventeen—gone for nearly a year at that point.

I was still thinking about her when Charlie asked, "Aren't you curious, though?"

I stopped spinning and stumbled to the ground, right on the double yellow lines. Charlie lit another cigarette and held the smoke in his lungs.

"My dad says boys are only ever after one thing."

"Right."

"He says that I shouldn't even think about boys until after college."

"Huh."

I didn't know what else to say, so I got up slowly and tried to get my balance.

"But what do *you* think?" he asked, reaching out to help me steady myself.

"I think—" Before I could finish, Charlie was kissing me on the mouth and holding me tight, and when I opened my eyes, the moon was shining on his tender eyelashes, damp with cold moisture. He dropped his Marlboro in the road and smushed it out with his boot. He moved his hands to my waist and I caught them and slipped my fingers in between his. It felt good, his tongue moving in my mouth. Then I remembered. This was Charlie. My best friend. Not a boy. I remembered that I was my mother's daughter—fighting this very destiny. (Fighting it and losing, because nothing ever felt more right in my life.)

When I could finally untangle myself, I said, "Dude! What's up with that?"

He shrugged. "I dunno." He kicked his feet around and said, "Figured we could both use the practice."

A BRIEF WORD FROM THE DEAD KID

I regret everything that happened with Vera. Even back in grade school when I cut up that leprechaun picture. It's hard to explain. As far as I was concerned, I didn't have a choice. I was born to a man like my father and a woman like my mother, and I had to save Vera from myself.

This didn't stop me from sneaking behind my own back a few times. The time I kissed her on the road on New Year's Eve or the time I sent her flowers on Valentine's Day were tests, I guess. Loving Vera Dietz was the scariest thing that ever happened to me. She was a good person from a good family. She could spell big words and remember to do math homework, and her father didn't swear or drink like my father did. I know her mother was a stripper once, but that didn't matter. Vera was classy.

The thing you don't see while you're still there on Earth is how easy it is to change your mind. When you're in it and you're mixed up with feelings, assumptions, influences, and misconceptions, things seem completely impossible to change. From here, you see that change is as easy as flicking a light switch in your brain.

I spent a lot of time on Earth wishing I could be as classy as Vera. I thought if I was, maybe we could have a future together. But I assumed I'd never be classy. And it was that feeling, and the helplessness and anger that come from a destiny like mine, that drew me to Jenny Flick—the girl who landed me here.

FRIDAY—FOUR TO CLOSE

Friday nights perk up around eleven. We close at one. There's usually a run or two to Fred's Bar at midnight, and parties—sleepovers with giddy preteens or drunken college dropouts who have access to beer.

Two orders come in before we shut the ovens off. Marie is already tossing toppings from the translucent containers into the trash, counting receipts, and double-checking them on the computer. By the time I'm back from the final run, she'll have my totals ready, and James will be doing the dishes. Jill has already done the prep work for tomorrow, which is my day off, so all I will have to do is mop the floor, start the washing machine before we lock up, and go home.

When I leave, I stack up my orders in the car and have to run back in for a six-pack of Coke for the first stop. In the glass, I see James staring at the back of me, and I wonder has he daydreamed about me the way I've daydreamed about him. Maybe my father was right and a full-time job does mature a person. Maybe I'm twenty-three in my brain. Just old enough for James. Or maybe, since he dropped out of state college and started working at Pagoda Pizza, he's more like eighteen. He waves as I stick the car in reverse, and I act cool and pretend I don't see it.

First stop—a bachelor, half drunk. Doesn't even look at me. Needs the Coke for more rum and Coke. I doubt he needs the small pepperoni at all. He tips me a dollar, and I get back in the car and feel Charlie there again.

He makes me put on heavy metal music. He tells me to drive places I don't want to go, like Zimmerman's. He warns me, too, not to take Linden Road or else I'll die in a bad accident. I mean, I don't know this for sure, but that's what it feels like, so I do what he says just in case. Even in death, Charlie is frustrating as hell.

In life, the minute he seemed like one thing, he'd change and become another. No matter what the fad—music, clothing, hairstyles, hobbies—Charlie remained this indefinable rebel. His number one priority was smoking his next cigarette. Always. Which is why he had so much detention last spring. And though he'd joined with me in dogging the school's Detentionheads and Potheads since I could remember, his time in detention brought him closer to them, and further from me. Which was how I ended up hating Charlie.

I think back to last April Fool's Day, when Jenny Flick told Charlie that I talked about him behind his back. Which was where everything started to go wrong.

"I heard you were talking about me," he said. He was livid. Every muscle was tensed.

We were at the pagoda, and I was flying paper airplanes. He reached for his cigarettes in his breast pocket. I said, aware he seemed angry but thinking he was just putting on an act for April Fool's Day, "Oh yeah? What did I say?"

"Are you saying you weren't?"

I looked at him and smirked. "You're my best friend. I can't even figure out what I'd say if I wanted to."

"Oh really?" When I realized he was genuinely pissed off, I got a little frightened. "So you weren't the one passing around the whole school that my dad hits my mom?"

"What?"

"You're acting surprised, but I know you know."

What could I say to this? I'd kept the Kahns' secret for my whole life, against my own better judgment, and I'd never said a word.

"Of course I *know*, Charlie. I've only been your best friend and neighbor for seventeen years. But I've never said a word about it to anyone. Ever. Like *EVER*."

"So how does the whole school know, then?"

"Who says they do?"

"Jenny."

With that, the shitstorm began.

I had a hundred arguments that made sense. I had a hundred proofs. I had a hundred truths. Nothing worked. Charlie believed Jenny Flick.

"But you even know she's a mythomaniac!" I said.

"Stop using those big words. You sound like a fucking geek."

"Maybe I am a fucking geek."

"Maybe you're more than a geek."

"What does *that* mean?"

"I don't know. What goes around comes around, I guess."

I could hear our friendship dying right there. Hit by a truck so big, going so fast, there was nothing left. Not a shred of our childhood, not a splinter of our tree house, not a bit of our New Year's Eve kiss. Nothing. Jenny Flick had managed to take from me the only person I ever let in and replace me with beer, sex, and pot.

So now I had no mother and I had no best friend.

But, I assured myself, one day Charlie would come to his senses. One day he would see how he'd been led to the dark side by a lying little creep. I actually thought that this conversation at the pagoda was the worst that would happen.

I had no idea what was coming.

I think of a quote in Dad's bathroom Zen book. "The willow is green; flowers are red. The flower is not red; nor is the willow green."

Same went for Charlie.

Charlie was my friend; he was very nice to me. Charlie was not my friend; nor was he very nice to me.

FRIDAY—FOUR TO CLOSE—LAST STOP

Here's me using *mythomania* in a sentence.

Jenny Flick suffers so badly from mythomania, she believes her own lies. I could never understand what Charlie saw in her. I've known her since middle school, when I bumped into her at the bathroom mirror while she layered on eyeliner.

"What's your problem?" she said.

"Sorry."

"Yeah, you *are* sorry," she answered.

She wore too much eyeliner then, at age thirteen, and now, at eighteen, she wears so much black under her eyes, she looks like a slutty linebacker raccoon.

Jenny Flick could lie about anything. She'd tell you that she met the lead singer from your favorite band and dropped acid with them. She'd say she was screwing the biology teacher, or that her stepdad snorted coke with the principal. She drew pictures on herself with thin Sharpie marker and told everyone they were tattoos. I heard that she lied to her dad, who lived in California with his new family, about wanting to kill herself, and about an eating disorder or cutting or whatever else she could dream up to move in with him, but all that did was get her hooked on an array of antidepressants and land her in a shrink's office once a week. She lied the same way to her friends. She had the entire third-period study hall convinced she was going to die of leukemia in freshman year. Some of them even bought her cards—even people who she'd lied and gossiped about.

I'd managed to stay off her radar, for the most part, and maintained my invisibility. But once she started liking Charlie and wanted me out of his life, things changed. I became her target, and he became her prize.

Now that Charlie is gone, she ignores me again. I think she thinks she's safe now, because it's been three and a half months and I haven't said anything about what really happened on the night he died. But she's not.

My last delivery of the night is a four-pie stop in the old burbs. These are the small single-story brick places that are stuck so close together you can hear your neighbor peeing through the concrete alley between, though they do have front and back yards to litter with more Tacky Glowing Christmas Shit.

556 North Gerhardt Lane. A red brick bread box with a red and green doorbell that plays "Jingle Bells" when I ring it, and a sign to the right of the door that reads WELCOME TO OUR HOME with two spotted fawns on it. Eight cars stuck

multi-directionally in the driveway. Two on blocks. The sound of a party spills out into the sleeping neighborhood. One of the cars has a blue and white football jersey taped to the back window and the words GO PANTHERS painted above it. From the sounds within, I'm guessing we won the game tonight.

The door jerks open and the music and smell of pot smoke hit me. I open the flap on the hot bag and say, "That's thirty-four ninety-nine, please." Then I look up and I see Jenny Flick, arms folded, glaring at me, and Bill Corso, the school's semi-illiterate star quarterback, standing behind her. "Look who it is," she says.

I take the four pizzas out of the bags and hand them to Bill, and then I stash the hot bags under my arm, which is weak from the mix of fear and anger I'm experiencing right now, and get my change bag from the pocket of my black combat pants. Jenny is still staring at me with a scowl on her face, eyeliner drawn around her eyes like she's a character in a Tim Burton movie.

"Thirty-four ninety-nine, please."

She digs into her pocket and pulls out a wad of bills. Then she peels them off one by one and lets them float to the door-mat. Two of them land on my feet.

"How much was that, baby?" she asks Bill, who is too fucked-up to notice that she's been tossing out handfuls of cash.

"I don't know, Jen. You know I can't do math when I'm high."

She starts giggling and tosses the rest of the wad of bills

into the air above my head, and then slams the door in my face. I look around at where the money landed, kick it all together into one place, and bend over to pick it up.

The door opens. Jenny Flick appears again, and behind her, Bill Corso has a professional-looking slingshot, aimed at me. "And here's your fucking tip," she says.

He shoots a penny that hits my shoulder and stings like a mother. They giggle like a pair of ten-year-old girls and slam the door shut again.

In the car, I count the scrunched-up money and find that Jenny Flick has just unintentionally given me a thirty-three-dollar tip. Probably the best thing drugs will ever do for me. Before I take off, I look back at the house. A bunch of football guys have lined up in the bay window and are mooning me. Raised middle fingers fill the spaces between them. I can't lie. There are parts of me that want to blow the house up right now. There are parts of me that would laugh while the whole lot of them burned. My shoulder, where the penny hit me, is throbbing and hot. I reach under my seat and grope around for the cold glass. Drink, anyone?

HISTORY—AGE TWELVE

The summer after my mother ran off with the bald podiatrist in the convertible, Charlie Kahn's dad let him build a tree house. Even though I knew Charlie wanted to do it himself, he called it *our* project and *our* tree house. I think it was his way of trying to help me through a hard time.

His dad bought him a bunch of supplies the week school ended—lengths of two-by-four, pulleys and screws, and sheets of weather-treated plywood—but Charlie didn't choose a tree for three whole weeks. We walked around the woods between our houses and emerged covered in ticks and scratches to eat lunch, and then we dove back in. I asked Charlie what was taking him so long.

"The Great Hunter needs to approve," he said, then scribbled something on a small napkin and shoved it into his pocket.

Half an hour later, Charlie told me that my asking him about the tree every five minutes was pressuring him, so he asked me to leave him alone for a week. Sounds harsh, but he meant well. I think he needed space to be eccentric, and he was driving me up a wall with all that "spirit of the Great Hunter" bullshit.

We were twelve. Old enough to just pick a tree already.

This was the summer my father stopped renting the office in town and moved his desk and filing cabinets into the spare downstairs bedroom that my mother used to use for peace yoga and forgiveness meditation, which apparently didn't work out so well.

This was also the first summer I convinced Dad to let me volunteer at the adoption center inside Zimmerman's Pet Store at the Pagoda Mall. This was hard for him, because it was completely against his nature to care about pets. It wasn't that he was heartless or cruel or anything like that. Dad just isn't an animal person. He'd hated every single time I'd dragged him into Zimmerman's as a kid to look at the hamsters or the puppies. When I'd nag him about getting something fluffy to cuddle, he'd show me on paper how much money it cost to keep a pet, and point out that kids my age were going hungry all over the world. "I think they could use four grand a year more than a dog could," he'd say.

But he must have realized that summer that I was different than him—and that his coldheartedness was only making me worse. I loved animals. Partly because he didn't and had denied me one, and partly because it's in the manual. What twelve-year-old girl doesn't daydream about nurturing a puppy or a kitten? What twelve-year-old girl whose mother just walked out doesn't want a companion who loves her no matter what happens? So he helped me fill out the volunteer application, shelled out ten bucks for a purple volunteer T-shirt, and drove me down to the store one day a week, which was the maximum I was allowed to be there, because I was only twelve. I *loved* it. All of it. I loved the adoption people, who rescued animals and found them good homes. I loved the pet store and Mr. Zimmerman and his wall of exotic aquarium fish. He had a gray parrot who talked and sat on a perch by the register and would make phone-ringing sounds so accurately that none of us could tell if the phone was really ringing or not.

My first day volunteering, I took care of three Old English sheepdog puppies that had been rescued from one of those houses where crazy people have too many pets until their neighbors complain about the smell or the noise. I bathed them and brushed them and helped the visiting vet nurse apply lotion to their over-scratched flea bites. It was a feeling I can't really describe. I felt like I had purpose or something— like I was doing something *bigger*.

For the rest of the week, while Charlie still searched for the perfect tree for his tree house, I hung around and watched TV. I drank lots of yogurt smoothies and ate lots of low-salt no-frills tortilla chips.

"What are you doing?" Dad asked, openly annoyed that I was on the couch with the remote control before noon on a weekday.

"*The Price Is Right* is on in a minute."

Before he could start giving me a lecture on how I should be doing something more productive with my time, like weeding the vegetable garden or inventing a board game that would sell for millions, Charlie walked through the kitchen door.

"I found it!" he said.

I turned off the TV, then turned to Dad and shrugged. "Gotta go."

He nodded and went back into his office.

We walked out into the forest. Charlie said, "The Great Hunter picked this tree. What do you think?"

It was a great tree, no doubt.

"We start with the ladder, and then the floor." Charlie reached into his back pocket and pulled out a tattered and taped piece of lined spiral notebook paper. "This is what I want it to look like."

I studied the paper. There were two distinct rooms. One had a bed, the other a small futon couch. Up to that point, I'd envisioned a tree house Dietz-style. A piece of old plywood, a rope, and a great imagination.

"Are you planning on living here?"

"Yeah."

I looked up through my bangs. "Over winter?"

He looked at me as if I was making fun of him. I wasn't.

"Why are you always trying to make me feel stupid?" he asked, pulling the napkin out of his pocket that he'd scribbled on earlier.

"I wasn't."

He glared at me—testing. I looked as serious as I could and didn't laugh, even though I wanted to because when Charlie got testy, it was funny. He added something to what he'd already written and ripped off the corner where the writing was.

Then he popped the paper into his mouth, chewed, and swallowed.

"Let's get to work on the ladder first and then stop for lunch."

We were ten minutes in, me holding a two-by-four's end while he sawed perfect thirty-inch segments on a pair of carpenter's horses, when a car stopped in the gravel shoulder of the road. We were so deep in the woods, I couldn't see much, except that it was white.

Charlie said, "Hold up. There's something I have to give this guy for my dad."

I waited for ten minutes and tried to creatively visualize the tree house. This was Dad's new thing since Mom left—creatively visualizing everything from making dinner to the weekly grocery shopping. He made me do it for tests, too. (And I had to admit, it worked. Though it did *not* work for getting him to let me adopt a puppy.)

Charlie arrived back out of breath and red-faced.

"You didn't have to run," I said.

"I'm just pumped to get this thing up, you know?" He leaned back against the tree, and balanced the wrinkled paper napkin on his knee again, and scribbled something else on it. He'd been doing this since we were kids, and it annoyed the hell out of me. It's one thing to be purposely mysterious, but it's rude to be scribbling stuff right in front of someone. It's like whispering or something. So I reached over and grabbed it off his knee.

"Give it back!" he screamed, instantly losing all control. "It's mine!"

"Dude, I—"

He grabbed my arm roughly and twisted it behind my back, which made me drop the stupid napkin onto the forest floor. He kept hold of my arm while he leaned down to pick it up.

"Holy shit, Charlie." I didn't know what else to say.

"Don't ever do that again," he said. "Some stuff is private."

"Sure," I said. "Of course. Me too."

"Everyone is allowed to have secrets," he said.

"Yeah," I agreed, though I never knew anyone like him, who scribbled those secrets on napkins and ate them, or stuffed them in their pockets, or burned them ceremoniously on the rocks around the pagoda.

"Just don't do it again," he said, then he grabbed the saw and quickly cut three more step segments, kicking the scraps into a pile at the base of the trunk. He was like an angry machine, shaking as if he'd just eaten those caffeine pills my mother used to take to stay skinny.

HISTORY—AGE TWELVE—MID-AUGUST

From the finished tree house, we could see both our houses and the road. Charlie kept a pair of binoculars by the west window, next to his bed. He started to sleep out there, and had screened in the windows and made shutters for when it rained.

Only after Dad had climbed up and checked the tree house out did he consider allowing me to sleep there one night. I know he had to think about it because Charlie was a boy and I was a girl, and I tried to explain to him that it wasn't ever like that. I didn't understand yet that I was fighting my own destiny and Charlie was fighting his. I just wanted to sleep in the tree house.

"Charlie doesn't like girls," I tried, only hearing myself after I said it, and then correcting. "I mean, Charlie and I are only friends—like, ew, you know?"

"I know."

"So can I?"

"Veer, I think it's time we had a talk about this stuff," he said, visibly uncomfortable. "Boys Charlie's age can sometimes think and do things that you don't expect. You have to be careful."

"Charlie is twelve, Dad. Just like me."

"I know, but twelve can be—uh, it can be a confusing . . . ," he stuttered.

I tried to creatively visualize him shutting up. It didn't work.

"I know you know about sex. And I know you're smart. But you're about to enter a whole new part of life where things aren't as simple as they once were."

We stared at each other, silent. I was frowning; he gnawed on his lower lip. A minute ran by.

"So can I sleep in the tree house or not?"

He sighed. I could tell he was really broken up about it, so I added, "Really, Dad, you've got nothing to worry about when it comes to Charlie Kahn. He's about as interested in me as he is in combing his hair."

He leveled his eyes with mine. "I think you know why I don't want you near his house, right?"

I nodded. "We won't be *in* the house. We'll be in the tree house."

"I know, but what if you have to pee during the night? Or what if you need a drink of water?"

I thought about it. "Okay. I got it," I said. "The tree house is halfway between our house and theirs. So if I have to pee, I'll just come here."

He smiled.

"So can I? Tonight?"

"Let's see if we can dig out your sleeping bag," he said, and I was jubilant.

Charlie and I ate popcorn and drank soda and talked about stupid stuff, like kids from school and what we day-dreamed we'd be when we grew up. (Me = vet, him = forest ranger.) We listened to the radio a little. Then we snuggled into our sleeping bags and said good night—and after that, all we could hear was the loud screech of cicadas and crickets. It was awesome. Until midnight, when a car barreled up the hill and stopped in the gravel of the blue trail's parking area. Then Charlie snuck out of the tree house and didn't come back until dawn.

HISTORY—AGE THIRTEEN—SUMMER

The summer between seventh and eighth grade, Dad put me to work stuffing envelopes for an advertising campaign he was doing to get more customers. He had me doing most of the garden work, too. He still allowed me time with Charlie (we'd become Uno masters and had an ongoing ten-thousand-point tournament), but no more tree house sleepovers.

He said, "I hope you know you can never date Charlie," and claimed he was saying this to save me from a destiny like his and Mom's. He said, "Charlie isn't like us, you know?" and I knew what he meant, but somehow it was that not-like-us that made me love Charlie more.

I had too much on my mind to digest this. I was still digesting the whole mother-was-a-stripper thing on top of the mother-never-coming-back thing. I felt a deep resentment toward Dad that summer. I think part of me blamed him for her leaving and part of me wanted to leave him, too. I got two half days a week at the adoption center at Zimmerman's, which was my way of getting away from him.

The pet store had been renovated with easy-to-clean tiled floors, and each type of animal had its own windowed area now so dogs and cats for sale and rescued animals for adoption could have their own space. We even had a rescued reptile room. In contrast to the previous summer's mishmash of metal cages and confusing signs to differentiate between the store and the adoption center, there was now just one long wall of windows, and shoppers could just as easily adopt from us for free or go farther along and pick up a purebred puppy.

The memories I have of that summer at Zimmerman's are all scratched, like old films. I see myself leaning over the stainless-steel sink in the back room, scrubbing a large Labrador retriever with flea shampoo and plucking fat ticks from her skin, while she shook and whimpered a little. I remember feeling bad that I'd accidentally hurt her—because my mother used to hurt me that way, too. She hated removing ticks, and claimed my father was no good at it and would leave the heads under the skin to become infected. So if I didn't sit still, she'd kneel on me and pin my arms down while I freaked out, screaming, and she'd forcefully remove them. No patience. No kisses. No hugs. Just a tweezers and some rubbing alcohol, and a stinging sensation that never goes away.

VARIOUS TIMES SATURDAY
MORNING—DAY OFF

When I get home from work, it's one-thirty in the morning and I can smell something weird the minute I walk down the hall to my bedroom. I only figure it out once I open the bedroom door. A mouse died in the wall and the stench is overwhelming. This happens a lot in our house because it's an old hunting lodge and there's no way to control where the mice die, and no way to get them out once they do. The only thing we can do is cover up the smell somehow, and avoid the area until the thing rots completely. This happens faster in summer than it does in winter.

Dad's snoring so loudly that the house is rattling and he doesn't hear me rooting around the kitchen pantry for scented candles. Mom bought them—that's how old they are. She went up to the Poconos one afternoon before Christmas and came home with two cases of scented candles.

"It's the candle capital of the world!" she said.

That's what they'll call anything if they want you to buy stuff there. People believe it because people are stupid. Apparently, that's adequate now. There are kids in my class who can't locate Florida on a map and they're going to get the same diploma I'm going to get. They're going to get accepted to college and become physical therapists or kindergarten teachers or financial analysts and they still won't be able to locate Florida on a map. They spend gallons of cash on tacky Christmas crap, and they drive sixty miles to buy candles because someone made a sign that says CANDLE CAPITAL OF THE WORLD when really, their local store sells candles just as nice.

I finally get to the case of scented candles in the back of the pantry, dig out three vanilla ones, and snatch the lighter from the shelf. I go back to my room, run in, light them, and run out and close the door again. Then I go to the kitchen for a snack. My shoulder is killing me. I stop in the downstairs bathroom to look at it in the mirror and there's a big red welt. Seeing it makes me feel delayed embarrassment. I wonder did I handle it okay? Did I look like an asshole? Should I have told Jenny Flick to fuck off, or thrown her pizzas on the ground? Dad is snoring so loudly, I can hear him over the crunch of my cornflakes. I remember that tomorrow is the second-to-last Saturday before Christmas and we're going to put up the tree.

When I arrive back to my room, it smells like a dead vanilla mouse, which is a bit better than just plain dead mouse, and when I close my eyes to sleep, I see it behind my eyelids, in a state of decomposition—legs stiff, eyeballs drying out— and suddenly I'm strangled by visions of what Charlie must look like now, nearly four months dead and underground, rotting. Maybe this makes me crazy or weird, but I can't stop myself from thinking it.

I tell Dad about the stench in the morning, but he says he can't smell anything. "Not like we can do anything about it anyway, Vera. If it's that bad, sleep on the couch," he says. It's almost noon. He's already gone out and bought a Christmas tree, which I'm staring at.

"Wow, Dad. That's one ugly-looking tree."

"It cost me twenty dollars, too," he says, still pissed off about it being too expensive.

"We putting it in the living room again this year?"

He looks from the kitchen into the dark and unused living room. Times like these, I think we both realize that the house is too big for just the two of us. Times like these, I can see how much Dad loved Mom and how much we both miss her. It's as if we left the living room there, dark and empty, like a parent leaves a child's room after they die.

"I was thinking we could change tradition and stick it in the den. What do you think?"

"Cool."

"Good."

"I'm going to take a shower," I say. "When I'm done, we'll put on some of that corny Christmas music you like."

In the shower, I note that I'm reshaping. Again. I thought this was supposed to be over by now. It's not like I can ask Dad about it. I bet if I did, he'd suggest meditation or come out with some Zen koan to counteract it. ("Breasts grow. Breasts shrink.

The farmer still plants corn in rows.") Just getting him to buy the right brand of tampons is difficult enough. I don't have any girlfriends to talk to, so I don't know how other people deal with things like this, but I think it's about time I told Dad that I'll buy my own. I make enough money. A few bucks a month won't eat too far into my college savings. Part of me feels bad for cutting him out, though. I still remember the day I got my period, and how he looked at me with proud eyes, hugged me, and then drove me to the drugstore down in the Pagoda Mall.

Thinking of this reminds me of Charlie and the day I had to change my tampon while we were hiking Big Blue—the six-mile-long extension of the blue trail. It was only two years ago. I was sixteen.

We were halfway up Big Blue when I asked him to hold on for a second and ducked behind a tree.

"It really must suck," he said.

"What?"

"You know—bleeding."

Geez. What a thing to say. "You get used to it. Not like I can make it go away, right?"

"I guess."

I took the used one, flung it deep into the brush, and ripped the wrapper off the new one.

"Does it hurt? You know. Putting it in?"

"No," I answered, now feeling awkward about the whole thing. He must have felt funny, too, because he got quiet. Then he sighed.

"My dad won't let my mom use them," he confessed—which was probably the weirdest confession I ever heard.

"That's weird."

"He says it's like her having sex with another person."

"That's gross. He's fucked-up, Charlie," I said, standing up, trying to un-hear what he just said while I pulled my jeans up.

"Yeah, I guess."

"I mean, you don't think I just got some kick out of that, do you?"

"I guess not."

"Well, do you think wiping your ass with toilet paper is like having sex?"

"Ew. No."

"Well, it's the same thing. Your poor mom. Geez. Why does he think he has any right to tell her how to deal with her period?"

"That's just how he is," he said, and I knew we both knew that already, so I buttoned up and came out from behind the tree and continued up the trail, realizing that Charlie's dad was ten times worse than I already thought he was.

"Where'd we put the spike last year?" Dad asks from the bottom of the stairs when he hears me open the bathroom door. The spike is the funky 1960s green thing we put on top of the tree instead of an angel or a star. My mother hated the spike, so Dad makes a huge deal out of it every time we decorate.

"With the lights, I think."

"I can't find it."

"I'll be down in a minute," I say, inspecting my Jenny Flick penny welt in the bathroom mirror. It's less swollen today, but the bruise is red-blue and dark.

I dry my hair and put on a pair of sweats. Saturdays are better now than they ever were before. Working full-time has given me an appreciation for days off—sweatpants and slippers and skipping breakfast.

When I get downstairs, Dad is untangling the lights and making three straight lines from the socket across the den floor. He's knocked over his stack of self-help books, and they lie like shallow steps between the couch and the radiator. I watch him secretly from the kitchen, where he's left a blueberry muffin for me on a small plate. I see what my mother saw in him. He's handsome, smart, and fit, which is a miracle in this part of the world, where everyone is spilling over their edges. His only flaw seems to be linked to being cheap, which really isn't that bad of a thing. So what if he buys the discounted cans of dented tomatoes at the grocery store? So what if he wears socks until they've got holes in them? He's raising me while my mother is off in some flashy hooker town with some retired bigwig doctor who likes to play poker. He's reading self-help books and learning new things about himself and the world. Only last week he learned how to make vegetarian lasagna and tried a new dish at the Chinese place. Back in October, I got him to try pineapple on his pizza, and got him hooked on Walt Whitman. What's not to love about that? As far as I'm concerned, Mom must be an idiot. If it were me, I'd marry him in a heartbeat. But I don't mean that in a gross way.

"You know, I think you're cool, Vera," he says out of the blue.

"Why?" I ask, blueberry muffin crumbs shooting out of my mouth.

"I can tell you're really growing up since you listened to me and got a job."

Forget everything I just said. Clearly, the man is an idiot.

CHRISTMAS BREAK

Christmas was all about clothes, mostly. A card with $100 in it. Three vintage Funkadelic albums—with the original record sleeves. Dad says I'm old enough for the lyrics, as if I hadn't already looked them up on the Internet. Dad tells me a few more times, between my holiday shifts at Pagoda and his new meditation routine, that he thinks I'm cool. He says, "You know, most kids these days are getting drunk and screwing boys. I'm so glad I raised you right," which makes me feel partly like never drinking again so I can continue to make him happy, and partly paranoid that he looked under my driver's seat and found my stash.

PART TWO

NEW YEAR'S EVE

Marie brought in two drivers from day shift, every part-timer we've got who would come in, and three extra pizza makers—including ex-cheerleader-turned-food-service-worker Jill, who can't stop making suggestive remarks about me and James.

"You two would make a cute couple," she says as she passes by with a full dough tray in her arms. I don't know why she says it. We aren't doing anything but folding boxes with the other drivers and telling dirty jokes.

But we would.

We would make a cute couple.

First run of the night is in the rich part of town—Potter Farms, where the houses are huge and geometrically pleasing to the eye, but the tips are not. Three stops, six bucks, and once I get back to the shop, the night becomes a blur of pizzas, garlic bread, six-packs of Coke, doorbells, kids in pajamas, adults tipping more than they should, leftover glowing tacky Christmas shit, drunk people in party hats, and confetti.

Every time I come back to the store, Marie has a new stack of orders to go out. She may have crazy-looking teeth, but man, can that woman run a pizza delivery store. Holy shit. I don't think there's one backup all night, which has to be a miracle on New Year's Eve.

Around 11:45, a customer at 362 Lancaster Road asks me when I get off work.

"We're having a small party, as you can see," he says. Yeah. All six of you. Playing Monopoly. Excellent. I decline.

At midnight, I ding-dong while a house on McMann Avenue erupts with cheers and party horns and "Auld Lang Syne." I ring again a minute later and a tall kid I used to know answers the door. He's swaying, and his eyes are bloodshot.

"Don't I know you?" he asks as he hands me the money.

"I don't think so," I lie. We had film class together when I was a sophomore and he was a senior.

"You look familiar, though."

"Have a nice night," I say, turning back toward my car.

"You should come back later! When you get off work!"

"I'll think about it," I say. And I do. For about three seconds, and then I drive to the next house. On the way, I whisper "Happy New Year" to Charlie.

At 12:10 I knock on the big green door of 21 Thirty-fourth Street. Two kids from my school answer it. Math geeks. They give me exact change and don't say thank you.

Last stop. 12:17. A loud party at the apartment complex where Jill lives. They are unprepared. I hand them their six pizzas and they take a drunken collection for cash, but can't count it. I help them. They are a dollar short.

"Come on! Pete! Pete! Where's that cheap son of a bitch?" People look around for Pete.

"I already chipped in, you asshole!"

"Who has an extra dollar? We're a buck short!"

I say, "And a tip. You're a buck *and a tip* short."

I watch them all dig deep into jeans pockets and shrug at each other.

"Shit, man. I'll have to spill out the penny jar," the guy says. Behind him, two girls pass a smoking bong between them. Someone yells "Happy New Year!"

I hold up my hand. "It's cool, man. Don't worry about it."

He stops searching his pockets for the third time and smiles at me.

"Hold on. I have your tip, though," he says, and he runs into the kitchen and returns with a four-pack of vodka coolers. "Something for when you get off work tonight," he says.

"Thanks, I—" I know I should give them back, but I don't. Instead, I pop the trunk and secure them between my gym bag and the cardboard box for groceries (one of a hundred Ken Dietz practical ideas—never have jars of mayonnaise rolling around the trunk again!) and cover them with the sleeping bag I keep in there in case of emergency. I think of my mom. Is this how it started with her? Are there baby steps toward complete loserdom, and if so, how many are there to go?

It's 12:25. As I wait for the traffic light on Bear Hill to turn green, I can't stop myself from reaching for the bottle that's under my seat. I've gone all night without a sip, but it's not about being addicted. It's about being told what to do my whole life and doing it and then losing everything anyway. Let me explain.

The night of Charlie's funeral, I took two shots of chilled vodka that someone had left at their table. I don't know what possessed me, but something did. (Probably Charlie.) The glasses were sitting there, I was walking by on my way to the bathroom, and no one was looking. So I picked one up in each hand and knocked them back one after the other. I had no idea how much it would hurt my throat, but loved the way it made me feel a minute later as I sat on the toilet, pondering the tiled floor. Warm. Happy. Safe. Now, on Bear Hill, I take the last shot left in my bottle, I think of my father's lifelong alcoholism warnings, and I say, "Am I not destroying my enemies when I make friends of them?" (Abraham Lincoln said that.)

1:02. Another trip to Potter Farms and a teenage party with chaperones who look vacant and are dressed in neutral, catalog-bought clothing. I have to walk across a bridge that spans an indoor koi pond. The father is foreign and very nice, and escorts me over the bridge. The mother is clapping a lot to get the kids to come to the kitchen. They intentionally tip me ten bucks, which is my biggest intentional tip of the night. When we're halfway back over the bridge toward the door, the father says, "Want to toss in a penny?" and sticks a penny in my hand.

I turn to the pond and eye a bright pink fish the size of my forearm shimmering his way from shadow to shadow, and I toss in the penny and make a wish. I wish for world peace, because it's about as likely to occur as anything else I can wish for.

● ● ●

At two, the phones stop ringing and Marie cashes the part-time drivers out. All the store help are gone but Jill, who's doing prep, and a girl I know from school named Helen, who needs a ride home. There are three or four runs left, and James says if I wait a few minutes I can take Helen home and drop off a big order at the same time, so I wait.

Halfway to her house, she says, "How are you doing? I mean"—she sighs—"uh, since Charlie died?"

"I'm okay."

"It must be hard. I mean, I'm sad about it and I didn't really know him."

"Yeah. It's sad."

"Did you know about the animals?"

It's weird. Nobody really talks about the animals. The minute she mentions them, my heart pounds and the images come rolling back behind my eyes. Damn brain.

"No," I lie.

"I just couldn't believe that, you know? That such a nice kid would do that to innocent animals."

I think of what Charlie had seen. How his father beat his mother. How he pulled her hair out sometimes. I think about what it must be like to want to stop a thing that you can't stop.

"It's pretty easy to blame the whole thing on the dead kid, isn't it?"

"I—uh—I guess."

We get to her house. "Don't believe everything you hear, you know?"

She cocks her head and thinks about it for a second. "Happy New Year, Vera."

As I watch her walk to the door, I realize that she's just another person who probably can't locate Florida on a map.

I deliver my last run, get a five-dollar tip, and stuff it into the bag behind my seat. Then I get back to the shop and start mopping. It's already three-fifteen and I want to be drinking the bottles in my trunk by four. James has stocked the cooler, Jill has done the dishes, and Marie has cashed me out. I hand her my money bag and she hands me my double commission in cash, with an extra twenty-dollar bill.

"A bonus for my full-timers," she says, and winks.

The mix James made in the mop bucket is bleach-heavy. It sticks in my nose and as I mop myself into the back kitchen, Marie's cigarette smoke thickens and mixes with it and I feel light-headed.

I finish, dump and rinse the bucket, and clean the mop-head. I go into the bathroom to change, and toss my shirt into the washing machine, and start it.

James is still here, in his car, in the parking lot. He motions me into his passenger's seat and lights a cigarette.

"You going anywhere special?" he asks.

"Just home," I lie.

"No party? No boyfriend to kiss?"

There is no doubt that James is flirting with me.

"Nope. No party. No boyfriend. But some geeks over on Lancaster Road invited me to their all-night Monopoly party. Wanna go and crash it with me?"

He feigns consideration. "Nah. Something tells me I won't get any kisses there."

"Kisses, eh?"

"Uh-huh."

He leans in toward me and my stomach does a bunch of flip-flops.

"Is that all you're after?"

"Uh-huh."

So, I kiss him and it feels really nice, and I really don't care that James is twenty-three, or a college dropout, or that he smokes. I wonder if this is step two on the baby-steps-to-loserdom trip I seem to be taking tonight, but I simultaneously don't care. I'm eighteen years old and I've never had a real boyfriend. I've never got past first base or gone to the prom or got detention for PDA. All this time I thought that if I avoided all the slutty shit my mother must have done, I would be a good person. I'd be safe. I'd be better than her. But while James is kissing me and holding the back of my head with his strong fingers entwined in my hair, I realize I don't really care about my mother and how she became a shallow loser capable of leaving her husband and kid. I realize that this feels nice and I really want to keep doing it. We stay there for about ten minutes, kissing, until I say, "I have to go." James's hand is under my shirt, around my waist, and part of me hates myself for making him stop.

His cigarette has burned down to the filter in the ashtray, so he lights another one.

"Happy New Year, Vera."

"Happy New Year, James," I say.

"You working tomorrow?"

"Yep. You?"

"Yep."

We smile at each other for a few seconds and then I push myself out of his car. It's cold out, but I don't feel it.

Six a.m., two hours later, and I'm parked on a dirt track that leads to a dead brown cornfield on top of Jenkins's Hill. It's still dark. I need to get rid of the evidence. I open the driver's door and toss the bottles into the field, one by one, until all four empties are gone. I crush the cardboard holder flat and fling it like a Frisbee.

I know I shouldn't be driving, but how else am I going to get home?

Anyway, I'm only three miles from my house, and if I get home now, Dad will be sleeping and won't know I'm drunk. I think this, but my body is falling asleep right here in my bucket seat. I think, *Hey, Vera! Come on! Snap out of it and get your drunk ass home!* but my body has shut down. I'm already drooling. Who cares what Dad thinks? I'm getting good grades, working his stupid full-time job, and saving for college.

I think of James—how he kissed me and how I have to see him tomorrow. Then I think of Charlie and our first New Year's Eve apart, and how I miss him. I miss him so much, but it's confusing, because I missed him long before he was dead, and that's the bitch of it all. I missed him long before he was dead.

It appears that my body knew I was going to vomit, so it woke me up and got me outside of my car without telling me. I hold on to the back bumper and puke into the row of compressed cornstalks. Again. Again. Again. I dry-heave a few times, then wipe my nose and my mouth and look at the horizon. The light is just appearing—that bluey-violet color that my mother used to get up early to see.

Then, like an army lined in marching formation, they are there. The Charlies—walking toward me between rows of shin-high skeletal cornstalks.

They have needles? Are they needles? They aren't threatening. They seem friendly this time, but machinelike. They seem like a thousand android Charlies. Coming to get me. With what look like dental needles. They are going to shoot me up with the past and show me everything that led me here. They are going to inject me with outer space truth serum.

When I realize I can't run away, I try to glue my mouth shut. I refuse to tell them anything. I convince my brain that I am a mute, change-making, tip-counting machine, nothing more. A pizza-delivering android. I do not have emotions. I do not have truth. A thousand Charlies know better. They outstretch their arms and hug me tightly until I bawl and tell them what they want to hear.

If Mr. Jenkins, the owner of this field, was to walk onto his back deck right now to see the beauty of this bluey-violet morning, he'd see me standing by the side of my car, hugging myself, sobbing, "I couldn't stand you anymore!"

I couldn't. I hated him.

"I wished you were dead!"

A thousand Charlies know this.

But they don't have to come to terms with it. I do.

NEW YEAR'S DAY

We're at Uncle Caleb's house for our traditional New Year's Day meal. I'm sitting next to Jessie, my fluffy cousin, and her little brother, Frankie, who isn't paying attention to what's going on at the table because he's watching the muted football game on TV.

"I don't get it," my cousin Jessie says. "You could probably get into a good school, Veer."

"Yeah, but what does that *mean*, you know?" I ask, although I'm not asking. We've been through this before.

"It means you'll get a better job," Aunt Kate says while shoveling a forkful of mashed potatoes smothered in sauerkraut into her mouth.

"It means you'll look better on paper," says Uncle Caleb—Kate's husband, Dad's oldest brother.

"I don't care about how I look on paper." I am so hungover I want to die. My head is throbbing. My eyes are still bloodshot. Dad either noticed and is saying nothing, or he really is the most inattentive man in the world, like Mom used to say.

"Well, you should," Aunt Kate says.

I look down at my plate of pork and sauerkraut. This is proof that life is totally surreal here in our little Pennsylvania Dutch county. Who makes pork and sauerkraut a traditional lucky meal on the day after the year's biggest traditional drinking binge?

"I don't see what the difference is, as long as she gets a good education," Dad says.

The table goes quiet and we get back to eating our good luck for the year. We are maniacal about it now, since six years ago, when we tried to change the tradition and had venison stew instead. That was the year Mom left, Jessie got sick with appendicitis, and Maw-Maw died. Last year I skipped it because I had the flu and what happened? I lost Charlie. Twice.

Anyway, I think Dad's right. What difference does it make what college I go to? There are idiots at Yale whose fathers get them in. There are illiterate football players at all of the state schools. Bottom line—the only thing I care about is how much my education will cost. Because Dad has made it clear that I am paying.

Which may seem cruel, but it's not.

Sure beats being one of those kids at school who don't yet understand what "college loan" means. You know the ones. They think it's free money. Think their parents will cover it. Or they just don't think. Then suddenly, at twenty-two, they get the payment booklet and discover that they owe a hundred grand, and they can't buy groceries or health insurance because of the school they picked—all so they could look good on paper. (And they still can't locate Florida on a map.)

Sorry. Not me. I'd rather pay class by class at community college, and deliver pizza at night while I live cheap in Dad's house. Then, when I graduate, I can actually start fresh, rather than starting with a hundred-thousand-dollar stone around my neck.

Jessie has her heart set on Penn State. She's one of those college football fans who chant "We are . . . Penn State." She has no idea what she wants to do outside keg parties and blow jobs. I know that sounds harsh, but Jessie is just—Jessie.

Most of the family eats quickly and goes back to watching football on TV. I look at my watch and decide to save myself from any more unsaid criticism.

"Sorry to eat and run, but I've got to work at four and I need to do some stuff at home first."

Before anyone can say anything, I have my coat on and am out the door.

I pull into our driveway and sit in the car for a second. The woods are still covered in a shallow layer of snow, and though everything is dead and brown, there are birds and squirrels making it move and sing. Birds always remind me that spring will come, and the brown will be green, and the dirt will sprout a million blades of grass and scrub where ticks will live and crickets and cicadas and spiders. The stream between Charlie's house and our house will fill up with the snowmelt and then slow to a trickle. In summer it will barely be there, and the crayfish will hide in the wet mud under rocks until the next rain. Salamanders will dry out and die next to fish that never made it to the lake in time.

Something about death reminds me of birth, I guess. I have my own version of afterlife now that Charlie is dead. There is one. People there can see you and they live on in the things around us. In the trees. The birds. Like that feeling you get when someone behind you is staring at you—I get that all the time, but it's Charlie who's staring. From up there, or over there, or wherever it is that he went.

Since I developed this idea, I sometimes joke with him when I eat things. I say, "Charlie, if you're part of this Big Mac, I'm really sorry." Then I eat the Big Mac. Because it's possible, isn't it? Isn't anything possible? Charlie the pickle? Charlie the woodpecker? Charlie the raindrop?

I took three Tylenol at Aunt Kate's house and I feel better, but my mouth feels like something died in there, and I can't get it to feel normal. I've got an hour before I have to leave for work, so I stupidly go to my dead-rodent-smelling room and set my alarm for 3:45 and sleep.

When I get up three snooze alarms later, I feel worse.

I rush to the kitchen, scarf down a granola bar, tuck my hair into the Pagoda Pizza hat to hide how one side is plastered down with drool, and run out the door.

Right when the cold air hits and the door slams behind me, I hear it through the trees.

"You're a fucking idiot, you know that?"

"You're lucky I don't kill you right now!"

I don't know where they are. Back deck, where Charlie

and I used to play Uno? The front porch, where raccoons used to shit on the doormat because Charlie said it had some weird chemical that communicated "Shit here" in Raccoon? The upstairs balcony, where Mrs. Kahn would go every Saturday morning to beat the small sheepskin rugs they had in their bedroom?

I can see movement through the trees, but rather than think about it, I ignore it, like I should. As I drive to work, though, I wonder about every house I pass, because I've read the statistics—haven't you? Which of these houses hold the wife beaters? The child abusers? The rapists? The drunks and gamblers? Which of these houses hold the parents who hurt their own kids? Where are the signs? Wouldn't it be nice if there were big flashing signs to warn us about these people?

When I get to the main strip, I remember James and our kiss last night. He's not the kind of guy I can bring home to Dad and call my boyfriend. I can't take him to the prom.

Because I barely ate anything at Aunt Kate's, I go to the McDonald's drive-thru and get a Big Mac. Because Charlie could be a pickle, I say, "Sorry, dude," before I bite into it.

HISTORY—AGE FOURTEEN

Charlie and I were sitting in our normal spots in the Master Oak. The leaves were nearly all fallen now, and the forest allowed the autumn sun rays to press through. He climbed two limbs up and reached into a gnarled old knot that had doubled as a squirrel's nest. He pulled out a box pack of Marlboro Reds and swung back down into the crook where he usually sat, and unwrapped the cellophane. He banged the pack a bit on his hand, coaxed a smoke out of the middle of the front row, and popped it into his mouth. Fourteen, and I'd guess Charlie was already at a pack a day.

"Where'd you get those?"

"What?"

"You always have a new pack."

"I have my connections, I guess."

I thought he meant his father. After all, there was no one at school who could get that many packs in a week.

"Do you buy them by the carton, or what?"

"Let's go and check out the pagoda," he said. "I'm bored as hell." Then he pulled out a brand-new shiny Zippo lighter. It had his initials engraved on it: CDK. Somehow, I didn't think his dad would buy him that.

"Nice lighter," I said as he used it to light his cigarette.

"Come on," he said, starting his descent.

"I can't. I have a stupid essay to write."

He continued down the tree, and I followed him. When we got to the blue trail, he went toward the pagoda by himself and I went home. The essay was about *Romeo and Juliet*, our first journey into the mind of William Shakespeare. The assignment was: *Many writers and filmmakers have used the classic story of Romeo and Juliet as the theme for their works. If you were to write a modern-day Romeo and Juliet, what would make yours stand apart from these others?*

Pretty hot question for eighth graders, if you ask me, but I was excited by it, too, because I liked when teachers asked hard questions. It's safe to say that when all other students in the class said "Ugghhh!" it was an assignment I was going to enjoy. But this time, there was a problem. I couldn't picture Romeo and Juliet without picturing Charlie and me.

Part of me was repulsed by the thought. Dad had just told me, the year before, about Mom's old job at Joe's and had made it clear that Charlie Kahn was off-limits to me as a boyfriend. (Though to give him credit, he did it in a nice way and was nothing like Lord Capulet. I think his closing words were: "I hope you understand I'm saying this because I love you.") The other part of me was excited. Charlie was such a strange sort of attractive, it was hard to explain—I felt a mix of wanting to kill him and wanting to kiss him at the same time. When I thought of what true love must be like, I figured it must be a mix like this, and not the stupid eighth-grade infatuation most girls my age felt. True love includes equal parts good and bad, but true love sticks around and doesn't run off to Vegas with a podiatrist. Anyway, somehow, in my weird, mixed-up brain, Charlie was Romeo and I was Juliet. I wrote my essay about how in my version, Romeo was a total slob and Juliet was a tomboy, and they decided that the fake suicide was excessively dramatic, and instead, ran off to live in the forests beyond Verona. When Charlie asked me what my essay was about at the bus stop the next morning while he picked some old blue-trail dog crap out of the tread of his shoe, I told him it was about Shakespeare, and he made a yuck face before I had to go any further.

That winter, we fidgeted a lot because we were too old to do the stuff we used to do, like play card games in the tree house, and too young to do anything interesting. Charlie went hunting with his dad on the weekends, which was the only thing they ever did together, and I felt happy for him. The only tradition Dad and I had at that point was Friday-night pizza from Santo's.

When the forest sprouted in between our houses, and the brambles grew new bright green leaves, we took to spring-cleaning the tree house and Charlie started to talk about building The Amazing Deck. Charlie had found a book in the library about tree houses—real ones, like real houses all over the world built around trees. He said that he wanted to rip down the house he'd already built but his dad wouldn't let him, so he planned to add The Amazing Deck. He worked with the shop teacher to figure out how to support the thing, and they drew a plan together.

The first Saturday it was warm enough, he walked in circles around the base of the tree with a calculator and a cheat sheet of geometry equations. He'd stop and scribble some numbers down on a small spiral notepad and then measure again, and say something like "Better safe than sorry."

After that, he furiously wrote cut lists. All mitered cuts because, he announced, The Amazing Deck would be octagonal. Because with Charlie, nothing was ever easy. Everything was windswept and octagonal and finger-combed. Everything was difficult and odd, and the theme songs all had minor chords.

I helped him build the deck every day after school, but my spring weekends changed because, since I was fourteen, my father filled out my working papers and made me get my first job, at Mika's Diner as a busgirl.

Which sucked.

The pay was shitty and the waitresses hated splitting tips, so my ten percent would equal two bucks if I was lucky. And I had to wear the stupidest uniform on the planet—a brown 100% polyester apron-style wraparound skirt thing with a white blouse underneath. Thing was, the wraparound part was too short, so it only overlapped about eight inches in the back. This made bending over a problem, because busgirls have to bend over a lot. Which, I suspect, was Mika's point in making us wear them. I daydreamed constantly about working at Zimmerman's that summer to save me the embarrassment of the stupid uniform, but I knew Mr. Zimmerman didn't hire people under seventeen. I put my name in to volunteer at the adoption center again, but Dad stressed that a summer job at my age was about making money, and volunteering wasn't in the cards.

When I came home from work on a Sunday afternoon in late May, I looked into the woods and saw Charlie sitting on his newly finished Amazing Octagonal Deck, binoculars in hand. I waved. He waved back. Once I changed and walked out to meet him, though, he was gone. I could hear yelling from inside the Kahns' house. More than the usual amount. More than Mr. Kahn drunkenly lambasting Mrs. Kahn for missing a spiderweb in a dark corner or not beating the rugs properly. I could hear Mrs. Kahn yelling, too—a first—which meant it was Charlie they were yelling at.

NEW YEAR'S DAY—FOUR TO CLOSE

I'm the only driver in on time. Marie loves me. I still feel like something died in my mouth, even after a chocolate shake and a Big Mac. I still have a headache, too, even though I took two more Tylenol before I left the house.

There's a big order waiting to go out, so I don't get a chance to walk into the back room. Marie just hands me my change envelope and my Pagoda Phone and eight pies in hot bags, and rattles off four addresses.

The run takes me an hour, so by the time I'm back, the place is a madhouse. Dylan Pothead has called in sick, when everyone knows he's just hungover/still partying/hallucinating too much to drive. Tommy Pothead is working but must have done one too many bong hits, because he's unable to comprehend the map. James finally comes in and winks when he sees me, which makes me feel oddly all-over-the-place, even though last night was amazing. We're so busy, Marie is thinking about leaving ex-cheerleader-turned-food-service-worker

Jill in charge of the store and taking her old Ford out on a few runs to help us out.

Jill says, "I bet Mick will do it." Mick's her boyfriend. He's a skinhead Nazi. But Marie decides not to call Mick. Which is great, because nothing gives me the creeps more than skinhead Nazis.

I take another run, and when I get back to the store and stack my empty hot bags under the stainless-steel counter, there is relative calm. People have settled into their New Year's Day rituals. They've watched their football and eaten their pork for midday and their pizza for dinner. My next runs are normal, and by eight, the phones stop ringing. At ten, Marie actually checks the phone line, she is so surprised. She sends Tommy—who is staring at his own hand and giggling on the back steps—home, and asks Jill if she wants to go, too.

"I'm not letting *him* drive me home," Jill says.

"No shit, bitch," Tommy says. "Who said I would?"

"I'll take you home," I offer, stupidly. I think I said it so I wouldn't have to be alone with James, who has now slipped outside with Tommy to smoke a cigarette. The most we've said to each other tonight is "Hi," and I'm still not sure what to say after last night's impulsive . . . *thing*.

Five minutes later, I am driving into Jill's apartment complex and I have the music turned up so we don't have to talk. I have Sly & the Family Stone in. "If You Want Me to Stay." Mick is standing on the concrete porch with his arms crossed and no shirt on, to show off his trillion nasty tattoos. His head is completely shaved, and his jeans are riding so low, I bet they'd fall down if he didn't stand that way—with his junk pushed out. When I pull up to Building A, before she opens the door to get out, she turns the volume knob down all the way.

I find this annoying, and my face must show it, because she makes the "What can I do?" face and says, "Thanks for the ride."

James is waiting for me in the parking lot when I get back. Seeing him there, under the streetlight, breathing smoke and hot breath into the cold night, makes me forget about Jill and her asshole boyfriend. Makes me forget that I shouldn't be kissing a guy who's twenty-three. Makes me forget I'm supposed to avoid all boys and men or else I'll end up the pregnant loser my mother was.

He's so awesomely gorgeous and manly and hunky. His hair is grown out a little, so he doesn't look messy, but rugged. He keeps himself shaven, but sometimes leaves a stubbly goatee, which he's done today. He wears a Pagoda shirt that's a tiny bit small for him, so his biceps and deltoids are really defined and I can't help but want to squeeze them. But this isn't all physical. He says smart stuff. He's funny, sarcastic, and cynical. He can see outside this stupid little town because he's *been* out of this stupid little town. None of the guys in school have all this going for them. They might have muscles, but they don't have brains. Or they might have muscles and a few brains, but they still think the world revolves around them. The fact is, being twenty-three makes James even more attractive to me. If you think about it, it's only five years. When I'm thirty-five, he'll be forty. When I'm eighty, he'll be eighty-five. Doesn't seem like such a bad thing when I put it that way, does it?

I guess the next argument would be that James doesn't know what he wants to do with his life. That's true. At least he can admit it. I'd rather go out with a guy who's facing his shit than a guy who's running from his shit. Beats finishing college and hating what you do. Beats going to college just to please your parents, which is probably what half the kids in school are about to do anyway.

"Hey," I say.

He exhales a chestful of smoke. "I thought you were avoiding me."

"Had to take Jill home."

"Sure you did. Because she's your BFF, right?"

I hit him on his arm. "Her asshole boyfriend was waiting on the porch for her like some kind of prison officer."

"Yeah. I know him."

He puts his hand on my waist and the flip-flopping in my rib cage happens. "You mean you know him? Or you *know* him?"

"He goes up to Fred's Bar sometimes and I see him there. I went to school with a few of his buddies, too, I guess."

"Nice guys," I say, trying to remember if I ever saw Mick the skinhead Nazi at Fred's before.

"Yeah. They weren't quite as fucked-up when we were kids, you know?"

Marie knocks on the window and waves us in. James puts out his cigarette and grabs me by the hand before I pull the door open.

"Are we cool?" he asks, and stutters, "I mean . . . last night?"

"Sure."

He looks at me and smiles. "You want to go out after work?"

I think about what awaits me at home. My stinky-dead-mouse room. My snoring and oblivious dad. My fucked-up neighbor who beats the crap out of his wife. And somewhere— a thousand dead Charlies trying to make me find the proof that Charlie didn't kill those animals.

"Where to?"

"How about we go up to the pagoda and make out?"

This makes me so happy, I whistle while I do the dishes— which makes Marie wink at me—which makes me even happier, because she approves, and I stop worrying about what Dad would think.

HISTORY—AGE FOURTEEN

The day after Charlie finished building the deck (and I heard all that yelling), he arrived at the bus stop, seething. He lit a smoke while I asked him what was wrong.

"My mom is making me go to the doctor," he said.

"Are you sick?"

"No."

"Then why?"

"My colon or something."

"Your colon?"

"She thinks I shit too much."

"Oh."

I wondered how much shitting is too much.

"Why does she think that?"

"Because I keep throwing my underwear away."

The bus roared up the hill as I pondered this and Charlie fast-smoked his cigarette.

He wasn't on the bus home, so I assumed he'd caught a

ride to the doctor's office. I sat in our seat—number fourteen—with my earphones in, listening to a mixed Motown playlist I made from Dad's old vinyl. It was in that stack of old records (that he got from his mom) I discovered Marvin Gaye and Tammi Terrell. I was on my third way through "Ain't No Mountain High Enough" when Tim Miller, a senior who lived down by the lake, jumped into the seat next to me and pulled my earphone out.

"What you listening to?"

I was startled. I'd been taking this bus for two years, and never had anyone from the high school talked to Charlie or me. We were eighth graders—bottom of the Crock-Pot. Plus, I knew what Tim Miller would think of Marvin Gaye and Tammi Terrell. He threw the n-word around like it was a conjunction.

I pressed STOP and stuck the whole thing in my pocket. "Nothing. Just some oldies."

He looked me in the eyes and slipped his arm around the back of my neck, pulling me closer. "You want to know a secret?"

"No." I pushed myself into the cold metal seafoam green bus wall so hard I could feel the rivets press into my arm.

"I know something about your boyfriend that you ought to know."

"I don't have a boyfriend."

He put his hand out. "A dollar will buy it."

"I don't have a dollar."

"A little rich bitch like you? Don't have a dollar?"

"I'm not rich."

"Sure you are."

The bus driver put on the yellow flashers. Tim's stop was fifty feet away.

"You need to know this. I'm telling you," he said, his hand out.

I pulled my earphones out of my pocket and stuck them back in my ears.

"He can't be your boyfriend if he's a fag, can he?"

I pressed PLAY while he strutted off the bus, hitting a few younger kids on the back of the head. I comforted myself with the idea that any high school senior who still takes the bus home is a pathetic loser.

That day was the first time Charlie couldn't come out and play—like, the first time ever. Ever. I went to his front door, rang the doorbell, and waited on the bench on the porch until his mother came out.

"Sorry, Vera. He can't come out. He's got diarrhea."

"He's sick?"

"It's nothing serious, dear," she said, her voice quavering a bit. "He'll probably be in school by Wednesday."

But he wasn't. He wasn't in school Wednesday or Thursday. When he didn't come on Friday, and I'd finally moved to the front seat of the bus so Tim Miller couldn't get anywhere near me on the way home, I decided I'd call.

Mrs. Kahn answered, and after much coaxing, she let me talk to him.

"Veer?"

"Wow, Charlie. You must be really sick."

"Veer—you have to score me some smokes, man. I'm dying here."

"I'm fourteen. I can't buy cigarettes."

"Walk to the APlus. Tell Kevin they're for me."

The APlus was two miles away. I was not allowed to walk that far. Plus, walking alone on Overlook Road gave me the willies.

"I can't. I'm sorry."

After a small chunk of silence, he sighed. "I know you would if you could. I'm just dying for a cigarette. It's been like four days."

"Are you really sick?"

"Nah."

"So what's going on?"

"My mom's just being a worrywart."

Suddenly I realized what might be going on. I felt so stupid for not realizing it sooner. My heart broke.

"Can you—uh—can you come to the tree house this weekend?" I asked.

"I don't know. We'll see what she says."

"Get better soon, okay?"

After I hung up, I went to Dad's office and sat in the orange retro chair until he was off his business phone call. I couldn't say anything at first, because the thought of Charlie getting beat up by his dad just made me want to cry.

"Vera? You okay?"

I looked at him and made that face that says "Not really."

"What's up?"

"You know how we've always ignored what goes on next door?"

He stared at me over his reading glasses.

"Would we still ignore it if Charlie started to get hurt,

too?" A wave of tears came then, and sobs. Dad didn't know what to do, so he handed me a tissue box and organized the paperwork on his desk.

"You have to be sure of these things, Vera. You can't just accuse people without proof."

"He was out of school all week," I said.

"A lot of kids get the flu this time of year, because the weather warms up."

"He doesn't have the flu."

"It's just not as easy as reporting it. There's just so little we can do. The guy's a jerk, and if we get involved, it'll only make him worse."

Maybe the adults around me were too cynical and old to do anything to help innocent people like Mrs. Kahn or Charlie, or the black kids who were called nigger at school, or the girls Tim Miller groped on the bus. Maybe they were numb enough to blame the system for things they were too lazy to change. Not me. As I sat there watching Dad tidy his paperwork, empty his pencil sharpener, and blow the dust off his glass paperweights, I vowed never to become a heartless, blind-eye hypocrite like him.

HISTORY—AGE FOURTEEN

At the bus stop on Monday, Charlie opened a brand-new pack of Reds and smoked two, lighting the second off the first. He hadn't come to the tree house on Saturday and I'd had to work on Sunday, cleaning up dishes after the church crowd at Mika's, so it had been a whole week since I'd seen him.

I looked for bruises. Anything out of the ordinary. But he was always disheveled and messy. I saw a small cut next to his lip, but it looked like a razor cut. I noted that his cheek and lip fuzz was missing and his eyebrows were now separated by a stark white space of skin rather than the unruly mess of hairs that had been there before.

"What're you looking at?"

"Nothing," I said.

He paced.

"I'm just glad you're back."

He took a long drag of his cigarette. "Why?"

"Tim Miller was bugging me last week on the bus home."

This was the fastest thing I could think of that didn't reek of bullshit.

"The senior?"

"Yeah. He's a creep."

"Huh," he said, and inhaled the last of his cigarette deeply.

The bus came and we went down the hill to Tim Miller's house, where the Confederate flag flew on a pole in the backyard, but he didn't get on.

About a minute before the bus pulled up in front of the school, I decided to ask Charlie straight out about his health. If I wasn't going to be a hypocrite, I would have to learn to ask hard questions, I figured, and this was as good a time as any. "So hey, how'd the—uh—doctor's appointment work out?"

"I have to take pills now."

"Last thing I knew, your mom thought you shit too much," I said. "Did that turn out okay?"

Charlie got visibly agitated. His muscles twitched under his skin. "Yeah, well, it's none of her goddamned business. I know what I'm doing. It's not illegal."

"What's not?"

He turned to me and crouched into the green vinyl seat.

"Charlie? Is everything okay?"

"Can you keep a secret?"

"Of course." I rolled my eyes.

"Are you sure?"

"We've only been best friends since we could walk."

"I know a way you can make thirty bucks a week."

I squinted at him. "How?"

The bus pulled up to the curb outside school and Charlie told me how. He told me he was selling his used underwear to some rich guy who lived down in Mount Pitts. "I get five bucks for each pair. Double if I toss in my socks."

Before I could scrape my jaw off my lap, he was walking down the center aisle of the bus, laughing his ass off.

A BRIEF WORD FROM THE PAGODA

I know that guy. He drives up here all the time in his dirty white New Yorker and peeks into the steamed-up make-out cars. It wasn't always this way, you know—a sleazy spot to get laid. Back when things were still civilized, the rich folks from town used to come up and stay their weekends in grand hotels, and ride on the gravity railroad. Ladies in long skirts, with parasols, and strong men in striped three-piece suits with gold pocket watches. When I was built, I was supposed to be a top-of-the-line resort, but the owners never secured a liquor license, so I became an instant disappointment. A shame. I would never be a temple, or a resort, or a hotel. I didn't have a ballroom or billiards or a back room to gamble money away. I had no other use but to sit here and look pretty. I was almost demolished during World War II on account of my seeming Japanese. I was a restaurant for a while, but went bankrupt. I nearly burned down in 1969. But they keep saving me because they know I stand for something. They're just not sure what yet.

NEW YEAR'S DAY—AFTER WORK

"You want anything?"

We're outside Fred's Bar and James is asking me this. I can feel myself split in two. Part of me, the part who knows what's good for me, wants to ask him for a ginger ale. The other part of me, the one who's been thinking of another drink since I woke up this morning, answers.

"Some of those vodka coolers. The black ones."

James raises his eyebrows and disappears past the green door with the three diamond-shaped windows. As I sit waiting, the creepy vibes from Fred's pinball room ooze out and surround me. I realize this is the first time I've been in a boy's—uh—man's car and been out of control of a situation. I guess, technically, this is the first time I've been on a real date, too. If that's what this is.

I wonder what might happen to me and give myself a good dose of the date rape heebie-jeebies before I stop and remember that James is a nice guy. I've known him from the very first day I started at Pagoda Pizza last summer.

I was still seventeen and wasn't allowed to do delivery yet, so I answered phones, mostly, and made pizzas. James worked the day shift full-time. In at ten, out at four, seven days a week, so on weekdays I'd only see him when he was leaving. Even then, he treated me like an equal and not some kid.

Now, here I am, in his car, and we're going to make out at the pagoda. (But I'm equally excited by the vodka.)

He bursts out the door with a brown paper bag and a grin. He puts the booze in the trunk and hops into the driver's seat. As we pass the lake and twist around the S curves that lead up the mountain, I push thoughts of Charlie out of my mind. Of course, this is impossible. Every square inch of this road, of that lake, of these woods, is Charlie. I ask James to go the long way to avoid Overlook Road. It takes us past the old tower and the view of the city.

"Did you ever see what the lights spell?" James asks.

"I grew up here, remember?"

"Oh, yeah."

If you stop at the tower lookout spot at night, the lights of the city unintentionally spell ZERO.

But as we pass by tonight, we see a cop car parked behind the little electric company shed, so instead of stopping to read the lights, James drives on and we act like innocent kids on their way to make out—which is easy, because we are.

An hour later—around one o'clock—James and I are making out after a few drinks and I'm in Vera Heaven. I'm starting to think I love James. Already. I know this makes me stupid, but I don't care. Every song he puts on is perfect. Everything he says is clever. Every place he touches me feels awesome. Not creepy. Not pushy. He does not try to touch any warning spots, and, as if we are all born rebels, because he is not touching them, I want him to. This makes no sense to me, because I have never gone this far with a guy before, so I really don't know why my brain is telling me to want him to go further. But it is.

After my third vodka cooler, I straddle his lap and drape my arms around his strong neck and whisper things in his ear that I shouldn't be whispering. I say things I shouldn't be saying. He puts his seat back and we make out some more. The windows are steamed, Led Zeppelin is in the stereo, and when I lift my head up to fling my hair away from my face, I open one eye and gasp.

They are in the car—all thousand of them, stacked like paper. They are curved into the backseat, pressed up against the back window. Pressed against my back, my sides—staring at me. Today they're wearing Charlie's favorite blue-and-white-checked flannel shirt—the one with the tattered cuffs. His red bandanna—the one he wouldn't take off during our last summer together. They have his combat hiking shorts on.

James doesn't know what's happening and holds me at my waist, his eyes still closed. I struggle to breathe and can't inhale at all, so I reach for the door handle.

He opens his eyes when he feels me panicking. "Veer? You okay?"

They are squeezing him from every angle, but he can't see them. They are not sucking the air out of his lungs.

I open the door and stumble out onto the gravel. In front of me is the red neon pagoda—a reminder of what happens when we act and don't think. I breathe deeply and James arrives behind me, and wraps his arms around my shoulders.

"Veer?"

"I'm okay," I say. I look back at the car. A thousand Charlies are drawing something in the steam on the window. They are drawing pictures. They are spelling something.

A childish stick figure of a dead dog, legs up. A dead fish, floating. A dead rodent with a pointed nose and a long tail.

The letters T-E-L-L.

The dead rodent reminds me that it's a school night and I should be home by now, sleeping in my vanilla rotten-corpse room.

"Do you see that?" I ask, pointing at the pictures in the car window.

James can't see them. He's looking at me, concerned. Great. Now I look like some immature drama queen. A few drinks and I'm seeing shit. He's probably writing a mental restraining order right now.

"You want to call it a night?" he asks.

"Sure. I have a Vocab test in the morning and I didn't learn any of the words over break," I say. He helps me back into the car, now void of tissue-paper Charlies, and drives us back toward the store. When we pass by my house, I see the downstairs lights are still on and I realize I might be in trouble. Then, just after we pass by, the cop behind us puts on his lights and things get about twenty million times worse.

A BRIEF WORD FROM THE DEAD KID

I was an idiot. I was an idiot about Vera and about Jenny
Flick. I don't know what I was doing. I don't know who I was
trying to impress. I've asked myself for months now, and I can
only tell you what I *wasn't* doing.

I wasn't trying to hurt Vera.

I wasn't trying to impress the Detentionheads. I didn't
really even like them.

And let me set the record straight—I did not kill those
animals. That was Jenny.

But I did send the cops.

You're surprised? You had a different idea of the afterlife?
This goes against your religion? Well, what did you really
know anyway? No one living understands dying, and no matter what they dream up—from harps and heaven to pickles in
Big Macs—they can't prove a thing until they're on this side.
Which, if you can, you want to avoid until it's really your
time to go. You might want to leave some time to fall in love

and have a family. Stay healthy so you can meet your grand-children one day. I can guarantee you this: you do not want to die by asphyxiating on your own puke and get kicked out of a car onto your front lawn.

I spend most of my time watching my parents. You'd think I'd get as far away from them as I could now that I'm free, but seems I'm here to learn something. Not sure what. I never liked either of them. He's just a bully, and she's a doormat.

I spend the rest of my time trying to communicate with Vera. I want her to know I'm sorry. I want her to find the box and clear my name. I want her to fall in love and have a nice life. In a way, I feel like I was the one standing in her way, so I'm glad I'm dead. I would have never made a good enough man for her. But she deserves better than a college dropout pizza delivery guy, too.

So I sent the cops.

No, I'm not omnipotent. Of course not. But I can make things appear to those who want to see them, and small-town cops are always looking for trouble, aren't they?

NEW YEAR'S DAY (NIGHT)

"Step out of the car, please."

Oh shit. I can see the porch light go on at my house and the living room curtain move at the Kahns' house. Can't they turn off the flashing lights now that they've stopped us?

James and I get out of the car. James hands them his paperwork when he gets out. I just stand there and try to disappear while chewing spearmint gum violently to get rid of my vodka breath.

"I'll need to see your license, too," the fat cop says to me. I reach into the car for my purse and see the bottle caps on the floor of James's car. Oh man. We are in big trouble.

I hand him the license and my school ID in case he might take pity on the fact that I'm still in school.

He looks at it, mumbles "4511 Overlook Road," and looks down the street at my house. "That your house?"

"Yep."

"Well, let's walk you home, then."

"Uh—I—uh—have to pick up my car."

He laughs. "You're not picking up anything tonight, Miss Dietz. Except maybe your coat from the backseat there."

I look to James and he smiles, with confidence. I'm unsure why he's so confident. He could lose his license. He could lose his job. He could go to jail for buying an underage high school senior vodka coolers, right?

Before I know it, I'm walking to my house with the cop. A thousand Charlies are in the air, walking with us, reminding me that I could tell the cop everything I know. That I *should*. When we get to within view of the porch, I see Dad, arms crossed, his reading glasses shoved onto his forehead and his concerned face on.

"Please don't tell him I was drinking."

"I don't think I need to tell him."

"Please don't take my license. I need to keep my job."

He stops me at the end of the drive and turns me to look at him. "Look. Don't screw your life up. There's plenty of time to get drunk and hang out with boys. That guy's too old for you."

"I need my job. It's full-time. I can't lose it."

He inspects me. "Tonight you get your one and only warning from the Mount Pitts police department. After this, you don't get a break."

Then he waves to my dad from the end of the drive and turns back toward the car. Dad looks confused, but concentrates on me. I pray for his crappy sense of smell. I pray I'm walking straight.

"What was that about? Where's the car?"

"It's at the store. We can pick it up tomorrow." I walk past him through the front door as if it's not two in the morning on a school night.

He catches my arm. "Vera? What's going on?"

"Can we talk about it in the morning?"

"No," he says, grabbing his coat from the hook and looking as if he's going to ask the cops.

He's only bluffing and I know it. But I do have to tell him something. Something.

"I went out with a guy from work tonight. That's all. He was driving a little fast on the way home."

"So where's the car?"

"I told you—it's at the store. I'm working four-to-close tomorrow anyway."

"Who's the guy?"

"James."

"James what?"

Of course, I have no idea what the answer to this question is.

"Vera?"

"Yeah. James—uh—I can't pronounce it. Starts with a K."

"James Starts-with-a-K?"

"Can I go to bed now?"

He leans in and inhales. I am so up shit's creek.

"Yeah. Go to bed. I'll see you in the morning." He puts his coat back on the hook and looks out the front window. The flashing cop car is gone, and so is James's car. I go to the bathroom and wash the feeling of getting caught off my face. I'm feeling more like my mother every day.

A BRIEF WORD FROM KEN DIETZ
(VERA'S FRUSTRATED DAD)

Vera thinks I don't know she's drinking. As if my past is just a vocabulary word (alcoholic [noun] 1. a person who habitually drinks excessive amounts of alcohol) that will stay in the past. She has no idea what it means to be me. She has no idea that when she came in the house stinking of liquor, part of me wanted to hop off this seventeen-year-old wagon and tap into her veins to suck out the booze. In one way, I hope she never understands this. In another way, I wish she'd look beyond herself once in a while. But that's a side effect of alcohol, isn't it? Stopping to think about other people is not on the bar menu.

I had my first beer when I was ten. My teenage brother Caleb and his friends were having a tent sleepover party in our backyard and one of the boys brought a six-pack of Michelob. I stole a bottle and drank it in the shadow of our brick bi-level.

It didn't make me feel drunk. It made me feel a little bit sick. From my bunk bed a half hour later—where our brother Jack slept above me, seemingly immune to the low self-esteem Caleb and I inherited from our father walking out when we were kids—I could hear the boys fighting over who drank the last beer, but no one ever figured it was me, because I was ten and still messing around with cap guns and frogs.

But from that night on, all I ever wanted was the next drink. Which was easy to get, because my brothers and my mother always had something in the fridge I could steal.

In junior high school, I became good pals with the truancy officer in the area. He'd pick me up from home a few mornings a month when I'd oversleep from a hangover and bring me to school in the back of his cop car.

"You know, son, I think I know why you're oversleeping."

"So?"

"So I think you should know that if you get caught drinking at your age, you won't be allowed to get a driver's license."

"So?"

"So don't you want to get a car and drive the girls around? Don't you want to get a job and grow up and make some money?"

"No."

He sighed. "Well then, you'd better get used to sitting in the back of squad cars," he said. "Because I've got my eye on you."

Mostly, I'd steal liquor from my mother, or from her friends' houses when I went to mow their lawns on the weekend. Then I'd go to the 99¢ noon matinee and drink up through whatever movie was playing at the time. I was a complete drunk by the time I was in tenth grade. I got a part-time job at the Burger King at the end of our road, and started stealing from the till once I found a manager who would buy me a fifth of Jack Daniel's at the state liquor store. That job lasted three months. Then I got a job at the Snappy Mart across the road. Rather than steal from the till, I started to give wrong change to customers for my booze money. It worked, too. I got really good at reading people to see if they'd count their change or not. The best were distracted mothers who either had kids with them or left them in the car, with one eye always toward the window. They never checked their change, and if they did, by the time they noticed I'd shorted them five bucks, they had the kids strapped into the car and wouldn't bother coming back in.

The worst, of course, were old men. Old men always count change.

That job lasted a while. Almost two years. I'd short-change enough people each night to pay Caleb for a trip to the liquor store or beer distributor. My boss didn't mind me working drunk, and ~~Cindy~~ Sindy, my girlfriend since junior high, didn't mind me not buying her anything. She'd say, "I don't love you for your money."

I dropped out of high school after Christmas my senior year. The vice principal had it in for me and gave me detention every day for not making it to detention every day before that. But I told him I had a job and couldn't miss it.

"If you felt the same way about school, you wouldn't be in this position in the first place."

"I work until midnight and I'm tired," I'd say. But really,

I'd work until midnight, drink until about four, and then pass out until noon, when I'd decide, ultimately, that I'd missed too much of the school day to go in. My mother had given up on me long before the vice principal did. Our last conversation about school, while she signed the forms the vice principal gave me to drop out, went something like this:

"Why couldn't you be more like Jack?"

"I don't know," I said. "I wish I could be." Jack loved school. Loved dissecting frogs, doing word problems, going to football games, and dating cheerleaders. He was already in college, learning how to make money off money.

"At least Caleb got a trade. At least he got something."

"Yeah. He was lucky." Caleb was a cabinetmaker and worked in a shop making kitchens.

She looked up from signing and slapped the pen down on the table. "Damn it, Kenny! When're you gonna stop blaming everyone else for your shit? Caleb isn't lucky! He's responsible!"

What I'd meant was, Caleb was lucky to land a job and keep it while being a closet drunk. Because he had my father's drinking genes, too.

In the end, I went to AA first, after one night babysitting Vera when she was seven months old. She wouldn't stop crying and it started to drive me crazy and I thought, just for a split second—a split second that would turn out to be life-changing—that I should shake her or stuff her head in a pillow or something to make her stop. The only reason she was crying was because I was too drunk to remember to feed her. Lucky for both of us, ~~Cindy~~ Sindy came home from the club and found me half nuts, pacing the house, hugging the baby, crying like Vera was. I remember she said, "Ken, look at you! You're worse than *her*!"

The next day, I went to my first meeting. Caleb followed me eight years later, after losing three of his fingers to a table saw because he was drinking on the job.

I've warned Vera about the drinking genes, but she acts like it's funny. She jokes about stripper genes too, but she's too young to understand the situation ~~Cindy~~ Sindy was in when she was born and I was drunk. Plus, youth is judgmental. With time, she will experience enough shit to free her own demons. I just wish I could give her a ticket to pass Go faster.

KEN DIETZ'S FLOW CHART OF DESTRUCTIVE BEHAVIOR

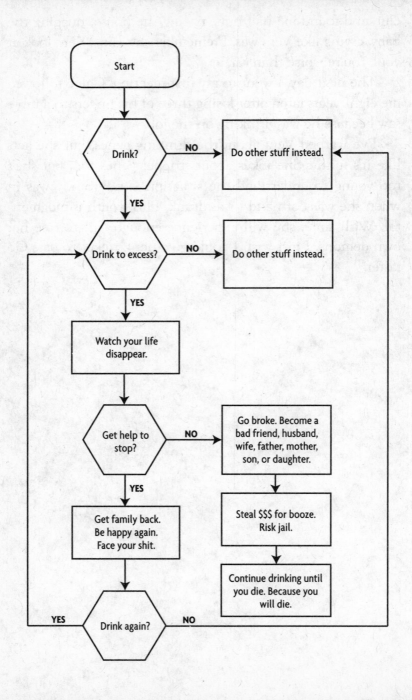

MONDAY, JANUARY 2ND

Here's me *not* using *fainéant* in a sentence.

My Vocab teacher, Mrs. Buchman, looks concerned. I failed. I didn't even try to guess. My head hurts and no matter how much gum I chew, my mouth is like a highway in lower New Mexico.

"Vera, I'm concerned," she says.

"I just forgot. I don't know what got into me," I say, but what I mean is: *Who gives Vocab words over Christmas break?*

"This might lower your grade," she says. But I don't care, because all I can think about is James and whether I'll ever see him again. I imagine him in the small police station over in Mount Pitts getting his mug shot taken. I imagine him having to leave Pagoda Pizza. I imagine him leaving me no note, no number, no word. Like, maybe the universe is trying to save me from my destiny now that I've given up on saving myself.

Still, I walk around cocky all day. I have a secret life. All these idiots are caught up in their stupid sports or their college choices. They're caught up in trivial fashion or who's getting laid or who's snorting coke or who likes what music or who's going to the prom with who. And I have a full-time job, a twenty-three-year-old boyfriend, and a secret binge-drinking problem.

I arrange a ride to work from Matt Lewis—my Vocab partner. He drives a VW Beetle—a vintage one. He has self-decorated the entire interior with Sharpie marker manga-style drawings and it is the coolest thing ever.

Right before the end-of-day bell rings, the secretary comes on the intercom and makes the usual announcements. All the kids who did something dumb to get detention today (Bill Corso and Jenny Flick and their minions) are called to the assistant principal's office. Then she says, "And will Vera Dietz please report to the office. Vera Dietz to the office."

As I approach the glass-enclosed office, I see Dad there, waiting, leaning over the front counter, talking to the secretary. When I walk in, he turns to me and says, "Are you ready to go?"

"Go where?"

"Work."

"I have a ride, Dad. Really—you can go."

"Go and get your things. I'm here." He's cold and weirdly robotic.

"But I have to tell Matt not to wait for me."

"That's fine. I'll be here."

So I go to Matt's locker and tell him I don't need a ride. Then I go to my own locker, pull out the books I need, and head back to the office. I see Dad through the glass wall, still talking to the secretary, and I sit down on the padded bench outside the door until he's finished.

When we get to the car and I click my seat belt into place, he says, "I got you the night off."

He's freaking me out. He's too chipper. He's like a happy maniac.

"From work?"

"Marie says she'll see you tomorrow."

My whole body goes a little bit numb when I hear that he talked to Marie. I want to ask him if he asked Marie about James. I want to ask him if he knows where James is and if he's okay. But I don't ask him anything, because he's driving with that weird fake-happy look on his face, as if he's about to chop me up into little pieces and feed me to a tiger.

When we get home, he gives me a bowl of dried fruit and granola and a glass of milk. Talk about weird. This was my favorite after-school snack when I was a little kid. Before I can comment about how weird he's acting, he hands me the phone and a phone number scrawled on a sky-blue piece of notepaper. ~~Cindy~~ Sindy—702-555-0055. My mother. She changed the C to an S when she left us.

"I'm not calling her."

"Yes you are."

"How is this a good idea?"

He puts his hand up, as if nothing I say will change his mind. Because nothing I say will change his mind. "I'm going outside to clean up some branches. You talk to her. She's smarter than you think."

Smarter than I think? Do I think she's dumb? Huh. Yeah.

I guess I do. Wow. Well, let's see just how smart she is, then. 1-702-555-0055. Rings once. Rings twi—

"Vera?"

"Hi, Mom."

"Don't you 'Hi, Mom' me. What the hell are you doing? Trying to kill your father?"

"Whoa. Hey. Happy New Year to you, too."

"Don't be impudent."

Wow, she just used *impudent* in a sentence. Awesome. Now I don't know what to say. I haven't talked to my mother in six years—since the day she left—and now she's yelling at me as if she cares?

"Did you hear me?" she says.

"Yeah."

"So? Let's hear it. I don't have all day."

I can't seem to harness my hate for her, and it seems she's having the same problem. I am instantly aware that she left us because she never wanted to have me. I am instantly aware that I don't want her to come back, either.

I say, "What did Dad tell you?"

"You were out drinking with a twenty-three-year-old man last night and were lucky not to lose your goddamn license because of it."

"Oh." So he knows I was drinking, and he knows how old James is.

"He also told me you were planning on driving yourself home. Is that true?"

"I guess," I answer, still computing the information that my dad knows way more than he lets on.

"Are you that stupid?"

"Charming, Mom."

"Seriously, Vera. Are you that hellishly stupid?"

I don't say anything.

"Are you there?"

I don't say anything. I notice I'm tearing up a little.

"Look, I know when your boyfriend died it was hard on you, but—"

"Charlie wasn't my boyfriend."

"Well, whatever he was. I know you took it hard."

I don't say anything. I hate her. She doesn't even know me. She doesn't know what happened. She doesn't know about Zimmerman's. Or about Jenny Flick. Or about the screaming parakeets. Or about any of it.

"You don't know anything about that, Mom."

"I knew Charlie, Vera. I *did* live there for twelve years."

"Not like that counts anymore," I say.

Surprisingly, she doesn't answer this. There's silence on the phone, and I munch on the dried fruit Dad gave me. Is it just a coincidence that I am eating a ten-year-old's snack and simultaneously feeling like a ten-year-old because I'm talking to my mother?

"You may hate me for saying this, Vera, but don't make yourself a slut this early in life."

I do. I do hate her for saying that.

"Vegas is full of girls who thought putting out a lot was a high idea once, but now they're just washed-up jokes sliding themselves around oiled poles."

She is comparing me to Las Vegas strippers. Who told her I was making a slut out of myself? Who told her I was doing anything more than drinking occasional vodka?

"Some of them think this is a really hip way to live, you know. Freedom from the oppression of men! Sexuality personified! Morons, Vera. Morons. I met one the other day reading Whitman. She said it made her smart even though at night she's taking her clothes off for money. Making a joke out of herself. Making a joke out of all of us. Don't make a joke out of yourself."

"Okay, Mom. I get the point. No stripping or turning into a hooker—intellectual or otherwise. Gotcha."

"I'm serious. These girls used to think it was no big deal to down a few drinks at the pagoda with a college dropout, too."

I'm irate now. There is no other way to describe it. If she were in the room with me, I'd pick up sharp things and throw them at her.

"Okay, I'm done," I say. "I really don't give a shit what you think. And thanks for the fifty bucks on my birthday every year. I'm sure it will make a huge dent in my college tuition. You're the best mom ever." I hang up, roughly.

Before she can call back and yell at me (though I doubt she will, because she was as forced into that call as I was) I pick up the phone and get a dial tone, and then leave it off the hook.

HISTORY—AGE FOURTEEN

I sat in homeroom that morning thinking about what Charlie told me on the bus. I thought back to all the times I climbed the Master Oak with him, and all the times we hiked the blue trail. Suddenly, every time I ever saw his buttcrack rushed back at me in a vivid slide show I never wanted to watch. I used to think Charlie just wore low-riding boxers or something. He was skinny, and his jeans and shorts often landed right around his hipbones. I just figured, like everything else about him, this was another way Charlie could be sloppy. But now it was different. This was not the same as greasy hair or ripped-up flannel shirts. My mental list looked like this:

- Every day in the cafeteria while we ate lunch, when he leaned forward.
- Every day on the bus, when he leaned forward.
- When we built the tree house and the deck (at least two hundred times as he ascended and

descended that ladder). Especially the time I asked him as a joke if he was going to be a plumber. He was so mad!

- When he leaned forward for handfuls of chips on the glide-o-lounger at Sherry Heller's New Year's Eve party.
- The time we went canoeing on the lake.
- The time at Santo's Pizza after Dad dropped us off. Charlie leaned over the table to snatch my purse to get the dumb picture of him from fourth grade that was in my wallet.
- Every time we sat on the big rocks at the end of the blue trail to scrape the dog crap off our shoes.
- The time he got that buck behind our houses and dragged me out of bed to see it lying there, dead. I remember thinking, *Who forgets to put on underwear when it's twenty degrees outside?*

The more I thought about it, the more I realized that Charlie had been without underwear a lot over the last few years. I tried to remember when he was missing his socks, too, but then the thought of the pervert in the white Chrysler popped into my head. Surely he hadn't been doing this since we were eleven. Had he? Everything rushed back. The night in the tree house when he disappeared. The times I heard a car turning around in the gravel at night. The times Charlie had new things—not just cigarettes. The Zippo. The pair of fake Ray-Ban sunglasses. The turquoise and silver ring he wore. Only the week before, the new MP3 player. Not an iPod, but close enough. Could dirty underwear really buy a new MP3 player?

When I saw him at lunch that day, I had a bunch of questions.

"So—you just give him your underwear?" I asked.

Charlie laughed and laughed. "Yeah."

"And what does he do with it?"

"I dunno. I just give it to him. I don't really care what he does with it."

He was embarrassed and wouldn't look me in the eye, but he was laughing, too. He really thought this was funny.

"What about the night you left me in the tree house?"

"What about it?"

"You were gone for hours," I said.

He laughed. "John and I just sat around and smoked and talked about the world," he said.

John. John and I.

"Is he the guy from the day when we were eleven? In the white car, who said my pigtails were pretty?"

He nodded, still smiling. "Yep."

"Are you sure he's not—um—dangerous?"

He leaned toward me and said, "He's harmless, Vera. He's loaded—he inherited millions from his parents—and he has a thing for underwear. I've been to his house. He has it in Ziploc bags, labeled by date and piled up in his computer room. I think he might sell it on eBay."

"On eBay?"

He laughed again. "Well, pervert eBay or something."

"How do you know he's harmless?"

"I don't know how to explain it, but I—uh—I trust him." He was so confident about this—about this trust—that I saw clearly the hole in Charlie's process. What does a boy who's witnessed what Charlie's witnessed know about trust? How does a boy like that discern right from wrong?

Charlie moved into the tree house as soon as school was over in June. Now that he had his deck and his screened windows, he looked for other ways to improve it, so since he'd just finished his eighth-grade shop class introduction to electricity and had a wad of underwear cash, he decided he'd get some sort of electric out there so he could run a fan on hot nights and listen to his radio without having to use up so many batteries.

The summer was unbearably sticky. When I walked anywhere near the forest, the gnats stuck to me and flew into my eyes, mouth, and ears, and it drove me crazy. Dad finally shelled out for central air-conditioning, now that he worked at home, and it was too easy to stay inside and comfortable rather than go and help Charlie wire the tree house. Plus, electricity scared me. Always had, ever since I'd stuck the tip of a dinner fork into the toaster to pry out an Eggo whole wheat waffle and got a little zap from it.

Mika's Diner closed three months after I started working there, and because of the up-and-down economy, regular people were taking summer jobs that used to be saved for students. Even college students were having trouble finding decent jobs that summer, so Dad agreed that I could take the volunteer position at the adoption center on Wednesdays and Fridays. I hoped to see more of Mr. Zimmerman so he could get to know me better and like me enough to hire me to work in the store one day, but he was so busy between the store and taking care of his wife, who was at home with cancer, we rarely saw him. When he did take the time to visit, the adoption center ladies fawned over him.

I asked him, on a hot Wednesday in July while we all ate ice pops, "Did you know I've dreamed of working in your store since I was five?"

He laughed. "Since you were five?"

"Yep."

"That was probably back when we only had one unit. Remember that, Elle?" Mrs. Parker, the volunteer manager, nodded. "How old are you now?" he asked.

"Fourteen."

"Come back to me when you're seventeen and I might make your dreams come true," he said, winking.

Mrs. Parker told me that he always hired seniors the summer before their last year in school. She hinted that if I kept volunteering, I'd have a better chance and he'd "remember my face." Of course, Dad probably wouldn't allow me to volunteer if there were paying jobs around, but it was nice to daydream.

No matter what I did in summer while I lived under his roof, I knew that when I could, I wanted to work with animals, whether Dad liked it or not. Humans just couldn't love unconditionally like animals could. Humans were too complicated. Mrs. Parker had the perfect bumper sticker on the back of her ugly Subaru hatchback. THE MORE I KNOW PEOPLE, THE MORE I LOVE MY DOG. When I told her how much I liked it, she got me one, too, and when I showed it to Charlie, he plastered it on the door of the tree house before I could tell him not to. I mean, wasn't it stupid to have that on the door when neither one of us had a dog? Plus, the tree house had always been more his than mine, and that summer, though I still considered Charlie my best friend in the whole world, I kind of wanted to have a bit of individuality or something. I wanted the bumper sticker for myself.

We both would turn fifteen that fall. He was starting to grow fluff on his chest. I was starting to feel attracted to him more than I ever had before, and I felt totally lame about it. There was no way, now that we were going to go to high school, that I was going to have a real crush on Charlie Kahn—especially if I wanted to slip through high school quietly, with no one noticing I was an ex-stripper's daughter.

Plus, one day in August, I went out to the tree house when he wasn't there and I found a few porno magazines sticking out from under his bedside milk crate. From then on, I couldn't picture Charlie sitting there contemplating the spirit of the Great Hunter. I couldn't see him drawing plans for his next octagonal addition or a crazy idea for how to make his own solar panels. From then on, I saw him more like a real boy, and not a superhero.

I had promised myself to avoid my mother's destiny by staying boy-free until after college, and I knew that once I went looking, I'd need a man like Dad—dependable and respectful toward women, and *not* into porn or weird rich old guys who bought teenage kids' underwear. But promises aside, Charlie Kahn was still the most exciting boy I had ever met, and part of me (the part we learned about in biology class) wanted nothing more than to run off with him the minute I could, and leave Mount Pitts behind us where it belonged.

PART THREE

MONDAY, JANUARY 2ND—NIGHT OFF

The phone makes that beeping noise once it's off the hook for too long and I can hear it from the sliding door, where I'm standing, watching Dad pick up winter debris. I feel an urge to escape, but then I remember that my car is still at Pagoda Pizza. And really—is there any realistic way to escape how much I hate my mother right now? (Which Zen guy said, "Man's main task in life is to give birth to himself"?)

Dad sees me and raises his chin to acknowledge me. My need to escape inflates exponentially and the beeping on the phone is getting annoying, so I walk over and hang it up. But I want to know what happened to James last night, so I pick it up again and call Pagoda Pizza, and Marie answers.

"Hey, Marie—it's Vera."

She laughs a bit. "Hey, Vera. You okay? Your dad said you're sick."

"I'm fine," I say. "Is James there?"

"Yeah. Hold on. He's in the back."

I hear her yell for him and I feel relieved. He didn't go to jail or lose his job. Everything is fine.

"Hey," he says.

"Hey. What happened to you last night?"

"They let me go with a warning. I only had two beers. You working tomorrow?"

"I think so. I have to convince my dad to drive me over there to pick up the car."

There's a brief, awkward silence as I realize that this is our first phone call. For some reason, this causes me to realize our age difference again. I remember what my mother just said to me. I wonder if James thinks I'm making a joke out of myself.

"I had a great time last night," he says.

"Me too."

"I hope we can do it again soon."

"Me too," I say.

Dad's still outside, finishing his lawn cleanup, so I go upstairs. Thirty minutes later, after a hot shower and a quick run through half my vocabulary words for the week (*incandescent*, *contumacious*, *ingratiate*, *chawbacon*, and *banausic*), I find my father on the white den couch, reading the *New Yorker*.

"Dad?"

"One second."

I go to the kitchen and fix myself a plate of cheese and fruit. This is a novelty. Another snack, time to study, an extra shower. It's like I'm a normal kid or something. The view from our breakfast bar is dead forest. It reminds me of Charlie, so I usually eat facing away from the window, but today I want to think about Charlie. I look out to where he showed me his first buck and I remember his smile and the way he'd look up through his unkempt bangs, how he'd look at me that flirta-tious way, and how I'd ignore it. I pop a grape into my mouth and think about how maybe the whole thing was my fault. Maybe if I hadn't been so hell-bent on not becoming my par-ents, I could have saved Charlie. Maybe I would have been his girlfriend. Maybe we could have gotten married and been happy, regardless of who our parents were and what they did to each other.

We have a bird feeder out there that every squirrel in the forest is trying to infiltrate, which drives Dad crazy. Now, there's a red-headed woodpecker making the thing swing, and cardinals dot the forest scrub with red coats, waiting until the bigger birds have their fill.

Dad sits down across from me and folds his hands to-gether. "We need to talk," he says.

I nod and chew on my mouthful of cheese.

"I talked to your manager today and she told me that you and James have been working together for months."

"So?"

"Is that how long this has been going on?"

Oh man. What a dork. "No. Last night was our first 'date,' if that's what you mean." I brought my fingers up to make the quotes around *date*.

"He's twenty-three."

"And I'm eighteen. And he's a nice guy, so who cares how old he is?"

"I do," he says. "And before you get all high-and-mighty—'I'm eighteen and can do what I want'—with me, you might want to consider your options." He's so calm, it's starting to spook me out.

"My options?"

"You live under my roof, which means you still have to do what I say."

"Geez. Are you going to take away my allowance next and ground me for a month? For liking a boy?"

I push my plate aside and stare at him. He's serious.

"My main concern at the moment is your work schedule. Can you work with this man and stop being friendly with him?"

"Oh my God—can you *please* stop being so weird?"

He sighs. "I'm not being *weird*. I'm your father and it's my job to make sure you—you, uh"—he looks around the kitchen for his next word—"it's my job to make sure you don't make any mistakes."

I laugh. "Oh, come on! Who doesn't make mistakes?"

"I didn't mean it that way. I know everyone makes mistakes," he says. "But you know. The same mistakes we—your mother and I—did."

I really can't believe he just said that. "I can't believe you just said that."

He shrugs. Inside my head, there are a million angry monkeys.

"No. Seriously, Dad, think about it. Was Mom working a full-time job and saving up for college when she was eighteen? Was she making good grades? Or was she too busy picking dollar bills out of her G-string to study?"

"Don't—"

I cut him off. "I'm not YOU. Okay? I'm not MOM. I'm ME."

He breathes deeply through his nose. I see his diaphragm move. In. Out. In. Out.

"You didn't answer my question," he says.

I stare at him until he repeats it. "Can you continue to work with this man and control yourself?"

Inside, the monkeys are Kubrick monkeys. Inside, I'm saying, *Control myself? CONTROL MYSELF?* But when I open my mouth, it says, "Okay—fine. I won't hang out with James anymore. No problem. For God's sake, Dad. I'm not some sex-crazed tramp. He's just a friend and we grew to like each other."

"Stop making it sound innocent."

"It *is* innocent."

"Not if he's twenty-three, it isn't."

He walks over to the coat rack and pulls something out of his coat pocket—a handful of pamphlets—and brings them over to the table. Two cardinals balance on the bird feeder behind him.

Teen Drinking. Talking to Your Child About Alcohol Abuse. DUI. Drinking and Driving. Making Responsible Decisions. Peer Pressure. Teens and Drugs.

"Will you read these?"

Is he serious?

"Vera, I don't know how long you've been drinking and I don't know if you understand how bad it is for your body or how susceptible to alcoholism your genes make you, but more important to me, you planned on driving home last night. You can never do that. Never. Do you understand me?"

"Yes, Dad."

"You're smarter than that."

"Yes, Dad."

"Especially after that Brown kid last year." Kyle Brown. Fifteen. Killed by a drunk college kid while he walked home from his neighbor's house.

"Yes, Dad."

"I'm not raising another one of these senseless, irresponsible idiots!"

"I know. I don't know what I was thinking."

"You *weren't* thinking. That's the problem," he says. "You can't ever let that happen again."

"I won't."

"And you can't drink anymore. Obviously. I mean, you're not even legal, Veer."

"I know. It was stupid."

He takes a deep, disappointed breath and it's over. *Thank God.* He putters around the den, tidying, and I read the brochures. Stuff I learned in grade school, when the D.A.R.E. cops used to come around and teach us about the so-called war on drugs. Alcohol kills brain cells. Alcohol causes depression. Alcohol causes memory loss. Nowhere does it say, "Alcohol causes your dead friend to show up in the form of inflatable two-dimensional aliens."

Nowhere does it say, "Alcohol numbs the pain." But I know it does.

Two hours later, after dinner, after I memorize the rest of my Vocab words (*ephemeral, exacerbate, jettison, vacuous, gumption*) and after I vacuum the upstairs and clean both bathrooms, Dad takes me to Pagoda Pizza to pick up my car.

"Can I tell Marie that I'll be back to work tomorrow?" I ask this because I'm really not sure of anything. He seems to be a new person. Robo-Dad. I ask this because James's car isn't in the lot, and he could be back any minute, and I want to see him.

"Of course."

"You can go," I say, before I shut the door.

"Nah," he says, "I'll follow you home."

So I tell Marie that I'll see her tomorrow while Dad watches me, and then I get into the car and drive down the hill and onto the main strip. Dad drives behind me the whole way home. I ask Charlie, "If I tell him now, will you leave me alone?" not knowing what I want the answer to be.

FOUR WEEKS LATER—SUPER BOWL NIGHT— FOUR TO CLOSE

Every driver we have is here, even drivers I never knew existed. This is the craziest day in pizza delivery.

We've been folding extra boxes all week, but still, all the part-timers are back on the steps folding more. Marie is sweating, but that's only because BMW-driving Greg is coming in—to help. Oh boy. Last time he came, he snafued half the runs because he didn't know there was a road connecting Butter Lane and Lisa Avenue, and he got upset when he splashed sauce on his beige preppy dickhead wide-lined corduroys.

When I see him pressing the lock button on his keychain for the Beemer in the parking lot (where it would never get robbed), a bunch of recent Vocab words come to mind.

Here's me using *exacerbate* in a sentence. Greg thinks he helps on busy nights, but really, he only exacerbates the problem.

Here's me using *dickwad* in a sentence. Greg is such a dickwad, he locks his car in the Pagoda Pizza parking lot. (No. That isn't a real Vocab word.)

The rest of the night is a complete blur of boxes and hot bags and change and six-packs and twenty-dollar bills. I see winning men and losing men. I see happy fans, sad fans, and mad fans. Did you ever hear the statistic about Super Bowl night? How there's a spike in wife beatings? I think of that statistic when I see the mad fans.

By midnight, we've slowed down. Greg struts out of the store like he's some sort of hero, even though he managed to drop two pizzas (no kidding) facedown onto the floor during the rush. I've never seen anyone do that—not even people who are on serious drugs.

The phones have stopped ringing and Marie is cashing out the part-timers who came in to help. I go out to my car, pull out the Dunkin' Donuts bag from the backseat, and count my tips. $109. James comes out and slips into my passenger's seat.

"You sly dog! That's more than I made tonight."

"Yeah—I kept getting burb runs. Tough luck, big guy."

He leans in and kisses me and I kiss him back, but only for a second. I don't want Marie to see us. I don't want anyone to see us. For the last four weeks, we've only made out in covert places. Like the bathroom in the back of the store, or behind the Dumpster. Once, we drove up to the pagoda again, but instead of parking where all the other morons park to make out, we went farther down the road to the old parking lot, and we didn't bring any booze.

I get my cash bag ready to cash out and scribble my total

on a napkin so I don't forget it. When we get inside and Marie starts counting cash, she asks us both, "You coming to the Christmas party?"

I look at her, confused. Christmas is a month gone. She explains that the annual Pagoda Pizza Christmas party has always been on the second Friday in February, because Super Bowl night marks the end of our busiest season.

"You have to come," James says.

"Sure," I answer. "Where is it?"

"Greg got us the fire company in Jackson," Marie says.

"They have a great bar," James adds, smiling.

Marie stops to look at us and then shakes her head and goes back to counting. She compares her numbers to the computer's numbers and punches in a bunch of decimals for our commission. She pays us that and a bonus, which makes my Super Bowl total $185 cash, plus the eight bucks an hour I'll get in my next paycheck. Not too shabby for one night's work.

James goes out for a smoke and I take a quick bathroom break before closing duties. I put my face really close to the mirror and try to see inside my brain. I try to get the Charlies to come and suffocate me. I breathe on the mirror and beg him to write something. He doesn't. I wonder why not. Is he using reverse psychology? Does he think I'll tell if he stops haunting me? Doesn't he know it's more complicated than that? That it's not all about *him*?

When I step out of the bathroom, James is at the big sink, filling the bucket. "Jill already did the dishes, so all I have to do is mop. You want to take off early? I know you have school in the morning."

Why isn't Dad here to hear this? He'd love James if only he gave him a chance. God. I mean, compared to some of the real creeps in school—the ones who cling to Jenny Flick as if she's some sort of rock star because she gives out—James is an angel.

SECOND MONDAY IN FEBRUARY—
FIVE DAYS UNTIL PARTY NIGHT

Sometimes just thinking about Jenny Flick draws her into my life, you know? Like that law-of-attraction stuff Dad's always talking about. When I drive into the school parking lot this morning, she's there, next to her car, putting lipstick on, waiting for the rest of her stupid little gang.

She glares at me as I drive by. She thinks she's intimidating me.

When she glares at me like this, I wonder if she's dreaming up new lies about me, even though Charlie isn't here to hear them. I wonder if she's inventing new ways to steal sympathy from her friends—new diseases to feign to make them more loyal. Maybe she's trying to scare me into disappearing. Maybe she's afraid I'll tell the truth about the animals. Maybe she knew all along that even dead, Charlie would like me more.

I hear giggling while I'm at my locker before my Modern

Social Thought class. It's Bill Corso. He's whispering to some other Detentionheads and looking at me. Of course, Jenny Flick sent him. He's like her horde of flying evil monkeys or something.

I shrug it off. Today is table two's day to read *Lord of the Flies*, and I'm looking forward to watching Bill Corso struggle through every word.

Here's me using *indolent* in a sentence.

My MST classmates are so indolent, they wouldn't read the book for homework, so the teacher is making us read it aloud to shame us.

We get there, and the bell rings, and everyone gets out their paperback and Mr. Shunk says, "Page twenty-five," and looks at his notebook. "You—in the black—read."

Mr. Shunk acts like a drill sergeant, but only because he has to. Dad knows him and says he's not like this in real life.

Gretchen, one of Jenny Flick's best pals, starts reading from the book. We're at the beginning, Chapter Two, where the kids are only just realizing that they're going to have to fend for themselves. They are discussing how there are pigs on the island. How they will have to hunt and kill.

"Next," Mr. Shunk says, and the quiet kid next to Gretchen starts.

While he reads the part where the little kid asks the bigger kids about the scary beastie in the woods, I daydream. I've read *Lord of the Flies* twice now. I know what's going to happen. (**SPOILER ALERT**—Piggy dies.) But I forgot about the little kid and the snake in the woods. How they told him that he was making it up, and how being called a liar freaked him out because he wasn't lying. I know that feeling.

"Next." The kid stops reading and Heather Wells starts. She's a nervous reader and reads too quietly, mumbling into her neck.

Bill Corso is sitting next to her and looks worried. He fidgets. Then, about a paragraph into Heather's reading, he gets up and grabs a lav pass from Mr. Shunk's desk. He sees me watching him and glares. When he's directly behind Mr. Shunk, he makes a V with his two fingers and wiggles his tongue between them.

Twenty minutes pass and Bill is still not back. The bell rings and we pack up for sixth period. I take my time because I have sixth-period lunch and I don't feel like rushing. With only four of us left in the room, Bill returns and hands Mr. Shunk a note.

"Sorry. Coach saw me and needed me to help him out down in the gym," he says.

"Put the pass back on my desk," Mr. Shunk says, not looking up from his notebook.

"'Kay, Teach."

"Tomorrow you'll read us Chapter Three, Mr. Corso."

Bill nods as if that didn't scare him, but I know it did.

SECOND FRIDAY IN FEBRUARY—PARTY NIGHT

Bill Corso skipped the rest of the week of school. I don't know if Gretchen or any of the other Flickites are telling him this, but each day, Mr. Shunk says, "I guess I'll have to wait another day to hear the dulcet tones of Mr. Corso reading Golding."

No one gets this but me, and I feel, even though Mr. Shunk doesn't know it, that he and I are on the same team.

Tonight is the Pagoda Pizza Christmas party over at Jackson Fire Company, which my dad says used to be the kind of place where you'd watch girls with tassels on their boobs dance. He told me Mom used to bust out laughing because there was always one girl who was new to it, and went off beat, like a washing machine with one lumpy towel. There are too many things wrong with this description for me to actually process it. I need to teach Dad the meaning of TMI.

"So what makes you think I'm going to let you go?" he asks.

"Because you trust me and you want me to have some fun in my life?"

"Are you even allowed into that place? You're underage."

"It's a private party. Even Barry's kid is going to be there. He's, like, fifteen or something."

He doesn't say anything.

"I think they're having a turkey dinner, too, so you won't even have to feed me before I go," I say.

He nods and starts reading the paper.

I have three hours to wait out at home before I leave, so I do some homework and clean my room. I'm on the deck, shaking out my throw rug, when I see movement in the trees. I stop. Stare. A blinding reflection, like a mirror makes in sunlight, is flashing at me. I know the thousand Charlies are there, calling me to the tree house. I can hear their faint whispering.

So I hang my rug over the banister on the deck and walk a few steps toward the woods. It's a quiet day. The road is through with school buses for the week and the rush home hasn't started yet. The sun is low. There are no aliens. No accordion dolls coaxing me into the trees.

I cup my hands around my mouth and yell, "Karma's a bitch, eh, Charlie?" Then I pick up the broom and start beating the dust out of the rug.

Dad stays in the den after his small dinner and doesn't give me the lecture about responsibility that I'm expecting. He just says, "Be smart, Vera. Have a good time."

I drive to Jackson, where I find James already at the fire company bar, and he orders me a vodka cooler. Next to him are two people I don't recognize at first. But then I realize the brown-haired woman is ex-cheerleader-turned-food-service-worker Jill (I'm just not used to seeing her without her uniform on), which means the tall guy in the black leather coat next to her is Mick, her skinhead Nazi boyfriend.

HISTORY—AGE FIFTEEN

Ninth grade was a blur. Charlie and I were separated by the plethora of new people we'd never met before who went to the other middle school. I was put in the advanced track and had some of my classes in the senior wing, which helped me achieve my main objective—getting through high school unnoticed by doing well enough to not draw attention, but not doing so well that I stuck out. I didn't want to get to know anyone, because eventually they would ask me about my parents, and I had to keep Mom's past a secret or I'd suffer the consequences. I liked pretending that I didn't have a mother, and that my father simply caught me when the stork dropped me from his crisp white sling.

Charlie and I still shared a seat on the bus. We'd press our earbuds into our ears and read or daydream or, in Charlie's case, occasionally scribble things on tissues or napkins and then eat them. On weekends, we'd see each other sometimes, but Charlie was busy between hunting trips with his father and dates. Girls swarmed him that year, impressed by his windswept attitude, his over-the-eyes haircut, and his Goodwill dress sense. By the time summer came, I think he'd had about four different girlfriends, but he kept them totally secret, and if I asked, he would deny it, as if having girlfriends wasn't cool.

He moved into the tree house when school ended and spent a lot of his time leafing through motorcycle magazines. We took an occasional hike on the blue trail and talked school gossip and career stuff (me = still vet or vet nurse, him = still forest ranger, but starting to lean toward more exotic things like roadie for a metal band or racing motorcycles). I thought about asking him to come with me to the licensing center when I finally got Dad to drive me there to pick up the rules-of-the-road study book, but he was keeping to himself a lot, and though we were still best friends, we were mature enough to give each other space. I'd be lying if I said I wasn't more cautious around him since he'd told me about John, his pervert underwear-buying friend. That year, I'd heard the car go up and down Overlook Road and turn into the gravel so much, I'd begun to recognize the sound of its sputtery engine from the bottom of the hill as it echoed off the Millers' clapboard house. It was so obvious, I couldn't believe Mr. and Mrs. Kahn hadn't figured it out yet. A few times, the thought of what that guy could be doing with Charlie's underwear crept up on me and made me want to tell Dad, but I didn't.

I volunteered Mondays, Wednesdays, and Fridays at the adoption center that summer. It took two arguments with Dad to convince him that these volunteer hours would count for something if I was one day going to be a vet. He was still hell-bent on me working fast food for minimum wage, because he said saving tuition money was more important. In the end, I was saved by the crappy economy again. Most fast-food jobs were taken by college students—or more accurately, by college graduates.

I slept late every day I wasn't at the center. At first, Dad would make sure I was out of bed by noon, but then he stopped arguing with me and let me do what I wanted. So I started to sleep until one. Until two. Sometimes I slept until four, the whir of the central air under my window blocking out the sounds of the world.

"Is everything okay, Vera?" he asked, around the end of July.

"Yeah."

"You're sleeping way too late."

"I think I'm growing a lot." This was true. I'd grown two inches in only a few months.

"So you're not depressed or anything?"

"No."

"Do you see Charlie much?"

"Sure," I said, sipping a glass of orange juice and wiping the sleep from my eye. "I think he has a girlfriend. I don't want to be in the way."

"A girlfriend?"

"I guess," I said. "I mean, isn't this when normal kids do things like that?"

He squinted at me, concerned. "And what about you?"

I laughed. "Not me. After what happened to you and Mom—uh, you know. No boyfriends for me."

He rested his chin in his hand. I could see the guilty thoughts tumbling down his wrinkled forehead. "Are you sure?"

"I'm sure. Boys only want one thing, Dad. And that's just boring."

"For now."

"What?"

"It's boring for now," he said. "One day you'll think it's great, I promise you."

Who changed the channel? What was with this wishy-washy crap? Wasn't this the same guy who'd been telling me to avoid my destiny my whole life?

"Yeah, well, I can't see that happening while I'm still in high school. All the boys there are dicks."

"Vera."

"Sorry. I meant jerks. All the boys there are jerks."

On Mondays at the adoption center, new animals arrived that the vet had spayed or neutered over the weekend, and it was my job to make sure that they recovered and to keep their paperwork up to date. On Fridays, we had to ready new animals for the procedure and get them organized for pick-up at five. In July, the day after my all-boys-are-dicks conversation with Dad, there was a long-haired Afghan hound who'd been found in the park, covered in dried mud/feces/who-knows-what. He was scheduled for surgery on Sunday. One of the younger volunteers washed him (twice) and then gave him to me to brush.

It took over two hours to comb out the knots, little by little, without hurting him. He sat still and quiet for the most part, but yipped when I accidentally caught his skin with the metal teeth. I was instantly reminded of my mother, who would comb my hair every morning while staring into space, never stopping to apologize when she pulled too hard or made me cry. She did so many things with that vacant look on her face—as if she was daydreaming of living somewhere else.

Most days I didn't think about my mother. She'd been gone three years, and a large part of me was happy about that. The older I got, the more I realized she'd never *really* been all there to begin with. The older I got, the more I realized that my happy-Mom memories were often fabrications invented to make me feel better about her being chronically unhappy.

Oddly, by midsummer, these sad realizations about my mother translated into a sort of talent. It started with a bet one day when a couple adopted a beagle I just *knew* they would return. Beagles are energetic, and these people looked like the type who liked constant calm.

When they left, I turned to Mrs. Parker and said, "I give them two days, tops." The next day, right before closing, they returned the dog and asked if we had anything older or more docile.

From then on, when people came to adopt, Mrs. Parker would walk them through the paperwork and then she'd refer them to me.

I liked this new interaction with people—asking seemingly innocent questions about how much they loved their furniture or wall-to-wall carpeting. I liked how Mrs. Parker trusted my judgment (she called me her secret weapon), and though it was sad to see an animal returned to us, I was elated when my few hunches turned out to be right.

In late August, we got a box full of rescued Shih Tzu puppies. They were crawling with fleas and covered in scars and cuts and scrapes from being kept in a tiny gerbil cage. One of their siblings had died from being suffocated by the others, who were piled in on top of it. Though they smelled like death and were covered in matted, sometimes bloody fur, I fell completely in love with them.

Mrs. Parker said they needed foster homes because they were too young to stay at the center on their own overnight. I volunteered to take one, even though I knew I shouldn't. She found two other homes and then dropped me off at my house after work with a Ziploc bag of puppy food and the usual how-to sheet we give out to adoptive families.

Dad was outraged. Seriously—a completely rational man turned to raging Hulk. Over a freaking puppy.

"You know how I feel about them," he said. Them. Like she was an it. Like she was a nothing.

"It's just for a few weeks," I argued, holding her in my arms, now washed and fluffy and sweet-smelling.

"No way, Vera. No way."

"I can keep her in the garage," I said.

He shook his head.

"In the shed?" What else did we keep there but hoes and shovels and rakes?

"No."

"Why not?" I finally asked.

"You know why not."

"Because dogs cost too much? Because they shed?"

"Actually, Vera, it's simple. You can't have the dog because I said you can't."

"Oh wow. Great." I rolled my eyes.

"It's my—"

"Yeah, yeah, yeah," I said, turning toward the hall and the front door. "I know. It's your house. I get it. Whatever." I went outside and sat on the front porch with the puppy in my lap for an hour. I figured the only way to keep her overnight was to pitch our old tent and sleep outside, which I did. It was one of the best nights of my life—cuddled close to the little thing, snuggling and listening to her snore. Even her meaty breath and the tiny pee she took on my sleeping bag were wonderful.

I didn't sleep much. I lay awake thinking about Dad and what it must be like to be a cold, heartless Vulcan. I wondered if he was like that *before* Mom left, or if that was what her leaving did to him. And if he was like that because she left, what did her leaving do to me? Was it possible that it turned him cold while simultaneously turning me warm? Beneath these thoughts I hid my biggest question. Did Dad realize he was treating this innocent puppy the way Mom had treated me my whole life? Like an unwanted extra responsibility? A pain in the ass? A mistake?

Around midnight, I heard the familiar car chugging up Overlook Road and pulling into the gravel. About fifteen minutes later, I heard footsteps outside the tent.

"Veer?" he whispered.

I unzipped and let Charlie in.

"What're you doing out here?" he asked. I showed him the puppy.

I didn't ask what he was doing out because we both knew what he was doing out.

"Are you gonna keep it?"

"I want to, but there's no way," I said.

"Bummer."

"Yeah."

It was dark and Charlie accidentally brushed his hand against my hip, and it caused waves of butterflies. I giggled under my breath.

"I guess I better get back to what I was doing," he said.

I nodded. "See you tomorrow."

The next morning, Dad drove me, the puppy, and the Ziploc of food to the adoption center and made me give her back. Mrs. Parker gave me a sympathetic look, and I felt the slap of irony hit—some secret weapon I turned out to be. I hadn't even judged *myself* accurately. When we got home, Charlie came over and invited me up to the tree house for lunch.

"I just got a fresh box of Noodle-o-Pak," he said, smiling. "Spicy."

I stopped in at Dad's office to tell him I was going. He was still in no-smiling mode from the whole puppy-hating Hulk thing.

I hadn't been to the tree house much that summer, and when I got up the ladder, I could tell Charlie had spent a lot of time working on it. He'd installed a pulley system to haul up a two-gallon water container he kept on the deck. There was a lot of new detail work. He'd started carving designs into the pine beams and had installed a homemade skylight in the roof, which was awesome.

"Holy shit!" I said. "That's so cool!"

He shrugged. "It leaks."

"I'm sure you can fix it, Charlie. You can fix anything."

"Meh," he answered. "What do you think of the rest?"

"Freaking awesome, man. The paint job. The posters. All awesome."

"And my kitchen?" he asked, gesturing to his electric kettle and a milk crate on its side that held cocoa mix, the box of Noodle-o-Pak Spicy, and two boxes of assorted-flavor instant oatmeal.

"Uh-huh. Great," I said.

After he filled the kettle and set it to boil, we sat on the octagonal deck. I noted the thinning leaves and felt a ball in my stomach. There is something about a dying forest that's sad, no matter how many times I reassure myself that it will come alive again in spring. And of course, autumn meant school. Our sophomore year would start in less than a week. Another 180 days of keeping my mother's secret. Another 180 days of sending out the PLEASE IGNORE VERA DIETZ signal so no one would even see me.

We swung our legs through the railing he'd made out of saplings. I had to admit my Noodle-o-Pak Spicy tasted extra nice that high up in the trees. Charlie told me about his new plan to do half days at the vocational school for either HVAC like his dad, or maybe carpentry, because he liked wood.

"Plus, it's not as boring as being at school all day. My dad says I'm a blue-collar guy, like he is." He sounded as if he was trying to convince himself more than me.

"Really? Huh."

"I like the idea of a Harley and a truck and a nice house one day. Working for a living, you know? Not like some accountant or— Oh. Sorry."

"I don't care," I said. "I'm not the accountant in the family."

"You know what I meant, right?"

"Yeah." He meant destiny, and I hated him for it. Because if we were all supposed to carbon-copy our parents, then I'd end up a brain-fried loser who runs away with a foot doctor, or a downtrodden Zen calculator. I was steering well clear of my destiny, thank you very much.

"Anyway, my dad said he'd buy me a bike if I went to Vo-Tech."

"A bike?"

"I have my eye on a little rice burner at The Corner." The Corner was a creepy car lot/gun shop with a small blinking sign on wheels that displayed a different Bible verse each month.

I wanted to ask him if this was his choice or his dad's. It didn't seem fair that no one had talked to him about college or any other options. It didn't seem fair that he'd get a free bike for doing what he was told rather than thinking for himself. It didn't seem right that he would be rewarded for turning into a trained monkey at the age of fifteen.

THE PAGODA PIZZA CHRISTMAS PARTY—
PART 1

"Tonight you will experience the snakebite," Mick says, and buys us all a round of shots. It tastes like sweetened lime juice and goes down smoothly. Except for the fact that a Nazi skinhead bought it for me.

But I'm trying to come to terms with it. It's where I live. God bless the USA, where you can love or hate anyone you want as long as you don't kill them doing either. I'm trying to see Mick as a *person*, you know? With a mother and father. As a baby—long before he got the word SKIN tattooed inside his lower lip.

The music starts after about two shots. Mick and Jill disappear into the poolroom and James and I sit at the bar, watching Marie and her look-alike husband step dance to country and western music. Fat Barry, the day manager from the store across town, joins in, and works up a red-faced sweat before the song is over.

James smokes a few cigarettes and orders me a beer.

"I don't like beer."

"You can't mix snakebites with vodka coolers, Veer. You'll hurl."

"But—"

"Just try it. It's not bad beer. He'll put a lime in it for you so it will taste fine after the shots."

The bartender brings me a Corona with lime and I monkey what James does with his. I push the lime past the lip of the bottle, into the gold beer. "What do you think of Mick?" I ask.

"You know."

"Yeah. Gives me the creeps," I say.

"Yeah. But he's here with Jill. And he seems to want to play friends, so why not?"

"Free drinks, right?"

He laughs. "Yeah."

An hour later, we're sitting at the plastic tablecloth–covered long tables, eating our plates of roast turkey. Thank God. Mick bought two more rounds in the last half hour, so I've had four snakebite shots, two beers, and a vodka cooler, and I was feeling a bit wobbly until I started eating this turkey. James keeps telling me to eat slowly.

The music starts again once the plates are cleared, and I make my way to the dance floor for "Black Dog" and bang my head, which makes James laugh. Marie pulls out her camera and snaps a few pictures of me. I'm certainly buzzed and I get dizzy moshing my head, my hair slapping me in the face, but I've still got balance. Though the turkey is sloshing around my stomach now, so I leave the dance floor before the song is over and go back to the bar, where James is working hard to fill the ashtray with butts.

"Another round for my friends!" Mick slurs.

I hold up my hand and smile. "No thanks, man. You can skip me this time around."

He gets in my face quickly and loudly. "Hey! What are you trying to say? You don't want my free drink?" I feel his breath. He's an inch away, with the angriest, most intimidating face I've ever seen. Ten times worse than Mr. Kahn.

I'm completely fucking scared. Then he laughs and steps back and says something like "I was messing around" or "I was joking" or "Take it easy," but I don't hear it because my adrenaline level has just tripled and all I can really hear is the blood going through my ears.

James puts his arm around me. "Don't worry about it. I'll take Vera's this time if she doesn't want it."

"Seriously, man. I was only kidding around."

"I know," I say. But they all know I'm lying.

"Two for the freaked-out chick, Keith!" Mick yells, and the bartender winks at him, which creeps me out even more. Suddenly I realize I don't know what they're putting in my drinks. I don't know if they have some skinhead Nazi master plan. I don't know anything. I'm a naïve eighteen-year-old girl who doesn't even belong in this bar.

I look around and see Marie and her husband hugging at the table, sucking down cigarettes, and occasionally locking crooked nicotine teeth. Fat Barry has brought his son, who is the only person in the room younger than I am. He looks like a stupid kid, sitting there between his mom and dad with his baseball cap on. I don't think he's moved all night, except when the dessert buffet came out. His mother used to be the playground lady for us when we were in elementary school, and I know she's an incurable gossip. Suddenly I want to play the rest of the night safe.

Actually, I want to leave.

An hour later, James has talked me into one slow dance, and has requested "Stairway to Heaven." We're acting like a couple, and everyone who comes around to talk to us is treating this like it's totally cool. Fat Barry even tells us we look like a cute pair—which is the kind of thing Dad would say if he'd just give James a chance. But of course, he won't. Because James is a whopping five years older than I am and he dropped out of college.

After the slow dance, my first ever, I'm in the bathroom—it's cruddy—and I look at myself in the mirror and touch up the small bit of brown eyeliner I'm wearing. I'm feeling more at ease than I was an hour ago, because these people can accept me for who I am. They can accept my feelings for James.

I'm even growing to like Mick, the skinhead Nazi. He tells funny jokes and has a very witty way about him. Better yet, he has a few set pieces about Corduroy Greg because he used to work for him, too, and hates the guy. When he sees a growing audience around the bar, he talks louder.

"What do the gynecologist and the pizza deliveryman have in common?"

"Dunno," I slur. I accept Mick's last snakebite shot because he's apologized for scaring me like ten times since he did it. He seemed sincere, too.

"They both get to smell the goods but neither one of them can eat it."

Though this isn't all that funny, I start to laugh uncontrollably, and I stumble enough for James to reach out and steady me.

"Veer? You okay?" he whispers into my ear.

"I want to get out of here soon," I answer, and he thinks I mean I want to make out. I know this because he winks at me, and it takes him all of thirty seconds to gather up his cigarettes and lighter from the bar and slip his coat on.

Mick sees this and quickly struts over with his mean face on. "Where do you think you're going?"

"Vera needs to get home, man."

"But the party's just starting!"

"Yeah—but we're going," James says.

"But I bought you all those drinks!"

"So what?"

"So, you were supposed to get the next round, asshole."

James reaches into his wallet, slaps thirty bucks on the bar, and nods to the bartender. "This should cover him and his girl for the rest of the night, okay?"

Mick walks over to me with his arms out, as if he wants to hug me, and I flinch into James's side. I do not want to hug a skinhead Nazi. Even if he might be okay. Even if he tells funny jokes. Even if he's really just a misunderstood nice guy who hates certain races of people.

"Aw, come on! You're not scared of little old Mick, are ya?"

I giggle because he's giggling. He has a huge smile. It

makes his lower lip curl out a bit, so I can see the very top of his SKIN tattoo.

He steps back like a 1950s sitcom dad and cocks his head, holding his arms out in the universal code for "Aw, come on, give me a hug!"

So I sheepishly separate from James and approach him.

He gets an excited look on his face and sweeps me off the ground before I can embrace him. He holds me around my hips, with my arms pinned down to my sides, so that my breasts are level with his forehead. And then he begins to wobble.

"Uh . . . uh . . . uh . . . ," he says. I wobble from side to side and try to get my hands free, but his grip is too strong. I start to kick my legs. I can feel he's losing his balance and I try harder to pull my arms free to catch myself.

But that doesn't happen.

He falls backward, and I see the hardwood floor coming at my face so fast, I can't even swear. Then, blackness.

HISTORY—AGE SIXTEEN

The first time Charlie got high school detention, it was for smoking. We were sophomores. I was an invisible sophomore and he was a Tech sophomore, just without the leather jacket yet. I told him a hundred times that he should wait to smoke until we got off the bus, but he couldn't help it. He had to take a few drags after lunch in the bathroom.

"This place doesn't understand addiction," he said. "They should pity me, not punish me."

Detention was a bore, he said, and he came back with stories of the regulars, who he called the Detentionheads, and he'd make fun of them. There was Bill Corso, a sophomore like us and the up-and-coming star quarterback. There was Frank Hellerman, a senior Vo-Tech kid who built souped-up cars on the weekends and was rumored to drag race out on Route 422. Last, there was Justin Miller, a junior—Tim's little brother—who was worse, Charlie said, than Tim was.

"A bunch of losers," he called them. "And the girls are

worse, because the only reason they're there is to follow the losers." He listed them. Jenny Flick, Gretchen So-and-so ("She's so dumb, Corso told her that humans mated with apes and created a half man–half ape and she believed him, Vera"), and some girl named Michelle who was a senior and always wore Deep Purple T-shirts. He said they all ignored him.

He got detention twice that month before he bought a pack of nicotine gum and chewed it instead of smoking because his dad said if he got detention again, no bike.

Meanwhile, I was busy bugging Dad for Mom's car, which had been locked up in the garage for four years at that point and was only taken out for an occasional run. It didn't make sense for a man so concerned with saving money to be wasting a car like that. Plus, I was sixteen and it was time for me to have it. He was reticent, and I reminded him that this was a step toward real self-sufficiency for me. I added, "You'll have to let me go sometime, right?"

He sat under the reading lamp, still pretending to read, and then turned to me. "Who's going to pay for the gas?"

"I will."

"With what?"

"I'll get a job."

We exchanged looks.

His look said, "Volunteering at the animal center isn't a job."

My look said, "Duh—who doesn't know that?"

"I'll think about it," he said.

"Can I take the permit test this weekend?" I asked. I'd been studying the rules of the road all summer, and my sixteenth birthday had passed two weeks before. (I got a savings bond and a gift certificate from Dad and the same lame fifty bucks my mom always sent me.)

Charlie got his bike a few weeks before Christmas. I got my license and a fast-food job, but Dad still wouldn't give me the car. Even when I got opening shift at Arby's and had to be there at 5:50 on Sunday mornings he'd get up and drive me. It sucked and didn't make any sense at all. Plus, I still had to take the school bus—now by myself, because Charlie would drive his bike to school, no matter the weather. I don't know how he got down Overlook Road, which was so full of grit, it made Dad slow down in his car, but he did, and it meant I had to sit on the bus by myself with all the other bus people. Most of them had cell phones and sat there with zombie looks on their faces, texting their friends in the next seat.

During Christmas break, Charlie arrived in our driveway clad in a full set of blue and red racing leathers. Up until then, I'd toyed with the idea of dating him, even though I knew I wasn't allowed. But seeing him in those leathers was the first time I really melted. I was a Vera puddle. I had to steady myself on the kitchen counter as he took off his full-face helmet, adjusted his bangs to the left, over his eyes, and walked to the door and knocked.

"Hey," I managed. The closer he got, the more liquid I became.

"Hey."

"You want to come in? Dad left me some real hot chocolate."

We went in and sat at the breakfast bar, stared out the window at the bird feeder, and talked.

"I don't see you much anymore. You liking school?" he asked.

"Yeah. Still invisible," I said. "Which is cool."

"Me too," he lied. I knew he was more popular than ever since he got the bike. Kids gathered around it in the student parking lot after school, and tried to look as cool as he was. I saw them every day from the school bus as it headed for Mount Pitts, and eventually Overlook Road.

"Nah—you don't have to say that. I know you have a ton of new friends. That's cool."

"But you're still my best friend, Veer. You'll always be."

"This is turning into a Hallmark vomit fest," I laughed. "Hot chocolate and all."

"Well, it's true. I don't know how I'd have turned out without you being my best friend."

"Me either."

We were quiet, aside from slurping our hot chocolate, and I decided to ask him about the pervert guy who used to buy his underwear. I was sure he'd stopped selling them, because I was sure he knew better by now.

"Can I ask you something?"

"Yeah?"

"Do you still—uh, you know. See that, uh—guy?"

He flashed his mischievous grin. This was why teachers passed him when he should have failed, and why the gym teachers let him wear whatever he wanted to gym.

"Do you want in?" he asked.

"Uh—no!" I said, laughing.

"It's easy money, man. All you do is take them off at night and put 'em in a bag," he said. "I know it sounds gross at first, but hey, man, at least he's not molesting little kids or any-thing."

"Do you know he's not?"

"No." He paused. "I guess not."

Dad walked in then, fresh from buying our Christmas tree. "Hey! There's my two favorite kids!"

"You are such a dork," I said.

"Hey, Mr. Dietz."

"I see you're still completely insane, Mr. Kahn, driving a motorcycle in this weather."

"I have to keep up my reputation, you know." Charlie turned to me then. "Thanks for the hot chocolate, Veer. You want that book?"

"Book?"

He gave me a signal with his eyes.

"Oh, yeah. The *book*."

"See ya, Mr. Dietz. Have a nice Christmas."

"You too, Charlie. Give my regards to your mother," he said, which had to be the most obvious thing he ever said in his boring little accountant's life.

When we got to his bike, Charlie hugged me tightly (Vera puddle again) and then held me at arm's length. "We're cool?"

"Sure," I said.

"Really? Like, you won't breathe a word?"

"About the—uh, no. No way."

"It's all harmless fun," he said, putting his helmet on and attaching the strap.

"Merry Christmas," I said.

"You too."

Watching him drive down the road, you'd never know he was a reckless boy. You'd never think a kid who knew his hand turn signals and used them even when the road was empty would be the same sort of kid who would sell his dirty underwear to a complete stranger. But again—that was the thing about Charlie. It was the thing we all fell in love with. He was the most exciting kid on Earth.

"I hope you don't think I was spying," my father said as I walked in the house, "but you two sure make one cute couple."

An uninvited anger boiled up inside me and raced out my mouth. "Jesus, Dad. Why would you want me to be with a kid you *know* will beat me up one day? What kind of sicko are you?"

He stood there, dumbfounded, while I rinsed the hot chocolate mugs and put them in the dishwasher, all the while thinking about Charlie and how good we looked together.

Spring was late that year. It snowed in April. Charlie had a job at the APlus, which Dad said was "too weird," seeing he got a job at a convenience store when he was in high school, too. I kept my job at Arby's and hoped to work a lot of hours in the summer to save up for my own cell phone—something Dad was vehemently against paying for, on account of him being stuck in the Dark Ages. (Best line from that argument: "I don't care who says it makes you safer. As far as I'm concerned, it's a marketing scam aimed at children who don't know any better." Sweet.) Also, he still wasn't letting me drive Mom's car, which was getting more aggravating by the day.

That summer, Charlie and I took a few walks to the

pagoda together, and climbed the Master Oak for kicks. I still loved hiking the blue trail with him, him in his red bandanna and combat shorts that I could smell from a yard away, but we didn't get to do that much. Both of us were working a lot, and Charlie dated a few more girls. He didn't tell me, but I heard.

I'd met Mitch, a private-school kid who worked the breakfast shift at Arby's with me on weekends and who asked me out to the movies twice. He brought his little sister, so I did not consider these real dates. More like babysitting. But I tried to act normal and spend time with a normal boy. We held hands. He smelled like onions. In the end, I realized he wasn't daring or cool, and I hated how he dressed up all the time. So after the two movies, I slinked into my manager's office and asked to be moved to evening hours on weekends.

I missed Mrs. Parker and Mr. Zimmerman and caring for the animals, but bringing home a paycheck was nice. I stopped by the adoption center a few times, and sent Mr. Zimmerman a card when I heard his wife died. Though I did that out of sympathy, I also did it because I *really* wanted a job in his store the next summer.

School started again. We were juniors. I was an invisible junior and Charlie was a very cool motorcycle-driving Tech junior. We'd occasionally see each other outside of school, but he quit the APlus and started work-study with the HVAC company his dad worked for, and often came home late. I bought myself a pay-as-you-go flip phone and we started texting each other sarcastic things about people in our lives. He'd tell me how lame some of the Vo-Tech kids were, and I'd tell him how dorky the geeks in my Trig class were and how they watched *Red Dwarf* on the Internet.

Dad had a busy autumn because he had to take two courses to stay up to date with some weird corporate tax return changes, and he asked me to tone down my work schedule on account of him not being able to drive me. I just couldn't believe he was going this far to deny me driving a perfectly good car that was sitting in the garage.

Before I could answer, he put up his hand and said, "Don't say it."

"But—"

"Don't."

I sighed and waited a minute, but couldn't stop myself. "It's so stupid!" I said, which wasn't what I would have said had he let me speak in the first place. Then I stormed to my room. I flipped open my phone and sent a message to Charlie about how much I hated my life. A minute later, I heard his bike on the road. When I looked out the window, he was parking it in the driveway and looking up at me. Even though it was getting dark, we walked up the blue trail to the Master Oak and climbed high enough to see the glowing red neon through the thin forest.

Charlie didn't say much and smoked a lot. I didn't say much, either. I wanted to flip open my phone and write *Kiss me*. But before I could, Charlie started to descend the tree. The next week I turned seventeen.

NO PLACE, NO TIME

I am in the dark forest and I can't move. I am lying flat on the forest floor. There are bugs. I feel wet. I smell gas. Above me is the Master Oak. It drops acorns on me, like hail.

The tree explodes into flames. I still can't move. The acorns are now flaming acorns, and I am wet with gasoline, bound to die. The strippers arrive.

Dancers with green sequins, G-strings, fishnet stockings, and garter belts dance around me. Tassels on their breasts go in circles, and fan the flames closer to me. One girl looks new. Her tassels don't synchronize. My attention is held by the lead stripper. My mother is taking off a feather boa and swinging it around with her lips pouted. She stares at someone in the audience, but I can't move my head to see who it is.

I am on a swing, swinging high above a river. I am a little girl again, holding on so tight, my hands hurt and the cold chain of the swing gnaws itself into my knuckles. I wiggle my legs. I yell "Stop!" but the swing won't stop.

Dad says, "But this is fun!"

I start to cry and scream like someone is stabbing me. I hope he will get the picture. Instead, he laughs and the swing does not slow down.

"Stop!" I cry. "Stop! Stop! Stop!"

There is a paper airplane floating on a current. I am riding it, wedged into the center fold, arms spread along the wings. I am flying over the town and up toward the pagoda. I zip down Pitt Street and then Cotton Street, full of Harley-Davidson motorcycles and American-made trucks. I hang on as the plane navigates around the S curves, and my hands grow stinging paper cuts. By the time we arrive at the pagoda, my fingers are bleeding, but I am overjoyed. It is beautiful up here. Flying is beautiful. Until I am thrown off, sent bouncing off the rocks to my death.

The strippers are now Nazis. I mean, they are in sexy Nazi uniforms—something out of a Mel Brooks movie. Fishnets and swastikas. The dancers' tassels are red and black, and behind them crosses burn. I look around and see no one. I look down and see I am back in the paper airplane. Parked. Someone has put bandages on my bleeding hands. My mother has been replaced by Charlie, who is twirling a pair of white briefs above his head. He tosses them to the nonexistent audience, and as I watch to see where they land, the pervert from Overlook Road appears an inch from my face. "What pretty pigtails."

Charlie is leading me through the dark woods. We are in real time—I somehow know this. Charlie holds my hand firmly and tugs. He is pulling so hard, my hand starts to bleed again. We get to a clearing and he stops and looks up.

"Look at that, Vera."

I tilt my head back and see a sky full of stars.

"Can you tell which one is me?" he asks.

I point to the brightest one.

He grabs my hand again and we arrive at the foot of the tree house ladder. Then we are in the tree house and Charlie is showing me his secret floorboard under the mattress.

He says, "You have to do this."

I say, "I know."

He says, "I'm sorry."

I say, "I know."

He says, "Do you forgive me?"

I say, "Not yet."

He says, "There's not much time left."

I say, "For who?"

He says, "People will get hurt."

I become annoyed.

He says, "What's wrong?"

I say, "I'm scared."

He says, "Just do it."

He hands me an old cigar box.

I say, "Why me, Charlie?"

He says, "You're the bravest."

HISTORY—AGE SEVENTEEN

The first time I ever rode on a motorcycle, Dad displayed a shade of fear I'd never seen before, and said, "Charlie Kahn, that's my only daughter you have on that machine."

"Be cool, Mr. D. I'll take good care of her."

We went to the pagoda. When we got there, I felt like a new person—a seventeen-year-old grown-up. When I pulled the helmet from my head, I felt, for the first time in my life, nearly as cool as Charlie. When he turned around and kissed me, gently, on my lips, I blushed and told him to stop.

But I didn't want him to stop.

Then we put our helmets back on and drove back down the hill—and when I put my arms around Charlie's waist, I held on tightly, like a girlfriend would. It was nearly Halloween. I had just turned seventeen.

We had a movie night every Friday that winter. Dad would make popcorn and then leave us alone. Our friendship hadn't suffered from the gaps of high school, like many did. Though we had our own lives, Charlie and I were able to come back to where it all began—just the two of us.

Sometimes Charlie would reach over and hold my hand, which made my brain explode so much I couldn't concentrate on the movie. All I know about *Apocalypse Now* is that it's about Vietnam. I can't even remember who starred in it. What I do remember is Charlie's hand and how strong it was, and how he rubbed my palm with his thumb and how he smelled of buttery popcorn.

I lost my job at Arby's in January because I had become so part-time, I was useless. I blamed Dad and his inability to cough up Mom's car, but he exhibited no signs of guilt.

Then, Valentine's Day came. There was a dance, and balloons and flowers and cheaply made rings and all sorts of lame teddy bears and stuffed animals, as if teenagers can be wooed with the same shit as five-year-olds. It was the Dietzes' most hated holiday of the year, too, because it dealt with the consumerization of something sacred. Mom and Dad had agreed never to buy each other anything on the day. It was a false, Hallmark holiday. A sham. A moneymaking sideshow for insecure couples who didn't have true love. I agreed with this, for the most part. (I disagreed that Mom and Dad were the poster children for true love, though. Obviously.)

So, when I got home from school and there were a dozen red roses for me on the kitchen table, I tried my best not to be cynical. Dad had put them in an old crystal vase we had, and left the sealed envelope at its base next to a note from him that said *Back at 5. Had to go to the notary.* I opened the card and Charlie's messy handwriting read, *Let's go out tonight. I'll pick you up at 8. Love, Charlie.*

Love? Love, Charlie? Out? Out where? You'd have thought I'd be used to Charlie and his spontaneous weird shit by then, but I wasn't. Not when it amounted to a hundred bucks' worth of roses and a date in three hours. Though he meant it to be sweet, all I could see was control and manipulation.

Over dinner, Dad said, "Nice flowers. Who are they from?"

I blushed. Sighed. "Charlie." I added, "But I don't know why he sent them."

He looked up at me from over his glasses. "Occam's razor, Veer."

My father was obsessed with Occam's razor, which, in short, says that the simplest solution is the best solution. (Meaning, Charlie sent me roses because he loved me.)

"We're going out tonight, I think."

Behind his eyes, I saw a thousand worried monkeys, knitting his eyebrows together into an indecisive frown. He'd told me a long time ago that I wasn't allowed to date Charlie, but in the years that followed, he'd said more than once that we were cute together. I don't think he knew what he really wanted anymore—and I wasn't sure what I wanted, either.

I came downstairs at 8:05, sat down on a kitchen stool, and looked at my reflection in the patio door until 8:15. I'd put on my favorite pair of jeans and a pair of Doc Martens boots I hadn't worn yet.

I should have known Charlie would be late. At 8:30 I called his house, feeling so stupid I can't even explain it. Mrs. Kahn answered in her usual chirpy hide-the-bruises sort of way, and when I asked if I could talk to Charlie, she told me he was out.

She didn't sound surprised that I was looking for him. Or that I wasn't out with him.

"Nice that he's doing something social, isn't it, Vera? After all these years of trying to be so different."

I wanted to tell her that it was okay to be different. That *different* made Charlie who he was. But she would never get it. To her, anything weird was scary or stupid. Something to roll her eyes at. If Charlie was the next Einstein, she would have told him to not be weird, to comb his hair, and to stop thinking about physics, while his father forced him to go to Vo-Tech and learn about HVAC.

"Will you tell him I called?"

"Sure. But let's not ruin his fun, okay?"

She hung up. I wanted to kill her. I wanted to kill him, too.

"Everything okay?" Dad asked.

"Yeah," I said. Right when I said it, I heard Charlie's bike buzzing up the road. When he arrived, he seemed distracted and upset by something. I figured it was just Charlie being intense.

I didn't know how to feel, wrapped around Charlie, driving up Overlook Road. While I bounced around on the back of his bike, I felt stupid for not asking him where we were going first—for allowing him to lead me, like I was some blind idiot disciple mesmerized by his coolness, like everyone else. When I talked inside the helmet, it echoed.

"Where are we going?" I asked quietly. And the echo asked, "Where are we going?"

He took the left toward the pagoda and carefully maneuvered around the S curves until we came to the straight part in the road, about a hundred yards from the parking area. He took his hand from the handlebars and patted my right knee. Because he was slowing down, I took this to mean that our first stop was the pagoda, which I thought was pretty romantic.

I thought back to the note he sent with the flowers. I said, "Love. Love, Charlie." My helmet said, "Love. Love, Charlie."

The place was deserted but for two cars, and I couldn't see any people.

Charlie slowed down and pulled into the first parking space, the one right in front of the pagoda itself, and put his feet down to steady us. I stepped off, and then he balanced the bike on the kickstand and got off, too. We took our helmets off, and I reached up and tousled my hair to feel better about it. Charlie smiled and opened his mouth to say something, but before he could, someone yelled, "Hey, Charlie! Over here!"

It was one of his Vo-Tech friends. He was down on the rocks, waving at us. Charlie waved back, then turned to me and said, "Come on." I gave an obvious scowl, but he didn't see it. As he walked, I saw him reach back for my hand, but I slowed instead and kept my arms to my sides.

There were six of them. Two couples curled up with each other and two extra guys, goofing around on the rocks. They had beer.

"Do you all know Vera?"

There were grunts of different answers. Yeah. No. Hey, Vera. Welcome. Nice to meet you. Weren't you in my gym class last year? Are you in Tech? Isn't she the one who . . .

I managed, "Hi." What I meant was: *Take me home.*

"Wanna beer?"

Charlie caught a flying can of beer. Then another. I declined and he stuck mine in the pocket of his leather. I was starting to get cold. The wind was bitter. This didn't seem like a date to me.

"You cool?" Charlie asked.

I didn't know how to say what I wanted to say, so I said, "Yeah."

The two couples sat at the very edge of the far rocks. They giggled and tossed their empty beer cans into the air and listened to them bounce off the rocks and land farther down the hill. Charlie guzzled down his beer really fast, then pulled the one meant for me out of his pocket and cracked it open.

"You want to sit down?" Charlie asked.

"I'm freezing," I said. What I meant was: *I hate you*.

Ten minutes later, the two couples who were on the rocks got up and walked over to us. They were Jenny Flick and Bill Corso, and Gretchen and her drunk boyfriend, who I heard was in college.

"She isn't drinking?" Jenny asked Charlie. I was standing right there, but she asked Charlie.

"I don't drink," I said.

This caused a chain reaction of snickering. Someone passed out more beers. Two guys headed toward the edge of the rocks to pee.

"You okay?" Charlie asked.

"Yeah," I said. What I meant was: *No*.

Bill Corso reached into his back pocket and pulled out a

joint. The rest of them circled around him to block the wind. My brain was sprinting through a trillion thoughts. Nothing made sense. They passed the joint around quickly, taking loud hits from it, and when it got to me, Charlie spared me by taking it from the person who was passing it. When she was done exhaling, Jenny said, "And she doesn't smoke, either."

Charlie looked annoyed. "So?"

Jenny shrugged and moved her eyes from me to Charlie, back to me, and then back to Charlie. I could see her brain working. Then, while the others passed the joint around again, her eyes undressed Charlie while I watched. It was so obvious, it made me sick to my stomach.

Charlie must have noticed I was shivering, because he put his arm around me and enclosed me in his leather jacket, next to his warm chest. This made Jenny sneer and put her arm tightly around Corso, and it made me warm enough to realize that I had to pee—which was a problem, because the pagoda was closed for business and there were no bathrooms.

When the stoner circle broke up, Charlie lit a Marlboro and the couples went back to making out on the rocks. I whispered in Charlie's ear about having to pee.

"There's a great spot down by the wall that Jenny uses sometimes. I'll stand watch."

I said, "Thanks." What I meant was: *You've been here before with Jenny?*

I walked down in the red glow, with my right hand on the stone wall to keep my footing. Charlie stopped at the top of the path. When I reached a dark enough spot, a few steps into the trees, I slid my jeans down, and once my body adjusted to the freezing cold, I finally peed. Above the sound of liquid on frozen ground, I heard Jenny say, "Why'd you bring *her?*"

Charlie said, "Vera's cool, man."

"You think?" one of the guys said.

I reached into my coat pocket for a tissue to wipe.

"Shut up. She's not deaf, you know."

"Isn't she a geek?"

"No," Charlie said, annoyed.

"I heard she was."

"I heard her mom slept around."

"That's kinda hot," one of the guys said.

"It's skanky," Jenny Flick said.

My heart beat in my chest as I zipped up and followed the wall back to the glowing red scene. Charlie held out his hand, but again, I didn't take it. I thought he could see things the way I was seeing them, and figured we were about to say goodbye and go wherever we were going next. But when we got back to the rocks, he walked over to the two Vo-Tech guys and pulled out a small bottle of booze from the inner pocket of his leather, took a swig, and passed it on.

They both drank, and when they passed it to Charlie again, and he tilted his head back to drink, one of them said, "Hey! Kahn brought the good shit!"

Charlie turned to me. "Want some?"

I said, "Nah." What I meant was: *Who are you?*

He reached into his cigarette pack for a smoke, but it was empty. He fumbled around his leathers and then turned to me. "Veer? Could you grab me the pack of smokes under the seat of the bike?"

"Sure," I said.

Jenny Flick said, "While you're at it, can you stop somewhere and find a personality?"

"Jenny," Charlie said.

"What? I was kidding."

"Wasn't funny," he said, and then turned to say something to me, but I was already walking up toward the parking area. I got Charlie's Marlboros from under the seat and stuffed them in my pocket. I stopped and sat on the wall, and faced the pagoda and appreciated its bizarre, out-of-place beauty. I thought if I stayed up there for a minute or two, Charlie would come looking for me, but instead, I smelled pot smoke again, and realized no one gave a shit.

I gave myself a real Ken Dietz pep talk. "Vera, this is what kids do in high school. You shouldn't be up here sulking. You should go back and be yourself. Cynical, funny, straight-up Vera Dietz."

It didn't work. It didn't work because I knew not to give the best of myself to the worst of people. So I decided to ask Charlie to take me home. But when I rounded the corner of the pagoda and saw him showing Jenny Flick and Bill Corso and the rest of his new friends how paper airplanes (this time, Corso's three interim reports to warn of his impending failure) soar in the fast, frigid current, I turned around and headed home.

I fast-walked down Overlook Road in the dark, thinking of Charlie, boiling. Fuck Charlie. Stupid asshole. Stupid roses. Stupid pagoda. Stupid losers. Stupid boots giving me stupid blisters. Stupid Vera Dietz.

When I walked in the door, up the steps, and into my room without a grunt, Dad noticed. He said up the steps, "Why don't you come down and we'll order pizza from that new delivery place and pig out?"

So we did—and he didn't say one word to me about Charlie. While I put on my flannel pajamas, he moved the roses to the windowsill by the sink, which was nice, actually, because our garbage disposal had gone funky, so they helped cover the smell of old water and rotten vegetables.

The pizza place had a little coupon pasted to the box top. Two dollars off a two-pie order with Coke. As my father cut it out for his fridge coupon organizer, he saw the call for drivers.

"'Must be eighteen,'" he read. "What do you think? That could be a fun job."

"I won't be eighteen until October. Anyway, I want to work at Zimmerman's this summer, now that I'm old enough."

Of course, Dad didn't like this idea, but he knew it was a paying position, because I hadn't stopped mentioning it since the first summer I'd volunteered at the adoption center.

After a second's thought, I added, "Hold on—are you saying you'll give me Mom's car if I do this? Because I can do part-time and still work at Zimmerman's if this means I get the car."

"I do a pizza delivery guy's taxes," he said. "The pay isn't bad, and he says tips are great. You won't get tips at the pet store."

"True. But I can't cuddle and love pizza, either."

The conversation took my mind off Charlie. It was nice. He cut out the "drivers wanted" part, stuck it on the fridge under a magnet, and said, "Heck, maybe *I'll* do it. Could be a fun moonlighting job. Plus, I'll be lonely around here if you start dating—or, uh, whatever it is you're doing."

I told him everything. The pagoda, the friends, the drinking, and the pot. I didn't tell him about the paper airplanes, though, because I knew it would hurt him that a bunch of assholes stole a sacred Dietz thing.

He sighed and clicked his tongue. "Well, that's disappointing."

"To put it lightly," I said.

He looked over at the flowers and back at me. "Veer, there's got to be some explanation. He spent a fortune on those. It doesn't make sense."

"This is the kind of thing I'd have to put up with if he was my boyfriend," I said. "Anyway, we're best friends. I don't want to ruin it. It's better this way."

He nodded and reached for my hand. "You're a real smart little cookie—you know that?"

Of course, I was lying to both of us.

A BRIEF WORD FROM THE DEAD KID

Jenny Flick and I officially met in detention in January of our junior year. I got caught smoking outside the wood shop loading doors, and even though Mr. Smith liked me, he had to write me up because the metal shop teacher was with him, and he's a hardcore asshole.

When I first got to the room, the Detentionheads were standing around, talking about a fight that was supposedly going to happen after school the next day. I didn't recognize most of the new kids because I spent half days at Tech, but I did recognize Bill Corso and his two best football buddies, who looked like inbred hillbilly twins, and Jenny Flick from my times in detention the year before. Jenny Flick was leaning back in her chair with her feet on the desk. She wore a pair of soft leather construction boots, tight jeans, and a black Led Zeppelin T-shirt, and was chewing gum and blowing bubbles. I sat in the back right corner and ignored everyone like I did every other time I had detention.

The Special Education teacher, Mr. Oberman, was the

detention teacher for the day, and when he came in, he wrote a quote on the board and as he was writing it he said, "We're here for an hour, ladies and gentlemen. If you choose to use this hour wisely and do your homework or class-assigned reading, that would be a very intelligent decision. However"—he stopped and eyed Bill Corso—"if you choose to just sit here like a bored jungle gorilla, you will have to write out this quote as many times as you can during the next hour. I have paper and pencils on my desk for those of you who have arrived empty-handed."

There was no doubt Mr. Oberman was gay. He didn't hide it. I'd venture a guess that he was overly gay in the detention room because it irked the Detentionheads so much. Bill Corso was not going to be told what to do by some fag—so Oberman put on his extra fagginess just to make kids like Corso squirm.

The quote said: HOW MANY CARES ONE LOSES WHEN ONE DECIDES NOT TO BE SOMETHING BUT SOMEONE.

"What the hell does *that* mean?" Corso asked.

"What do you think it means, Mr. Corso?"

"I don't know."

Corso sat at the desk, his legs open wide, straddling the entire thing, as if his crotch was the mouth of a giant whale, and had his arms crossed across his chest. He had no books, no pencil, and no paper.

"Well, maybe if you fill this paper with it a few times, you'll figure it out," Oberman said, dropping a piece of lined paper and a pencil on Bill's desk.

Bill shoved the things off his desk and onto the floor. "I'm not writing that shit. Heller and Frisk don't make us write."

Mr. Oberman stayed calm and smiled. "But I'm not Mr.

Heller or Mr. Frisk. I'm Mr. Oberman, and if you don't pick those up and watch your language, I'm giving you another month."

They stared at each other. The rest of us watched in silence. I already had my math homework out and tried to pretend like I wasn't watching because these kids were losers and no matter where I was from, I was not going to be a Detentionhead loser.

"I'm giving you one minute to pick those up, Mr. Corso. After that, you're out and facing possible suspension."

Bill didn't move.

At the fifty-second mark, he looked over his right shoulder at Jenny Flick and raised his eyebrows. She shrugged.

At the minute mark, Oberman looked up from his stack of paperwork and pointed to the door. "Goodbye, Mr. Corso. You'll be chatting with the office in the morning."

When Bill got about ten feet down the hall he yelled, "FAGGOT!" and Jenny Flick laughed, which caused the rest of the Detentionheads to laugh. Oberman continued doing his paperwork and I went back to my math homework and in another minute it was as if Corso had never been there.

The hour passed slowly. The minute I walked out the main doors, I reached for a smoke and lit it.

"I like rebels," Jenny said. I had no idea she was behind me, so she caught me completely off guard. Plus—what do you say to that?

"Yeah?"

"Yeah. Got a light?"

I lit her skinny girly cigarette, put my lighter back in my pocket, and didn't say anything.

"Wanna come to my house?"

"Nah."

"My mom works nights and my stepdad doesn't get home until eight."

I shook my head. "Nah. Thanks."

"I have pot."

I said, "I have to get home." When she didn't say anything, I added small talk. "What does he do that he gets home so late?"

"He's a manager. Tells people what to do all day. Then he comes home and tells me what to do."

"Oh," I said. "Like what?"

"What?"

"Like, what does he tell you to do?"

"The usual shit. Clean. Cook. Wash clothes. Walk the dog. Iron shirts. Shine shoes. All the stuff he's too lazy to do."

The minute she said this, I felt sad for her. I mean, I thought *my* dad was a dick, but I don't think he ever made my mom shine shoes. "That sucks," I said.

"Yeah. Same shit, different day, I guess." She adjusted her hair after a gust of wind blew it across her face. "Are you sure you don't want to come over?"

"I can't."

"I can give you head."

I acknowledged her offer with that facial expression that says, *Really?*

"I can," she said, dragging her cigarette deep into her lungs and then exhaling. I'm not sure how to describe what I was feeling. I was seventeen—and this was something out of a triple-X daydream. And yet, I could translate her language. In

Jenny's world, "I can give you head" meant "I like you a lot." And so, I took it as a compliment. Who doesn't like flattery?

At the same time, it stank of desperation and I didn't like it.

I said, "What makes you think I want head?"

She laughed overly loudly. "*Every* guy wants head!"

"Are you saying you give it to every guy who wants it?"

I admit it was probably not the best thing to say in that situation, but I wanted her to say what she really meant. I wanted her to say "I like you, Charlie," or something normal. Something classy.

She glared at me. "You watch your ass, Charlie Kahn. I know some pretty important people."

"Okay. I'll watch my ass," I answered, but she didn't hear me, because she'd already turned around and started walking back toward the school. I hadn't noticed, but the Detention-heads were about a block behind us the whole time, Corso (her boyfriend) included.

After that, she started showing up everywhere, and started being extra nice to me. When I stood around with my Tech friends, talking about bikes and cars and stuff in the student parking lot while we waited for the buses to clear out, she would join the crowd and smile at me. She must have figured I didn't respond to the hard-ass act after our walk from detention. Now, instead of playing the slut card, she played cute and smiled like a shy girl. In the halls between afternoon classes, she'd bump into me and apologize, or give a faint wave from a distance and mouth "Hi." The next time I got detention, I sat in the back and ignored her, but the more I ignored Jenny, the more she pushed. The more she pushed, the more I admired her, the more attractive she seemed to me, and the more I "accidentally" got detention. I can't explain this, except to remind you that I lived with a bully and a doormat. Also, I was seventeen and my hormones had taken note that Jenny was

- Easy
- Kinda pretty
- Really into me

Now that I'm here, I see that Jenny Flick was like Darth Vader, and that the dark side is enticing. But why did I turn on Vera? I don't know. Because I didn't want her to see what I was becoming—a sneaky person who couldn't stop himself from doing shit he shouldn't do. Maybe because I knew Vera was falling for me and I knew I was falling for her. Maybe because I knew she was fine and didn't need to be rescued, like Jenny and I did. Why do people think there are clear answers for things anyway? There aren't. Why does my dad hit my mom? Why does John have a thing for boys' dirty underwear? See?

A BRIEF WORD FROM THE PAGODA

Do you have any idea how old watching idiot kids drink and do drugs up here on the rocks is getting? The funniest part is, they all think they're more cool than their parents were, and their parents did the same crap. Also—tossing beer cans? That's a $300 fine. You're lucky I'm an inanimate object.

THE PAGODA PIZZA CHRISTMAS PARTY—
PART 2

The first person I see is Fat Barry's son, who is staring wide-eyed at my head. He says, "Have you seen your head?"

I'm still on the floor. I just came to. Of course I haven't seen my head.

James is here. "Vera? Vera? Are you okay?"

Everything is a blur except for the throbbing hotness on my forehead. I look up at James and the kid. I don't see Mick. I don't see Marie and her husband or Fat Barry.

"You need to go and look at your head," the kid says again.

So I get up slowly and walk to the bathroom. James has his hand under my elbow as support, and is jabbering a mix of garbled concern. "I'll take you home. Oh my God. I should kill that guy. Holy shit. Are you sure you're okay? Oh my God. Can you walk? Can you see okay?" Two steps from the bathroom door, I reach my hand up and touch it. It feels like I've just sprouted a Ping-Pong ball on my hairline. And there's blood, but not a lot. Just that familiar tacky feeling.

When I see myself in the old, peeling mirror, I sober instantly. When I emerge from the bathroom, James isn't by the door, and I make my way, like a ghost, to the parking lot.

Though I know I am driving drunk, I do not feel like I am. I am very aware that I should not be driving, and yet I seem to be doing this without expending any thought or energy. I have no idea how I got on the highway. I don't remember pulling out of the fire company parking lot. I don't remember saying goodbye to James or anyone else.

I am not driving the car. Someone else is shifting the gears for me. Someone has just put on my right-turn signal and turned me onto Pitts Road. I drive to the hill at Jenkins's field and I pull the car into my old stargazing spot.

Someone turns the light on in the car and I look at my lump in the rearview mirror. It's huge, and it's killing me. It could be the bad light, but it looks like there are bruises forming under my eyes now. This thought brings tears—the realization that I am going to have to explain this to Dad, who will surely pull some crazy shit when I tell him what happened.

I turn the light off.

Then, they are here. All thousand of them. Maybe a million. The field is wall-to-wall Charlies. They are glowing blue-white and I can hear them breathing. They exhale a word. *Rest.*

I can't sleep here. I don't even know if I can sleep, period. Maybe I have a concussion. Maybe I'll slip into a coma if I sleep. Maybe I'll die.

Rest.

I blink. A billion Charlies, glowing brighter. A trillion. Inhaling. Exhaling. *Rest.*

My head rests on the seat, and I curl slightly to my right, tucking myself into my coat. I make sure the doors are locked and close my eyes, and they are behind my eyelids, too. The Charlies. Infinite Charlies. Smiling, stroking my head, glowing blue-white light, and exhaling softly. *Rest.*

When daybreak hits, I wake up cold. I remember being woken up during the night. Hourly. I remember feeling Charlie nursing me, protecting me, making sure I wasn't dead. I lie there for a minute or two and then reach up to my head, which now feels like I've grown a baseball.

My father is going to have a shit fit.

Before the road starts carrying cars to Saturday shopping and work, I turn the key in the ignition and crank the heat up until I figure out what to tell Dad. There are good sides—I wasn't having sex with James all night. I don't even know where he is! There are bad sides—I have a concussion and probably need to see a doctor. I can't say how many drinks I had last night, I had so many.

Times like these, I wish my father was a long-haul trucker or worked in the International Space Station. I pull out of the field with a sigh, knowing I deserve whatever I get. Fact is, I feel lucky I'm not dead. I feel lucky I'm not beat up and raped and in a heap next to a Dumpster outside Jackson Fire Company.

Here's my father using *fuck* and *shit* in a sentence.

"Holy shit! What the fuck happened to you?"

I've never heard him swear before. He gets closer, sees the tears in my eyes, and his anger quickly merges into concern.

"Are you okay, Vera?"

"I'm fine," I say.

"Uh—um, I, uh—" He's panicked. He could never deal with medical stuff.

"Really, Dad. It's okay."

He's all mixed up. I can see it. Before I got home, he wanted to lay into me. He wanted to read the riot act and make me call my mother again, and book me into some home for girls who love twenty-three-year-old men and like to drink. But when I walked in looking like this, his plan collapsed. Now he's pacing and muttering to himself, tapping his fingertips together.

I get myself a glass of water and drink back three Advil. After two minutes, he takes a closer look at my head and says, "Get your coat on. I'm taking you to the hospital."

"Don't you want to know where I was last night?"

"No."

"Don't you want to know if I was drinking?"

He looks at me impatiently and rolls his eyes.

"Can I at least change?"

"I'm starting the car," he says, trying to hide how concerned he is.

I lock myself in the upstairs bathroom and turn both lights on. Oh man. I look like I got the shit kicked out of me. Did I? While I wash my face and brush my teeth, I think back to Mick the skinhead Nazi and how nice he was in between the intimidating Nazi stuff. Surely this was an accident. He hadn't meant to drop me on my head. No one would do that sort of thing on purpose—especially at a nice Christmas party with fifty people around to witness it. Or so I decide, here and now. No. Mick just accidentally fell over. He was drunk—like I was. I couldn't blame him.

But my memory has this little piece of information. A sound bite. The sound bite I have from when I was passed out on the hardwood floor. Maybe I was dreaming. Maybe I could hear while my brain took a minute to find consciousness again. But the sound bite won't let me forget it.

JAMES: What the fuck did you do that for?

MICK: That chick's a freak!

JILL: Jesus, Mick.

EXTRA #1: Is she okay?

EXTRA #2: Out cold.

JAMES: Vera? Vera?

MICK: (From a distance.) (Laughs.) Who's racking?

JAMES: Veer? Vera?

I hear Dad rev the car a few times and then open the front door.

"VERA! Let's go!" He sounds scared as hell.

PART FOUR

GROUNDED,
COMPLETELY AND TOTALLY—PART 1

Okay—here's me using *stultify* in a sentence.

My father, who won't let me go to school with a contusion the size of a baseball, has grounded me and banned me from working to stultify my life. I'm not even sure I used that right, but who cares? Being in the house all the time is fucking me up.

Plus, thanks to the stupid hospital consultant who called in a lab-coat-wearing guy from some unit called "Crisis" after my head X-ray and bloodwork came back, we have four insurance-covered "Family Meetings" with a local therapist before we have to start paying out of pocket.

Dad thought this was a great idea until halfway through the second appointment, when he realized we'd be role-playing and he wouldn't be allowed to hide behind his calm and cool Zen master bullshit anymore.

DR. B: Mr. Dietz, why don't you really act like you think Vera acts? I'm sure she isn't as subdued as you're making her out to be.

DAD: I don't want to hurt her feelings.

ME: Please, Dad. I think making me quit my job and locking me in the house did the trick. No need to spare my feelings. Really.

DR. B: See? Why don't you start with that? Can you capture that sarcasm?

DAD: Really, Dad, you totally SUCK for giving a shit about me.

I laugh.

DR. B: Perfect. Try some more.

DAD: Like, now I have to sit around doing nothing all the time, and my twenty-three-year-old boyfriend can't see me or bring me alcohol.

DR. B: Vera? Do you want to play?

ME: (Sits up straight, clears all emotion from face.) You will thank me, Vera, in a few years when you realize how stupid you're being.

DAD: I never call you stupid!

DR. B: Mr. Dietz. (Holds hand out.)

ME: Like I was saying, one day you will see how stupid and silly this is. It's simple.

DAD: What's simple about my having to work a full-time job while I'm a senior?

ME: You'll thank me for that job when you're older. (Eyebrows in serious knot, doing best Ken impersonation.)

DAD: (In annoyingly girly voice.) The only reason I even like my job is because of James! I love him!

ME: (Rolls eyes.) You don't know anything about love yet, Vera. If you did, you'd see that I grounded you this month out of real love. I'm concerned that you're throwing your life away.

DAD: It's all your fault, Dad. I would never be doing this if you really gave a shit.

ME: You have to learn how to give a shit about yourself, Vera. You're eighteen. You're soon going to go out on your own. I'm only teaching you responsibility.

DAD: I already *know* responsibility, Dad! Remember? The kid who keeps straight A's and a full-time job? The one who has always helped around the house? The one who helped you get over Mom?

ME: (Noticing twitch in Dad's eyes when he says "Mom.") You never helped me get over Mom, Vera. I'm still not over Mom.

The room goes silent and Dr. B can see that Dad and I are realizing something. We are realizing, simultaneously, that we have never dealt with Mom leaving. We pretended—like role-playing—but we never really did anything about it.

DAD: Well, I am. I'm completely over Mom.

ME: You are?

DAD: Aren't you?

ME: (Confused.) Hold on. Are we role-playing or not, now?

Silence. Dad still has a twitch in his eyes.

DAD: I'm not sure.

DR. B: How about for next week, you both write me a little something about Mom? I think this might be something we need to work on.

We both nod and don't say anything. Because we know he's right.

When we leave the office, part of me feels like holding Dad's hand and acting like I'm ten again. Like going back in time and remembering the warm love we used to have will help us. But then I remember I hate him now.

A BRIEF WORD FROM KEN DIETZ
(VERA'S HATEFUL DAD)

Vera thinks I'm a self-help book and a room full of crystals. She thinks I'm a yoga mat and a bowl of granola and fresh fruit. She's trying to figure out if I'm worth her time or not— a trustworthy grown-up, and not just some worn-out old alcoholic who wasn't good enough for her mother. Or who drove her mother away. Or whatever. It's all related to ~~Cindy~~ Sindy. But I guess that's fair. Losing your mother at twelve probably isn't easy. But whose relationship with their mother is easy?

I only discovered the truth about my mother at her funeral.

We were lined up in the receiving line—Caleb to my left, Jack to my right—and the people came through. Most of the people had known us since we were kids, but a bunch of people came up from Arkansas, where Mom had lived in a retirement village until she died. They'd tell Caleb how sorry they were. They'd make their way toward Jack, shake his hand, say something nice about Mom, and then move on to the buffet. They skipped over me like I was a space between words.

It wasn't until her best friend and neighbor from the Arkansas retirement complex came through that we figured out what was going on.

"Caleb," she said. "I'm so sorry to hear about your muthah. You were such a good boy to her."

He wasn't. To the last month, he was pinching from her Social Security checks.

She waltzed right past me to Jack. "I've heard so much about you. She was so proud."

That's true. Jack lives in London. He's an international banker. She was very proud. Bragged about him every chance she could. He's the family favorite—even though he hasn't been around since 1986.

Caleb kindly nodded to me, and she looked me up and down and said, "Now, who's this?"

"It's Ken," Caleb said.

"Who's Ken?"

"Our youngest brother."

"She had two boys. You and Jack."

"No. She had three. Me, Jack, and Ken."

"You boys are crazy with grief. Kitty had two sons, and I know it because we talked all the time. Why are you trying to confuse me on the day of her funeral?"

It hit Jack first. I saw his heart break for me.

"Mrs.—uh—ma'am," he said quietly. "I think you should move on now. The line is backing up."

Caleb figured it out then, and though he was always a total hard-ass, he put his hand on my shoulder and squeezed. She denied me. For all those years, as I paid her medical bills, as I filled in her 1040s and helped her with her Medicare paperwork and her will. As I bought her a hospital bed, an oxygen machine, and paid for the nurse who helped her at the very end. Even as I arranged to have her cremated—her final wish—she denied me.

I think I can safely say that finding out that my mother never told her Arkansas friends about me was worse than her dying. It was probably worse than ~~Cindy~~ Sindy leaving, too, which coincidentally happened earlier that same year. I stood in the line shaking the occasional hand for another fifteen minutes, keeping an eye on Vera as she sat talking with Caleb's daughter in the funeral home folding chairs, realizing that if my mother had denied me, then she had denied Vera, too.

Most people don't think past themselves. I know that. But I want Vera to see other people. To respect other people. To realize that the whole world is not here for her. I want her to see her duty to the world, not the other way around. Caleb let his girl walk all over him and gave her something for nothing her whole life. Now she expects him to pay for college when he has a sole-proprietor business and Kate's a receptionist at the car parts place.

When I was a teenager, my mother let me do whatever I wanted. Let me stay out all night. Let me smoke pot in her house. Let me drink openly as early as twelve years old, because she figured I'd outgrow it, which didn't really happen. But when she realized I was in trouble, rather than help me again my mother kicked me out and made me solve my own problems. Now, strange as it may sound, I see that it was the best thing that ever happened to me. Well, that, AA, and Vera.

KEN DIETZ'S SPOILED KID FLOW CHART

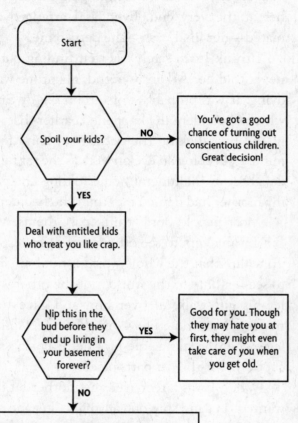

Start

Spoil your kids? — **NO** → You've got a good chance of turning out conscientious children. Great decision!

YES

Deal with entitled kids who treat you like crap.

Nip this in the bud before they end up living in your basement forever? — **YES** → Good for you. Though they may hate you at first, they might even take care of you when you get old.

NO

Get to know your local bail bondsman, your sheriff, and the security guy at Walmart. Turn that basement into an apartment for your kids, their spouses, and their children. Don't forget to stock their fridge with food, pay their health insurance, and arrange for your own eldercare. You know—in case something good is on TV while you need medication or anything important.

HISTORY I'D RATHER FORGET—
AGE SEVENTEEN—SPRING

During March, Charlie avoided me and I avoided Charlie. He was tied up with a Vo-Tech project and I was determined to stop loving him. He never explained why he sent me the flowers and I never asked why he took me up to the pagoda. He was getting detention again—weekly—for smoking and other rebellious acts, and hanging out full-time with the Detentionheads when he wasn't busy becoming his father.

The first time I realized things were going to get nasty was the first week in April, when Charlie broke our friendship off at the pagoda because he believed the lies Jenny Flick told him. First it was the one where I told the whole school about his dad beating his mom. Then, a few days later, she told him that I told people that his penis was small. Why he believed these things, I do not know. If he'd taken a minute to think about it, he'd have realized I never even saw his penis. But I guess when you believe the word of a complete liar, logic doesn't come into it.

Because I hadn't said any of these things, I didn't defend myself. I just waited for things to blow over, which I was convinced they would do on account of Charlie having a brain. But then, in late April, Jenny told him that I'd told the whole junior class that he was gay, and he finally retaliated by sharing the most obvious ammunition, which was the fact that my mother was once a stripper. Awesome. One minute I was Vera Dietz, invisible junior, next minute I was Vera Dietz, junior with a mother who used to be a stripper. People ate this up.

Inside, I died a little bit. I didn't know what to feel. On one hand, I hated my parents for being who they were. On the other hand, I hated Charlie. Most of all, I hated Jenny Flick. But none of that mattered, because I was faced with the harsh reality that the biggest secret I ever had was out, and I had to continue going to school, and sitting through Chemistry, and eating lunch. On the inside, I was so embarrassed, I could barely look up from my shoes. It was like walking around naked.

Somebody wrote SHAKE IT BABY on my locker, which turned my cheeks hot every time I saw it before the janitor washed it off. I got pushed or pinched by invisible hands in the crowded halls between classes, a few times by Jenny herself, but other times I looked behind me and saw no familiar faces. On the bus, kids who knew me sang that sultry song people sing when they're pretending to strip. Tim Miller's brother actually took off his shirt, twirled it around and flung it, and then started unbuttoning his pants until the bus driver told him to stop. I sat in the front seat after that day, with my earbuds in, and ignored them all.

While I quietly hoped it would all go away and sent my old PLEASE IGNORE VERA DIETZ signals into the atmosphere, the rumor grew. First they said that I also stripped, in town, at night. Two seniors told their gym class that they'd watched me and stuffed money into my G-string. Then, it was said that my mother had been a hooker. Also that my mother was *still* a hooker in Las Vegas. And also? Vera Dietz was a hooker, too. As crazy as these things sound, people *believed*. Within a week, Vera Dietz was a porn actress and had starred in films alongside her porn-star mother, who was also a hooker in Las Vegas. (If only she'd moved to Salt Lake City or Boise.)

I faced each day with a mix of dread, tears, and disappointment. I couldn't figure out why people (Charlie) had to be so cruel and why others were so stupid to just believe and tell their friends, who told their friends, until everyone knew ten versions of my story but didn't know which one to believe. I had thoughts of running away and changing schools. I even thought, once, how easy it would be to just die. It was as if living next door to the person who did this to me was a torment I would never shake. I don't think the word *betrayal* covers it—more like *high treason* or *defection* or *Iscariotism*.

But after two weeks, I realized that I was looking at things all wrong. First, who in their right mind would believe that a geek like me was really a hooker or a porn star? Second, as time went on, the only people saying this stuff were the mega-losers at school. Everyone else went on like normal. Essentially, by the time two weeks had passed, *I* was the only person who was thinking about it anymore. And I was slowly realizing that it wasn't the end of the world.

No doubt, it was hard to come to public terms with my mother's past employment at Joe's strip club, but confronting it made me feel a certain degree of freedom. I was not my mother. My mother did what she had to do. Anyone who didn't get that could believe what they wanted and I wouldn't care.

And soon enough, anyone who believed any of it would move on to Jenny's next victim, and forget about me.

Yeah, I had some pretty evil thoughts about telling Charlie's real secret—about the pervert in the white Chrysler—but I reminded myself that the high road is paved with positivity. I took deep breaths. I did homework. I ignored. Then I'd have thoughts about how to make people hate Jenny Flick by outing her lies about leukemia and everything else. But then I'd breathe some more. I'd do more homework. I reminded myself that the one thing Jenny Flick couldn't buy, no matter what she used as currency, was a ticket to drive on the high road next to people like me.

And then spring sprung. I missed being outside, so I started walking the blue trail. Since Charlie was doing work-study, I didn't have any fear he'd be around, and anyway, if he wasn't working, he'd probably be somewhere else drinking and smoking pot with his new friends, and nowhere near his sacred oak tree where the Great Hunter could see him. I bought myself a new pair of hiking boots and did the full three-mile circle every day. When Dad showed concern that I'd be in the woods by myself, I wiggled my cell phone and said, "I've got you on speed dial. Plus, I know those trails better than anyone."

He said, "Huh. I guess cell phones are good for something."

One warm day in early May, while I was walking, I heard voices coming from the trail ahead of me. Before I could turn around, I saw Charlie and Jenny Flick and Bill Corso, and a few other kids, hanging out around the Master Oak. Bill Corso had a pocketknife and was carving his initials into the bark.

"Hey! Look who it is!"

I turned and started walking back down the trail, so angry that they were in my woods. On my trail. Up my tree.

Jenny yelled, "Run home, little Vera!"

One of the boys yelled "Slut!" so I turned and looked back, and then something landed in my hair that smelled like dog shit. (Because it was dog shit.) I knew deep down that Charlie had thrown it, because he was the only one who was facing me, but I didn't admit it to myself. How was I supposed to do that? How was I supposed to admit that my lifelong best friend had just thrown dog shit at me? It was as if he had been abducted by aliens. That was *not* Charlie. Charlie would *not* let *anyone* carve the Master Oak. Charlie would *not* wear new clothes that fit him right, or have that new haircut. Charlie would *not* use hair gel. (Charlie would *not* throw dog shit at me, no matter who told him to do it.)

I stopped hiking after that and spent my free time inside, reading. As the nights grew warmer and the leaves filled the gaps in the forest, I started to sit out on the deck and look at the stars at night. One night, about two weeks after the Master Oak/dog shit episode, I saw the light go on in Charlie's tree house. I heard talking. More than one person. Then I heard giggles. Girlish ones.

No matter how hard I tried not to think about it, I knew he was having sex with Jenny Flick up in that tree house. It killed me, because that was *our* tree house. (Because it was *me* he was supposed to be having sex with.)

I felt evil again for a second. I felt like telling everyone that he sold his dirty underwear. But could I ever respect myself again if I stooped to their level?

By mid-May, it had become glaringly obvious that I needed a job.

Dad picked up an application from Zimmerman's and left it on the table with two others. One was from Martin's, the department store at the Pagoda Mall, where, at best, I'd be stuck behind a cash register all day, swiping cards and saying "Debit or credit?" The other was from the pizza delivery place we ordered from back on Valentine's Day.

"Why'd you get these?" I asked, holding up the extra two. I was sick of him manipulating me with his calm, innocent suggestions.

"I figured it'd be good to have more than one choice," he said.

"I'm not working at Martin's," I answered.

"Okay."

Why didn't he argue like a normal parent?

"If I apply for the pizza thing, will you let me have Mom's car?" It was worth a try. I was five months from eighteen. He'd said he'd consider it the last time we talked. Plus, we'd worked hard to get in all the driving hours I needed to get my license, and I'd passed with flying colors.

"Let's just see, first."

"But it makes a difference on the application, Dad." I waved it in the air toward him, rudely. "I have to tell them the make and model and insurance company."

He looked surprised, and confused, and he went into his office and pulled out the car's manual.

"It's a '99 Sentra."

"Make?"

"Nissan."

"Color?"

"Geez, Vera. You know what color it is," he said.

"Insurance?"

"Write in 'N/A' for now."

No matter how hard I tried to piss him off, it wasn't working. Anyway, I wanted to work at Zimmerman's pet store. I had *always* wanted to work at Zimmerman's pet store. I didn't want some stupid pizza delivery job, and I resented the fact that, like Charlie's dad, he was going to give me a reward for doing what he wanted me to do. *That* was unacceptable.

"So what should I write in the space where it asks me why I want the job?"

He sighed and sat down at the table. "Vera, I'm just trying to help you," he said. "If you don't want to fill out any of them but the one for Zimmerman's, that's fine."

"Okay," I said, pushing the other applications over to him. "There's no need to be a smart-ass."

"Then stop trying to manipulate me."

I could tell from his face that I'd hurt him, because he really was only trying to help. I remembered that this was the kind of thing Mom would have said. In fact, it's exactly what Mom *did* say. A million times.

The next morning as I waited for the bus, I saw Charlie pull his bike from the garage and start it up. He left it running for a few minutes, went into the house, then came back out and went into the garage again. When he came out with an extra helmet, the one I used to wear, I remembered our ride up to the pagoda back in January. How he'd kissed me, and how tightly I'd held him from behind on the way home.

Then Jenny Flick appeared at the forest's edge, her hair still tangled from sleep, and she slipped the helmet over her head and climbed on. As they drove by me—up the hill rather than down, which was not the way to school—she put up her middle finger.

GROUNDED,
COMPLETELY AND TOTALLY—PART 2

Family meeting number three out of four. Mom comes up again, even though neither of us did our "Write something about Mom" homework.

DAD: I just don't want you to make the same mistakes we did.

ME: You mean *she*, don't you? You mean you don't want me to make the same mistakes *she* did.

DAD: (Fiddling with the zipper on his favorite Cape Cod sweatshirt.) I want you to have a fair shot, Vera.

ME: Look at me, Dad. Am I *anything* like her? Do you really think I'd ever be so desperate as to take my clothes off for money?

DAD: I hope not.

ME: Hope? Hope?

DR. B: She's quite a responsible young woman.

DAD: (Still fiddling with zipper.) I don't want to fail her.

ME: Fail me?

DAD: Your mother was failed by her mother. By her father. By everyone in her life.

That means him. That means *I failed your mother,* which just isn't true.

ME: Not you.

DAD: (Silent.)

ME: Mom walked out on *us,* remember? Because she never got over her own baggage, not because of you or me, right?

He's silent.

ME: Seriously. I've been reading your self-help tomes, too, you know. The one on the breakfast bar—*The Power of Ownership,* or whatever it's called. Remember? The part about intellectualizing everything? How people who can't face their own negative emotions intellectualize things? Doesn't that remind you of her?

DR. B: (Raises eyebrows.)

ME: That's not your fault.

DAD: (Sighs.) How the hell was I supposed to know how to raise a girl by myself? How was I supposed to teach you how to be—uh—how to be—

ME: Honorable?

DAD: Yeah. And safe.

ME: I am.

DAD: (Silent.)

ME: You did just fine.

DR. B: She's a confident, smart young woman, Ken.

DAD: So why is she drinking and screwing a twenty-three-year-old?

I'm raging. I'm a tiger. I want to scratch his eyes out. I'm a shark and want to bite him with my five rows of razor-sharp teeth and twist him around in the water.

ME: (In the most disgusted tone I can muster.) I AM NOT *screwing* ANYONE, Dad.

Dad rolls his eyes.

DR. B: Ken?

DAD: (Sighs and kisses his teeth.) You're not, huh?

ME: No.

DAD: (Rolls eyes and smirks.)

ME: You know—I used to think you were different. But now I see you're just like every other jaded so-called adult I've ever met. You think you're so fucking smart.

DAD: Language, Vera.

ME: Oh, fuck off, Dad. You say I'm screwing a twenty-three-year-old and you're concerned with my language?

Silence, until I realize that I did, in effect, just tell Dad to fuck off.

ME: Sorry about that. I didn't mean it in the "fuck off" sense. I just meant, uh—that this is bullshit.

DAD: (Trying to look innocent, but failing.) I don't know what you mean.

I excuse myself and go to the small bathroom in the corner of the office to pee. I inspect the lump on my head, and it's still sore. My black eyes have toned down, so now I just look tired, and I figure I'll be good to go back to school next week.

I flush the toilet and wash my hands, and return to the pathetic scene. My father and Dr. B, talking about teen drinking.

DR. B: Why do *you* think kids drink, Vera?

Smooth.

ME: It's *there*, you know?

DAD: Not in our house, it's not.

ME: I don't mean *there* there. I mean, it exists. Just like all the other stuff kids try. This isn't a mystery, really, is it?

DAD: So you drink because it's *there*?

ME: I guess. (I'm lying.)

Dad looks really sad. I can tell he's got something to say.

DR. B: How do you feel about that, Ken?

DAD: Sad.

ME: (Raises eyebrows.)

DAD: That first night you came home drunk, I cried all night.

ME: You cried?

DAD: You're my daughter, for Christ's sake.

ME: But why'd you cry?

We look at each other until he speaks again.

DAD: I failed you.

ME: No you didn't.

DAD: I should have warned you more. More than just shoving brochures at you. I should have taken you to a meeting with me to see what it's like. So that you'd understand your responsibility.

ME: Uh, news flash. I'm not an alcoholic. I just had a few drinks, like a normal teenager.

DAD: But you're not a normal teenager.

ME: Sure I am.

DAD: I'm a recovered alcoholic. My parents were both alcoholics. It's different for people like us.

ME: That still doesn't make me anything but a normal teenager.

DAD: It makes you a teenager with addiction genes.

ME: But I'm not just my genes, Dad.

He looks up at me and finally stops fidgeting with his zipper.

DAD: Can I tell you what I think?

I nod.

DAD: I think you haven't gotten over Charlie.

Dr. B nods his head at this.

DAD: I think you've never quite accepted that he's dead or moved on to find new friends.

Dr. B nods again.

DAD: I'm sorry your friend died, Veer, but you have to find a time to move on and stop torturing yourself.

I'm wondering if anyone else hears the irony in this. Move on? Stop torturing myself?

ME: I think we could both benefit from that advice, Dad.

DAD: (After some fidgeting with his zipper.) Yeah. But at least you *know* that I'm struggling. I have a house full of self-help books and meditation tapes. I still haven't emptied your mother's clothing out of our closet. You? You just go on like nothing's changed. You need to let things out, Vera. Trust me. Drinking will only hide shit that you should be facing.

Here is where things get freaky for me.

As I try to stay the molasses pace of my father's remedial emotional purging, my mouth is now controlled by the thousand Charlies who are crowded in the small white room with the three of us. I bite my lips shut from the inside, but it doesn't work. He blurts out my secrets.

CHARLIES THROUGH ME: I know who burned down Zimmerman's Pet Store.

DR. B: (Raises eyebrows.)

DAD: (Leans forward.)

CHARLIES THROUGH ME: I know Charlie didn't do it.

There's a pause. They look at me as if they can see the Charlies, too.

DAD: Why didn't you say this when it happened?

ME: It's complicated.

Don't they know that regret begets regret begets regret?

DR. B: Vera, you need to answer the question.

ME: Because I loved Charlie too much.

DAD: Loved him?

DR. B: Is that all?

ME: Because I hated Charlie too much.

The daffodils are popping up in the beds. The view from my room is still brown and dead, but soon it will be new again, as if this stupid winter never happened.

Dad says I can go back to school next week and start part-time at Pagoda Pizza again, but only after our last visit with Dr. B, who we now make fun of during the ride home, as a sort of family bonding. Also, Dad has accepted that I swear, and I think I've convinced him that it's a fair trade-off. Swearing for drinking. He hasn't asked me again about clearing Charlie's name, and I'm hoping he'll let me do it in my own time. Because clearing Charlie's name is way more complicated than he thinks.

"Can we stop at McDonald's? I'd kill a Big Mac."

Dad makes that tiny sound that means *Oh please Vera*

don't make me go against every grain in my hippie freak body and make me give my money to those horrible corporate deep-frying bastards. Then he perks up and says, "I'd love a Quarter Pounder with cheese. God, I used to love them."

We pull from the drive-thru into a parking space, and we watch the traffic go up and down the main strip while we eat. Before I bite, I whisper, "Sorry, Charlie," soft enough so Dad doesn't hear over his chewing.

A BRIEF WORD FROM THE DEAD KID

What Vera doesn't know is: I'd kill to be a pickle on her Big Mac—ground to relish between her perfect white teeth.

I'd kill to be a bug she squishes with her holey Army-issue combat boot.

But she's too good for me. She always was.

Her parents were so nice. They said please and thank you. They had pictures on the walls. Paintings with frames. They had civilized furniture in neutral colors and daffodils around their flower beds. They had bird feeders. And Vera had responsibilities, something my father didn't think I should have because my mother should be doing everything for us.

One night, I tried to take my plate to the sink.

"What do you think you're doing?" my dad yelled.

"Just—uh—helping out."

"Don't make a woman out of yourself! Bring that back here."

"It's fine. I want to help."

"NOW!" He got up from his chair so fast, it toppled behind him and banged on the floor, making my mother and me jump. He grabbed my arm and took me to the sink. "Take it back," he said.

So I picked up my plate and glass, which still had an inch of milk in it, and took them back to the table. When I put them down, he let me go, backhanded the glass, which spilled the milk over Mom's favorite tablecloth, and picked up his chair.

"Son, if I ever see you being a girl like that again, I'll beat your ass."

I never tried again.

From here, on the other side, the truth wins. I can see what Vera and her family thought of us. How they never told. Never called the cops. Never interfered. Because we couldn't escape. My dad brought home our living money, and we were his prisoners. Which was why I lived most of my summers in the tree house after I built it.

I remember thinking, *If I distance myself, his crazy shit won't rub off on me. I won't become a wife-beating asshole.* I remember daydreaming, *One day, I will make enough money to rescue my mother. One day, I will come back and make him sorry he ever had me. One day, I will show him what a real man is.*

But then I got confused.

And I made some mistakes.

Which I didn't forgive myself for.

Which made things worse.

Because then I made more mistakes.

Vera and I had two fights before she stopped talking to me

completely. The first one was about what Jenny Flick told me—a lie—about how Vera was telling everyone that my dad was a wife-beating asshole.

The second was the night of May Day, when she found me in the bleachers by myself, with a bottle of Jack Daniel's in a paper bag.

I told her she was too good for me.

"Bullshit. You're my best friend."

"Bullshit yourself. I'm King Loser."

"No—Bill Corso is King Loser. He can't even read."

"Hey. Don't knock Bill," I said, trying to bait her. Like my father would.

"Sorry. I know he's your new pal."

"Why are you so fucking bitchy about my new friends? What did they ever do to you?"

"It's not what they did to me," she said. "It's what they're doing to you."

"What?" I took a swig out of the bottle for effect, but I knew what she meant. I'd been drinking every night for a month.

"Who are you doing this for? Is it Jenny? Is this about being in her pants, or what?"

Oh yes. I would kill to be a pickle on Vera's Big Mac. Because Vera gave a shit.

And she knew how to tell the truth.

And she loved me.

So I hit her. Right when she said that, I hit her.

THREE WEEKS OF VOCAB WORDS
AND OTHER MAKEUP HOMEWORK

Here's me using *bisect* in a sentence.

The night when Charlie hit me, I bisected. Half of me will never trust another living soul again. The other half already didn't.

Vicarious. The night Charlie hit me, I became Mrs. Kahn for a split second, in a vicarious body switch I had always feared.

Zoomorphic. The night Charlie hit me, he demonstrated his zoomorphic abilities by changing into a man-eating tiger.

Altruism. The night Charlie hit me, every ounce of altruism I had for him as a lost soul on a bad path dissolved.

GROUNDED,
COMPLETELY AND TOTALLY—PART 3

After our fourth and final meeting with Dr. B, Dad and I go out for ice cream and miniature golf. When we get to the third hole (par 4 through the windmill bridge), I see a new party of players behind us. It's Bill Corso and Jenny Flick and two other Detentionheads.

"Hurry up, Dad," I say.

He looks at me and shrugs, then chokes completely and misses the windmill. He sees me rushing and looking back at the Detentionheads and whispers, "Do you want to just go?"

I nod.

Only when we're back home, trying to figure out what dinner would be good on top of too much ice cream, does he ask me who they were.

"Just some assholes from school."

"You don't usually care about assholes from school."

The swearing trade-off is working out great.

"Jenny Flick is the girl who turned Charlie against me," I say, plopping myself on the stool by the breakfast bar.

"You never told me that."

"There's a lot I didn't tell you."

That night, we rearrange the living room and Dad throws Mom's clothing into a few black garbage bags for Goodwill. I round up her crystal collection, which has done nothing but gather dust for six years, and I box it up and take it to the attic. This is a very serious step we're taking—clearing Mom out of this house. Making my peace with her brings me one step closer to making my peace with Charlie. (Which brings me one step closer to making my peace with myself.)

FIRST DAY BACK IN SCHOOL—
MONDAY

It's been almost a month since I was in school, and Bill Corso is *still* getting detention for skipping Modern Social Thought. Mr. Shunk must know he can't read, but even though we have a remedial reading teacher, it's too close to graduation to help the kid. It's sad as hell, really.

Over at table two, three kids are listening to something on a pair of earbuds. Two others are doodling in notebooks. Rob Jones is doing his Calc homework. Three cheerleaders are giggling and whispering. I'm pretty sure if Mr. Shunk didn't stand at the front of class and clap his hands together, these people would just continue to do what they're doing until the bell rings, and then go to their next class.

This essentially makes Mr. Shunk a kindergarten teacher.

Which makes me a kindergarten student.

It also makes my father right again. How will I ever soar with the eagles if I'm surrounded by turkeys?

After we finish reading *Lord of the Flies*, Chapter Ten, the bell rings, and on my way to lunch I find Jenny Flick at my locker with Bill.

"How's your mom?"

How's my mom? WTF? Haven't we been through this already? "Fine," I say, tossing my books into the locker as fast as I can.

"She left you, right?"

"She left my dad, yeah."

"Where is she now? Is that where you were for the last month?"

I slam the locker closed, and turn away from them to go down the steps to the cafeteria. But Bill reaches out and grabs my arm.

"Where is she?" he asks. It's like he thinks he's the freaking mob.

"Las Vegas—not like it's any of your business."

"What's she doing in Vegas?" he says. "She working again?"

"I hear prostitution is legal there," Jenny says, still standing by the lockers.

I push my way through the reinforced glass doors and go down the steps. I can hear them laughing by my locker, though, and can't figure out why they think they can get to me with my mom. That's so last year. Shouldn't Jenny be avoiding me and hoping I don't tell the truth about Zimmerman's? Has she grown cocky now that it's been so long and I haven't told? Is she so crazy that she's forgotten that I *know*?

Here's me using *timorous* in a sentence.

There's a table of timorous kids in the back of the cafeteria, and I am one of them. They don't have any pre-assigned seating and they won't talk to you if you sit there, and that's fine by me, because I don't want to talk to anyone while I eat my soggy, too old, greasy grilled cheese sandwich that cost two hard-earned dollars. I make a mental note to pack my lunch tomorrow.

Until last year, when the shitstorm began, I sat with Charlie in the back booth on the east side of the cafeteria. Sometimes we let other outcasts squeeze in with us, but for the most part we ate alone, just the two of us.

And now he's a series of molecules. He's the wind. He's my shoe. He's your telephone and your eyeglasses. Now he's the pickle on my plate next to the cafeteria's limp grilled cheese sandwich. So when Jenny and Bill walk into the cafeteria, I pick it up and bite into it, hoping just a fraction of me can be as cool as Charlie was only a year ago.

Later today, I have a meeting with my guidance counselor, who is monitoring me for Dad. He's the only one in the school (that I know of) who knows what really happened to me during February. We told the rest of the administration that I was sick with mono. The family doctor even wrote me a note full of lies. It meant I didn't have to go to school with the lump on my head and black eyes. It also meant that no one found out about my weakness for vodka coolers and older men.

HISTORY I'D RATHER FORGET—
AGE SEVENTEEN—JUNE

The next time I saw Charlie Kahn, after the night he hit me, I was stopped at the APlus for a candy bar. Dad had loaned me his car (with an Earth, Wind & Fire CD in it, which I cranked to 10) so I could go to Goodwill for some new clothes for summer. When I emerged from the APlus already munching, I didn't see anyone else in the parking lot until I heard Charlie's voice.

"Hey, Vera! How's the stripper business?"

He was slurring drunk. Stumbling. He was standing next to his bike, now fitted with all sorts of expensive accessories, over by the bathroom doors. I wanted to slap him back to life. Slap some sense into him. I wanted to slap him so he'd know how it felt to be slapped. So he'd know how it felt to be zero.

"Shut up, Charlie."

"Don't tell my boyfriend to shut up," Jenny Flick said,

stepping out of the shadows, her cleavage hoisted up to bulge out of her scoop-neck tank top. Charlie took a loud hit from what must have been a joint. I'd heard in school that he was officially a druggie now, but I didn't know what to believe until I saw him.

I shrugged and walked back to the car. I don't know who threw the half-empty beer can at me, but it only skimmed my head and hit the car instead, leaving a small dent just under the driver's side window.

Dad smelled the beer. I didn't even notice my sleeve was wet. I'd driven home in a trance, with the stereo off, trying not to cry.

"Were you drinking tonight?"

"No."

"So," he said, and paused to look at my face. "Why do you smell like that?"

"Someone threw beer at me."

"Someone?"

"I'm tired, Dad. Can we talk about this tomorrow?"

He went back to his *Utne Reader*.

Around two in the morning, I could hear Jenny's souped-up Nova drop Charlie off outside his house. He opened the car door and a mix of laughter, loud, unintelligible words, and thrash metal music flowed into our forest and infected it with *them*.

I interviewed at Zimmerman's Pet Store on a Monday afternoon. I thought I had it made. Mr. Zimmerman—a man I'd known since I was five and who knew me from my volunteering at the adoption center for three summers—was a complete sweetheart and winked at me on the way out.

I drove home prematurely ecstatic.

I parked Dad's car and he met me at the door.

"How'd it go?" he said, looking past me at the car. He tried to hide it, but every time I came home from driving by myself after that night when the beer can dented the driver's door, he'd scour the paint job for scratches or dings.

"Said he'd let me know by next week," I said.

"But did it go well?"

"I think so. I mean, I didn't kill any of the animals I handled." He'd made me touch nearly all of them, too. Even the crusty old iguana and a gray parrot that bit me six times. "Anyway, Mrs. Parker will put in a good word for me."

By Friday, I was getting nervous. Dad purposely moved the pizza delivery application to the kitchen counter again and suggested I fill it out. "That way, you won't have all your eggs in one basket," he said.

Saturday, when no one called from Zimmerman's, I filled it out. Dad let me borrow the car to drive it down to the place, which was stuck into the side of a small, lame strip mall on the main strip of Mount Pitts. The place looked clean and the people who worked there seemed nice. But there was no point thinking about it. I was going to work at Zimmerman's Pet Store.

On my way back up the main strip toward my house, I stopped at a red light and heard the familiar buzzing of Charlie's bike. I looked around and saw him, with Jenny on the back, pulling out of one of the roads in the next block. So when I got to it, I took the right and tried to get my instinct to take me to where they had just been. I tried to convince myself this was detective work or simple curiosity, but really it was a mix of jealousy and payback, as if having information about them could make me more powerful. I guess I cared, even though I was trying not to.

About three blocks down Twenty-third Street was a dirty-looking house with the front curtains drawn and the old white Chrysler parked outside. 2301.

When I called Zimmerman's Pet Store and found out that I didn't get the job, I wanted to scream. I called Dad from school. It was finals week.

"I didn't get the job," I said.

"I'm sorry to hear that."

"Don't you want to say 'I told you so'?"

After a few seconds, he answered, "Don't sweat it, Vera. Everything happens for a reason."

The reason was: Mr. Zimmerman wasn't calling the shots anymore. The leftover medical bills from Mrs. Zimmerman's cancer had all but wiped him out. His store had been bought by a corporate group who allowed him to make it seem like a family-owned store when it really wasn't. The other reason was: They weren't hiring anyone under eighteen now, on account of a new community service program they'd set up with the high school.

During the early summer, I started work (day-shift pizza maker) at Pagoda Pizza at noon, while Charlie and Jenny were still asleep up in their tree house of lust, and I didn't get home until six, when they were already down on Twenty-third Street doing God-knows-what. Dad *finally* gave me Mom's old Nissan. He even put a decent stereo in it. (And even though I found it totally hypocritical that Mom had a PRACTICE RANDOM ACTS OF KINDNESS bumper sticker, I left it on to remind myself that I was not a low-road zero.)

My job at Pagoda Pizza was okay. It took me about three weeks to hate pizza.

One night after work, I drove over to Zimmerman's to say hello to Mrs. Parker and Mr. Zimmerman, if he was there, but when I walked in the door, it was a sea of new faces. I finally found Mrs. Parker back by where they kept the large dog breeds.

"Vera!"

"Hey, Mrs. P."

She told me she was sorry to hear I hadn't gotten the job. "Things have changed a lot around here," she said.

"It's all right," I said. "I was hoping to volunteer a few hours a week, but this new job is keeping me too busy."

"They're moving us soon anyway," she said. "The new boss doesn't think it's a good idea to mix business with—you know—charity."

"Huh. That's sad. End of an era," I said, scratching a black Lab mix under her chin until her paw started to move uncontrollably.

"We're going back to the old facility in town. Probably at the end of the summer. September, I think." While she said this, two girls grooming a dog behind the glass in the adoption area caught my eye. One of them looked like Jenny

Flick. She was wearing a volunteer T-shirt and had her hair in a ponytail.

"Is that Jenny Flick?" I asked.

Mrs. Parker shrugged. "I can't keep up with names. They send us new kids all the time. The community service program with the school is a mess," she said. "They spend most of their time screwing around and think they can get credit for it. Such a waste."

"Huh," I said, spotting Jenny's ample eyeliner as she turned around.

"It's so different from how it used to work," she said. "Half these kids don't even like animals."

Even though Zimmerman's wasn't my favorite place in the world anymore since I'd been denied my dream job, I was steaming mad about this. All of it. After so many years of Mr. Zimmerman's support, the adoption center would move back into town, where fewer people would get a chance to adopt pets that needed good homes. The mere thought of apathetic high school kids taking advantage of Mrs. Parker made me cringe. But of course it was more personal than that, because Jenny was working there—in my store, for my old boss. The only place in Mount Pitts that hadn't been touched by her was now hers. But while twelve-year-old Vera stormed around like a drama queen inside my head, saying things like "Charlie probably made her do it" or "I should tell Mrs. Parker she's a drug fiend," I tried to look at things like an adult (Dad) would. I *rationalized* and *used my head*. When I was done, I arrived at a *solution*.

I would *ignore* it. I would stop going to the Pagoda Mall. I would stop going to Zimmerman's Pet Store. I would stop thinking about being a vet. Maybe Dad was right. Maybe it was cruel to keep birds in cages. Maybe cats weren't meant to shit in a box. He always said human beings spent more money feeding their pets than they did feeding the world. He'd say children—some just miles away—were suffering from hunger and malnutrition while we spent our money on red-white-and-blue rubber bones, exercise balls, catnip mice, and hot rocks for iguanas who wouldn't even be living in Pennsylvania if they had the choice.

A BRIEF WORD FROM THE PAGODA

It's true. 47% of children in this town live below the poverty level. Many of them are hungry right now, while you're reading this. Some of them would be happy to eat one tin of that dog food you slop out twice a day.

MONDAY—FOUR TO EIGHT

When I called Marie to tell her I was coming back to work part-time, she told me that James had agreed to move back to day shift so my dad wouldn't freak. This, for a pizza delivery driver, is the ultimate sacrifice. He will lose approximately twenty dollars a day, probably forty on Fridays, which means James has made a $120-per-week effort to make my father (a man who would never give up $120 for anyone) more comfortable.

Going back to work without James there is weird. Marie found this middle-aged guy named Larry to work four-to-close on weeknights, and he's okay, I guess. Lazy. Can't mop the floor without leaving black, dirty streaks and puddles everywhere. Folds about two boxes a minute (so he doesn't get paper cuts) and smells like garlic.

Ex-cheerleader-turned-food-service-worker Jill quit the job while I was out, which is a surprise. Marie says she's chef-ing over at the local diner now, with the Greeks. I bet her skinhead Nazi boyfriend is thrilled about that.

Marie gives me nearly all suburban runs, since, while I was grounded, two pizza delivery drivers were robbed in town. Nobody from our place, but still, she's looking out for me, and I'm glad. Anyway, garlic man Larry can handle the town runs. He doesn't seem to mind.

"You going anywhere near Fred's Bar?" Larry asks, squatting a little to see all the pies and figure out what goes on whose pile.

"I hate that place."

"Well, I'm going into the east side," he says, with that look on his face that only the east side of town can give you.

"Yeah, okay. I'll take it," I say, although I know I shouldn't be going to Fred's Bar.

My farthest and final run is out to the government townhouses that they just built on Hammer Lane. Nice place—new, beige siding, nice landscaping with mulch. A great way to drag your family out of the stinking town and raise them up in the fresh air while maintaining an income from welfare and remaining unemployed. (You should hear what Dad says about places like this.)

I've only been here once before, so I'm unsure of the numbers. I slow down, find the even side of the street, and eventually find #224.

I am *so* not paying attention when the guy opens the door with his pants down that I hand him the four sodas before I see what's going on. Then, instinct tells me to ignore him. Keep eye contact. Do not look down.

I hand him the pies. "That's ten-oh-five, please."

He stands there, pants around his ankles, two large pizzas

balanced in his right hand and four Sprites in his left. He stares at me as if I'm supposed to do something.

It is erect and I wonder will this fuck me up for life.

He shuffles to the hall table and puts the soda down. As he shuffles back, it bounces, like a diving board. This is becoming one of the funnier moments in pizza delivery.

He reaches down into his back pocket, which is on the floor with the rest of his pants, and asks, "How much was that again?"

"Ten," I say, realizing that he has the use of his hands back and I just want to get out of here.

He hands me a ten and two singles and stays at the door with his pants around his ankles and his hard-on. When I back out of his little driveway, he waves. I tell the air, "See? This is why we need signs."

PART FIVE

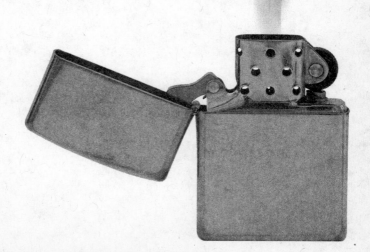

SECOND DAY BACK IN SCHOOL—
TUESDAY

I ask Dad over breakfast, "Do you think Mom stopped loving you before or after she met what's-his-name?"

He chews his granola slowly. It bugs me. Maybe it bugged Mom, too.

"I don't know," he answers. "I'm not even sure she did stop loving me," he adds.

I know the feeling. I don't think Charlie stopped loving me, either.

Now Charlie's dead and I'm here in the kitchen—on my way to school, and then to work. It's my senior year and I still have no idea what I want to do with my life. I am motherless, and in the last year, I lost my best friend twice, fell in love with a guy I shouldn't have (twice), got beat up by a skinhead Nazi, and had things thrown at me, including beer cans, money, and dog shit.

Oh. Yeah. And last night.

"There was a guy out on Hammer Lane last night who answered the door with his pants down," I say to Dad, who seems to still be chewing the same mouthful of granola.

"In his underwear?" he says, between chews.

"Nope," I say, slightly embarrassed to describe the details. "Um—fully, uh—you know. No underwear."

He looks at me and bulges his eyes out, chews fast, and swallows. "Did you call the police?"

I shrug. "What could they do about it?"

"Vera! What's *wrong* with you?" He's now pouring the rest of the contents of his cereal bowl into the drain strainer and rinsing the sink.

"I wouldn't have even thought to call the cops. He was just a weirdo." Right? Wasn't he? Harmless?

"You see? *This* is the kind of thing I was talking about when it comes to responsibility. You need to have a vision of *community*, Veer. What if that guy—what if—what if he does that when the Girl Scouts come around to sell cookies?"

I shrug again. I didn't expect him to freak out like this. We stare at each other for a minute.

"Can you remember the address?" he asks.

"Yeah. But what's the point in saying anything? What can they do about it?"

He looks at me, thoroughly disappointed. "Do you want *me* to call them?"

"No."

"Well, one of us will."

Okay. I admit it. The only reason I mentioned it was to

make him feel bad for making me work this job. I had no idea he'd freak. But now I'm looking at him and I'm thinking about what an enormous hypocrite he is. I'm thinking about how my guts told me a million times to help Charlie. I'm thinking about the million times Dad told me to ignore it.

"Let me get this straight," I say. "You want me to report some loser who answered the door for the pizza delivery with his pants around his ankles, but you've been telling me my whole life to ignore the boxing match—" I am so angry, I feel my hand shaking as I point to Charlie's house. "Right next door? What kind of person do you think I am?"

"I—"

"What about the Girl Scouts who came to the Kahns' and sold Thin Mints to the lady with the broken arm? What kind of *community lessons* did they learn from *that*, Dad?"

This approach is destined to backfire on me, so I decide to dump the rest of my cereal down the drain, too, and talk nonstop on my way to the door.

"All you ever said was, 'Ignore it, Vera,' and now you think this creep from last night is worth talking about? Get a grip, Dad. That's the most hypocritical thing I've ever heard. And that asshole is *still* beating her up. He's *still* getting away with it. You're *still letting him* get away with it."

I slam the door and walk briskly to the car. I see the bus coming up Overlook Road and remember how Charlie and I used to wait together, and how he'd smoke two cigarettes one off the other between 7:00 and 7:14, when the bus stopped. How he always made sure to exhale his last breath into the bus on the way up the steps.

I wonder if I'd called the police back when I was ten or thirteen or fifteen, would Charlie be alive now. I regret it. I regret every minute I lived keeping that secret. I regret every time I didn't talk to Charlie about it. I regret having parents who couldn't try to help or seem to care. I regret not being reason enough to *make* them care more. I regret never saying what I was thinking, never saying, "But what if that was me? What if I marry some loser who hits me? Would you care then? Would you help?" And I regret not calling the police that first day we met the pervert. Because I'm sure he had something to do with how Charlie was acting at the end.

I realize, sitting here in my car, watching my neighborhood wake up, that I can't let my regret stop me anymore. I say, half to Charlie and half to myself, "I'm so sorry. I promise I'll change this somehow."

As I back out of the driveway onto the road, I see Dad looking at me through the front bay window. He waves, which means truce, which means he still can't handle talking about anything remotely heavy and would prefer to ignore it. I think of the Post-it note he tacked near the sink. "Fundamentally, the marksman aims at himself."

Fundamentally, Dad is ignoring himself.

Fundamentally, Mr. Kahn is beating himself.

Fundamentally, then, I am delivering myself. I wonder if I want a six-pack of Coke with that? Garlic bread?

HISTORY I'D RATHER FORGET—
AGE SEVENTEEN—AUGUST

The summer wound down. I got good at ignoring Charlie and Jenny or whoever else he brought into the woods for pot parties and sex, or whatever he was into now. I got good at ignoring the Pagoda Mall and any leftover urges I had to work at Zimmerman's, now that I knew the adoption center was moving, and especially now that Jenny Flick had started showing up there to rack up community service credits for graduation.

I liked working at Pagoda Pizza, and even though I was dying to switch to night shift and start delivering once I turned eighteen, I got along great with Nate, the day manager, who said my love of Al Green made me an "honorary sister." I liked working so much, I was kind of sad to be going back to school to become Vera Dietz, the whatever-lies-Jenny-Flick-and-Charlie-told-people senior. There was a week left, and I hadn't bought any supplies yet. Or clothes. I hadn't even opened the envelope with my schedule in it, which had come in the mail two weeks before. I was thinking of these things as I pulled into the driveway after a ten-to-four shift. When I noticed something moving toward my driver's side window and then looked up and saw Charlie, I was scared.

"We have to talk," he said.

"Please, Charlie. Go away."

"I'm in trouble."

I looked into his eyes. He looked in trouble.

"Why should I care?"

"Will you take a walk with me?"

"No."

He stopped as I continued to the house. Dad was there, so I felt safe.

"Just to the oak?"

"Go home, Charlie."

"Vera, I'm serious. I need your help."

"I'm serious, too, Charlie."

We looked at each other.

"Jenny's crazy. She's going to hurt the animals," he said.

"Your problem. Not mine." I said that, but my heart twisted at the thought of it. Who hurts animals?

"She is," he said.

"Just go home, Charlie. Leave me alone."

"Can't you call one of your dog people and warn them?"

"Can't you?" I asked.

We stared at each other for a few seconds, silently, and I walked toward the front door.

"She's going to kill me," he said, dead serious.

"Your problem," I answered, rolling my inner eyes. Yeah, sure. She's going to kill you, Charlie. Right.

"But I thought you were my friend," he said, his voice quivering.

I thought about May Day, when he hit me. "I *was* your friend, Charlie. But I'm not anymore."

"When did you turn into such a *bitch*?" he screamed.

Dad opened the front door right then.

Charlie was still jittering next to the car as I walked past Dad and into the house. Dad stayed at the door until Charlie walked back into the woods, muttering to himself.

While I took a shower to wash the smell of grease and pepperoni out of my hair and skin, I had awful daydreams. I thought about Charlie coming back with one of his dad's guns and shooting us up. Or himself. I thought about what kind of trouble he might be in and hoped it wasn't too bad. Then I remembered that he was an asshole now. I'd probably been right to doubt him. Jenny and Bill Corso and Gretchen the squirrel-brained were probably all waiting in the woods, sad I hadn't fallen for their lies.

And seriously—the story about Jenny Flick hurting animals? What a sorry piece of bait that was. I wondered if it took all four of them to think it up. Morons.

Dad made dinner. Fettuccine Alfredo.

"What did Charlie want?"

I wanted to tell him everything. But Dietzes don't do drama.

"Nothing important," I answered. "Nice pasta."

"Thanks. I found the recipe in the paper."

I hadn't talked to Dad about what was happening with Charlie since Valentine's Day. He hadn't asked, either, and that was fine.

We sat at the breakfast bar, me facing the sliding doors, him facing me. I stared at the fading light, which was fading earlier these days.

I looked at the calendar on the fridge.

"Less than a week left," I said.

"Yeah. I went to the mall today to get some staples and the place was packed."

"Ugh. Shopping."

Dad laughed.

"Everything is overpriced crap."

"You make me proud, Veer," Dad said.

I did make him proud. I had become his mini-me—a parsimonious, self-sufficient Vulcan who pretended everything was great when it really wasn't.

A BRIEF WORD FROM KEN DIETZ
(VERA'S PROUD DAD)

~~Cindy~~ Sindy always said I saved myself like I saved money. Said I was emotionally thrifty. She used to tell me how bad it stank to go nowhere all day, and when I suggested that she take Vera with her, she said, "I can't take Vera to the places I want to go."

I never asked, but it occurred to me the night she left that she might have meant the grocery store, or the movies, or the hairdresser's, or just in the car by herself for a drive to nowhere special. Time alone. She meant she wanted a break. She wasn't even twenty yet. The least I could have done was give her a break after knocking her up and marrying her so young.

To say it was a shotgun wedding would not be inaccurate. Her father owned several shotguns, and he did refer to them twice the night we went to his place to tell them the bad news.

~~Cindy~~ Sindy told me she wanted to keep the baby, so before any mention of shotguns, I'd already prepared to marry her.

"You think the paychecks you get from the gas station can support a wife and baby?"

"Yes, sir."

"How much do you get a week?"

"One ninety-eight."

Her mother stopped crying for a second to say, "One ninety-eight? An hour?"

"A week, Janet," her father said, and then turned back to me. "Just how do you suppose you're gonna raise my grand-child on less than eight hundred bucks a month? Where you gonna rent a place for that kind of shitty money?"

"We'll move into my mother's house," I said.

After considerable silence and visible relief that we didn't choose *them* to leech off, he said, "And how did she take the news?"

"She's as shocked as you, but okay with it."

Mrs. Lutz cried louder. Mr. Lutz said, "I bet she is."

But I hadn't told my mother yet.

For three months, ~~Cindy~~ Sindy and I lived out of my bedroom, her sleeping a lot and puking occasionally, me drinking beer and watching bad sitcoms on the black-and-white mini TV I found in the attic. One Sunday morning, I woke up to loud noise right next to my aching head. I opened my eyes to find my mother in our room, cigarette hanging from her mouth, emptying my dresser drawers into black garbage bags.

"Did you think I wouldn't notice?"

"Notice what?" I asked, slipping on a pair of boxers under

the covers. ~~Cindy~~ Sindy rolled over, groaned, hugged a pillow to her chest, and kept sleeping.

"That you knocked up a teenager and moved her into my house?"

"Her name is Cindy."

"Her name is statutory rape, Kenny." She went back to emptying my stuff into a bag until I grabbed it from her.

"We're getting married. Her parents are fine with it."

She stared at me the way she had a million times before—like I was nothing but a regret.

"Then you can live with *them*."

I had to go to work in the afternoon, and when I got back to the house, she not only had all my stuff in the backyard, but there was a FOR SALE sign by the mailbox.

After a week in the Lutzes' basement, we found an apartment in town for $350 a month. It was infested with roaches and lacked air-conditioning. That's where we lived when Vera was born. Two months after that, we got married. A month or so after that, ~~Cindy~~ Sindy took the strip job at the club because I was drinking our rent. Five months after that, I quit drinking.

But quitting drinking didn't save my marriage, because quitting drinking is only what it is: quitting drinking. I had no idea how to be a friend or companion to ~~Cindy~~ Sindy. I never asked her how she was, because I didn't really think about how she was. I just thought about what she thought of me. And because I'd been conditioned to think I was an asshole by my chain-smoking mean-assed mother, I didn't know (or want to know) what ~~Cindy~~ Sindy *really* thought of me, because I was sure she thought I was an asshole, too.

When Vera turned one, ~~Cindy~~ Sindy stopped stripping and started waiting tables at the diner down the street. I'd watch Vera until three, when ~~Cindy~~ Sindy would come home, and then I'd go work the four-to-midnight shift at the gas station. ~~Cindy~~ Sindy seemed happier at the diner than she'd been at the club, but the money was less than half.

I went in one day before work and I saw the lunch guys flirting with her. I saw them leering and laughing, and something clicked inside me. I realized that I was the one in control of my being a loser. I realized that I wanted to give ~~Cindy~~ Sindy and Vera a better future. So on my way to work, I stopped at the community college and told them I needed to do something with my life. The admissions people were friendly and gave me stacks of information, which I leafed through all night at work. The next morning, I enrolled in the summer session for accounting. Just after Vera's fourth birthday, I passed my CPA exam and got a real job at a firm in the center of town. I tripled my salary and told ~~Cindy~~ Sindy to quit her job, which she did. But she didn't stop complaining about me. Because getting a great job didn't save my marriage. Because getting a great job is only what it is: getting a great job.

"You went from alcoholic to workaholic, Kenny. We never see you anymore."

"I just want to provide for my girls," I'd say.

"You just want to avoid me."

I said, "That's not true," but she was right. I was scared to come home. I was scared to explore the hole I still had inside myself.

She called it baggage. "You're scared to open your suit-cases and see what your mother packed."

That ~~Cindy~~ Sindy. She was so damn smart. But I never told her that. I also never told her that I loved her, or that I loved the two little stretch marks she got from carrying Vera. Or that I loved that freckle on her forehead. I never told her that I loved her lasagna or that I thought her views on politics were clever. I just kept my mouth shut because I thought that made me safe.

I see Vera doing this now. She hasn't said a word to me about Charlie, even though only a year ago, she was clearly in love with him. Before that, they were inseparable since they were four years old. She acts like I didn't see any of this. No. She acts like *she* didn't see any of this. I want to tell her it's no use hiding. I want to tell her that the only thing you get from walling yourself in is empty.

KEN DIETZ'S FACE YOUR SHIT FLOW CHART

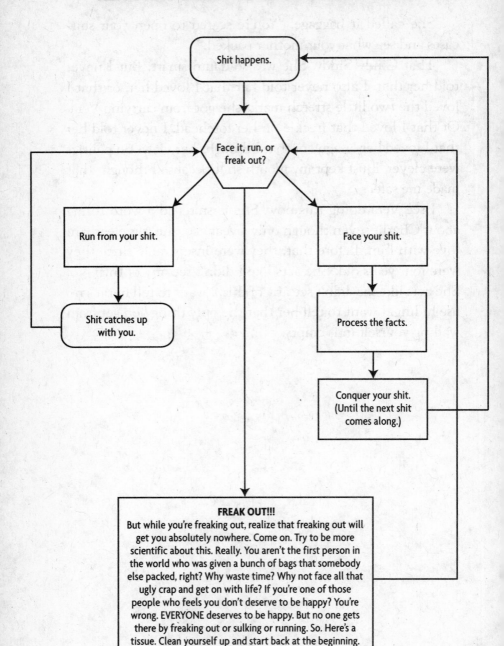

Shit happens.

Face it, run, or freak out?

Run from your shit.

Face your shit.

Shit catches up with you.

Process the facts.

Conquer your shit. (Until the next shit comes along.)

FREAK OUT!!!
But while you're freaking out, realize that freaking out will get you absolutely nowhere. Come on. Try to be more scientific about this. Really. You aren't the first person in the world who was given a bunch of bags that somebody else packed, right? Why waste time? Why not face all that ugly crap and get on with life? If you're one of those people who feels you don't deserve to be happy? You're wrong. EVERYONE deserves to be happy. But no one gets there by freaking out or sulking or running. So. Here's a tissue. Clean yourself up and start back at the beginning.

PIGGY'S REVENGE—TUESDAY

I have three minutes to get to Modern Social Thought and I am being pressed into the back corner of the library wing bathroom by a thousand Charlies. They are translucent enough for me to see the gross pink tiles behind them. They are heavy, though, and I feel the air being sucked out of my lungs. My arms instinctively guard my chest, crossways.

They are all talking at the same time. The noise is like a busy train station. No words are coming through. It's all chattering. But I know what they're saying. Their sole purpose is to push me to look for the note Charlie left me. The note that's haunted me from the moment he said, "I'm leaving something for you."

Through the thousand Charlies, I see the mirror steaming up. I walk slowly toward the sink, against the weight of them. I press through like I am battling a series of strong waves to where the breath is—without wondering how a hallucination/ghost/spirit/lost soul can even *have* breath. I am so busy surfing the Charlies that I do not see, until I arrive, that a message is scrawled—in Charlie's messy handwriting—in the steam.

The door squeaks open. Charlies disappear.

Gretchen, head Flickite, walks in, sees me hyperventilating, then looks at the mirror, sees the writing, and smirks.

"Freak," she hisses. "What are you? Some sort of baby?"

I look at the mirror. It says HELP ME.

When I get to Modern Social Thought, Bill Corso is there, and he's coughing a lot. Like the way I used to cough when I was in third grade and wanted Mom to come and pick me up from school.

The bell rings, and Mr. Shunk sits at his desk doing work for a minute before he gets up, sits on his stool at the front of the class, opens *Lord of the Flies,* and points to me. So I start reading the chapter where we left off.

A minute after I start, the classroom is quiet and Gretchen is back from her trip to the bathroom to smoke one of those stupid-looking long and extra-skinny cigarettes. Mr. Shunk says, "Corso. You next."

"I—uh."

"Pick up where Dietz left off."

He coughs and whispers, "I can't."

"Of course you can."

"Doc says that if I talk, I could lose my voice," he says. This causes a few Vo-Tech computer-programming geeks to snigger.

"That's odd," Mr. Shunk says. "I saw you last period in the gym playing badminton and you sounded perfectly healthy."

"I—uh, can't. I just can't," he says, getting up from his seat.

Mr. Shunk stands in the aisle between table one and table two. He leans into Bill Corso and says, "Mr. Corso, if you take one step toward that door, I'm failing you. You'll lose those precious few athletic scholarship dollars you have. Sit your ass down and read."

Bill sits down. He puts his finger on the book where I left off and he reads, slowly.

"You . . . are a silly little boy . . . said the . . . Lord of the Flies. Just an ig . . . igno . . ."

"Ignorant," Gretchen whispers. Bill kisses his teeth and glares at her.

Mr. Shunk says, "Continue."

Bill blinks. "Just an ignorant, silly little boy."

He stops and sighs before he stutters his way through another sentence. The room is still. I wonder if Charlie is here. In the bookshelf, on my pencil eraser. I wonder if he's spread himself through the air—as molecules of oxygen.

I wonder is he as sad as I am for Bill. What sort of future does the kid have? What's this place doing to ensure his destiny isn't for shit? Who taught him that football was everything?

During lunch, everyone is talking about it. I sit with the dorks in the center back, by the long, rattling heating and air-conditioning unit. I think about the fight I had with my father this morning. God, adults are hypocrites. Look at Corso. The only way Bill Corso got to be a senior in high school was by adults overlooking his reading problem in order to help our school make it further in the PIAA championships . . . which never happened. Now he's been accepted to a small college with a crappy football team, and he can't read.

"What do you think you're looking at?"

It's Jenny Flick and Gretchen. Jenny is looking especially nuts today—her eyeliner has curlicues at the edges.

"Nothing." I'm staring out the window. I'm looking at the huge oak tree out by the parking lot and creatively visualizing climbing it.

"So you think you need help?" Jenny says.

I look up through my bangs, now long and unkempt, like Charlie's used to be. "What are you talking about?"

"Gretchen saw you in the bathroom."

"So?"

"So this is about Charlie, isn't it?" she says. I think: *Isn't everything about Charlie?*

Jenny leans into my ear to whisper something and I get chills up my back and shiver. She says, "Too bad you never got to know him like I knew him."

I jerk away from her, pick up my books, and walk out of the cafeteria. Everything seems like *Lord of the Flies* now. We're all animals. Out to compete. Out to win. Out to kill. This means Charlie, in the end, is Piggy, right? I think about this through my next classes, because if Charlie is Piggy, then I should feel more sympathy for him. I know I do. Deep inside. I know he's sorry. He's been telling me he's sorry for nearly nine months.

Nine months is how long it takes to grow a baby. (Can

you tell I'm in eighth-period Health class?) When my mother was my age, she was just about to have me after I'd spent nine long months growing inside her. Now it's my turn. I am going to birth myself. I am going to be a better mother to me than she ever was. I'm going to stay faithful and stand up for myself. I am going to do more than send me fifty bucks on my birthday, and if I ever call myself on the phone, I'm going to act like I care, just a little, because I'm aware that I might need it. I will comb my own hair gently and never make myself get into bathwater that's too hot. I am going to be the kind of mother who shows warmth. A mother who would call the police when Mr. Kahn hit so hard, we could hear it all the way at our house—or who might drop in on Mrs. Kahn the day after to try to help her figure out how to leave that abusive bastard.

Today I am in control because I want to be. I can set Jenny Flick's future to zero. I can dial up Charlie's reputation to ten again, even though he's dead. I have my fingers on the switch, but have lived a lifetime ignoring the control I have over my own world. Today is different. On the night he died, Charlie said he left something for me. Today I'm going to find it.

I have twenty minutes before I leave for work, so rather than go inside the house, where Dad is probably waiting to lecture me about calling him a hypocrite this morning, I leave all my school stuff in the car and disappear into the woods between our house and the Kahns' house. I climb the ladder like I have a thousand times before and swing myself onto the octagonal deck that's covered in a mix of old, crackling autumn leaves and a layer of spring-green pollen. There are spiderwebs. I pull out my key and am surprised to find he didn't change the lock.

When I get inside, I see that nothing has been disturbed. The bed looks slept in. There are snacks. A mug with a ring of dried liquid at the bottom. I don't want to look around too much. The last thing this tree house saw was Jenny Flick and Charlie having sex, and I really don't want to think about that. So I shift the mattress to the right and find the floorboard that Charlie wants me to find. I can't pry it open without a tool, so I look back to his makeshift kitchen and find a teaspoon, still sticky, and insert its handle into the crack. After considerable wiggling, the board lifts, and I stick my hand in the dark hole beneath.

It's empty. I search the hole more and I feel stupid. I mean, seriously. Did I really think that images from a dream I had while passed out drunk would equate with real life?

Then my hand feels a crumpled napkin and I pull it out and straighten it. It's a Burger King napkin. My heart races. But all it says is *Hi, Vera.* I stick my entire arm in to see if there's anything that feels remotely like a box, but there's nothing. I fold up the note, stick it in my pocket, replace the foot-long floorboard, and hammer it in with the heel of my hand, then I shift the mattress over again. I back out, close the door, slip the padlock through the loop, and snap it closed. On my way down the ladder, I hear the patio door at the Kahns' slam, and it gives me such a fright, I jump from too high up and almost turn my ankle on the forest floor. Then I run home.

"Vera?" Dad calls from his office.

I poke my head in. "Yeah?"

"You want to talk about this morning?"

"I have to get to work, Dad."

"Are we okay?"

"I guess."

"I want you to be careful out there."

"I will."

"Don't let them send you into the projects," he says.

I say, "It's building character, remember?"

I wonder does he feel bad yet.

HISTORY I'D RATHER FORGET— AGE SEVENTEEN—AUGUST

I had Sunday off, so I went school shopping at the thrift store across town. It was the safest place I could think of to go—I wouldn't run into anyone from Mount Pitts, and I was guaranteed a good selection at a low cost. I already had my combat boots and jeans that still fit from last year. I only needed a few shirts and anything else I could find.

The bonus purchase of the day was a dark brown 1970s knee-length sweater with fuzzy fur around the collar.

On the bypass, Charlie passed me on his bike. Behind him, Jenny Flick raced her old Nova so fast, she wobbled a few times and nearly hit the concrete barrier. I couldn't tell if she was chasing him or if they were racing for fun. I slowed down to avoid any bullshit. Up ahead, I saw Charlie zig and zag into places Jenny couldn't keep up with. Then he took the next exit while she was stuck behind a truck and couldn't see him.

"Don't care. Don't care. Don't care," I said aloud, and then cranked up the funk.

Charlie was standing on my porch when I got home. I didn't see him until I got out of the car and got my bags from the trunk. I was surprised he'd come back after trying to talk to me the day before. Dad's car wasn't there, so I was nervous.

"Jenny's crazy," he said before I could climb back into my Parliament funk spaceship. "I broke up with her, and now she's crazy—like she's either going to kill herself or kill me or . . . I don't know. Something crazy."

"Your problem, Charlie."

"But I need your help," he said.

I didn't say anything and just shook my head.

"Fuck."

"Yeah. Fuck," I said, opening my car door. I tossed my bags into the backseat and got back in. He came to the window and put his two sinuous hands on the frame.

"You have to come to Zimmerman's tonight."

I glared at him. "Why don't you ask one of your new friends?"

"They're not my friends."

Silence. Then, "You let them carve the Master Oak, Charlie." He opened his mouth to say something, but I stopped him. "You took them to the pagoda and played paper airplanes with them. You fucked them in our tree house, Charlie. And now you tell me they're not your friends?"

"I could go to jail," he said.

"Your problem."

"I could die!" he said.

I rolled my eyes. "Oh, please."

He started pacing and muttering to himself.

"You have to meet me at Zimmerman's at seven. You have to help me stop her," he said.

"I'm working," I lied.

"Seven. You have to. My life depends on it."

Right then, I realized three things.

He was completely serious.

I still loved him.

There is nothing more disappointing than the coolest kid in the whole world turning drama queen on you. Really. It was downright depressing. So depressing that I figured, what harm could it do to help him one last time?

TUESDAY—FOUR TO EIGHT

The whole way to Pagoda Pizza, I think about where Charlie could have hidden something for me. I'm pissed it wasn't in the tree house, and half worried that it *was* in the tree house but that Jenny Flick already got her slutty little hands on it. But then I remember the note. *Hi, Vera.* No. Charlie was smart. The night when it all happened to him—and those poor animals—he *knew* Jenny was crazy. He'd have never hidden something where she could find it.

When I get in, Marie says James was looking for me, and that he might be back later. Middle-aged Lazy Larry is pacing around, avoiding work, and then goes out for a smoke. While I balance myself on the back step and place a stack of flat boxes in front of me, I notice the little logo on the back. It says "100% recycled materials" in a circle, around an image of a tree. I stare at it as I fold a box's side flaps and secure the tabs inside the slots. I fold another one, and then another—still staring at the logo. Until it hits me.

Charlie hid something in the tree, not the tree house.

I walk to the front and say to Marie, "I have to go. I'll be back in twenty minutes." I don't give her a reason, and I don't hear her response.

Ten minutes later, I pull into the gravel parking area for the blue trail. I wonder how many pairs of Hanes briefs did Charlie sell at this very spot? I get out of the car and jog up the path to the Master Oak. Though I'm taller now than when I last climbed it, it seems impossible to get to the lowest branch. I try to clamp myself around the wide trunk and shinny up, using the rough bark as steps, but it doesn't work. I scratch the inside of my forearms trying, though. I walk around the tree, look for knots, and remember how Charlie used to boost me up to them. I try the clamp/shinny technique again, aiming for a knot that will gain me a decent foothold. After several misses, I gently push myself higher, until I can grab a skinny limb and pull myself up.

By the time I'm twenty feet up, I'm out of breath. I look down and give myself a fright, knowing I still have about ten feet to go before I reach Charlie's favorite hiding spot. I sit for a minute and say, "If I fall and break my neck, it's totally your fault, dude."

When I have my breath and courage back, I continue up, branch after branch, until I'm standing with one hand reaching into the old hollow, groping around. I find an unopened box of Marlboro Reds and shove them back in the hole. I feel the other box—the cigar box from my dream—and grab it, and just as I'm pulling it out of the hole, I tip it against the edge and lose my grip. I do one of those crazy adrenaline overreactive catch things and secure the box, but not without almost tossing myself out of the tree in the process.

I have it. It's stuck in my armpit, and as I maneuver down the tree, I feel sad for the first time since Charlie died. Not angry or pitiful. Not hard-done-by or abandoned. Not sarcastic. Not protective. Just sad. I find myself hugging the Master Oak as I stop to balance on its strong, wise limbs. I find myself crying.

Which Zen guy said, "What is the sound of one hand clapping?" That's how I feel without Charlie. Like one hand clapping.

I stash the box under my driver's seat and drive back to the store. When I get there, I see Larry's car in front of the store and assume the rush hasn't started yet. So I park in the far end of the lot, outside the party store, and I pull the box onto my lap. I break the Scotch tape seal with my thumbnail and lift the lid. It's a small stack of messy, scribbled-on (mostly McDonald's) napkins—and under them, a sealed yellow envelope. Some of the napkins are stapled at the top, like a booklet. The cover page reads, in all caps, *DEAR VERA.* The writing on the envelope isn't Charlie's.

I start reading.

After you read this, you'll probably hate me.

"Impossible," I think. "I already hate you."

Valentine's Day, I was finally going to ask you to be my girlfriend. I sent the flowers—

"Whatcha readin'?"

It's James. His head is right by the car door. I drop the napkins in the box, close the lid, and move it to the passenger's seat.

"Nothing. Just some old shit from when I was a kid."

We look at each other.

"I miss hanging out," he says.

"Me too." I give him a quick peck on the cheek. "That's for switching shifts."

"How you feeling?" he asks, and points to his head.

"I'm fine," I say, instinctively rubbing the lump that remains.

"I wish I would have beaten the shit out of him, Vera."

"Why? It was an accident, right?"

"I just regret not doing something about it, I guess," he says. I can relate to that more than he knows.

We look at each other for a few seconds, until James says, "We can't hang out anymore, can we?"

I shake my head.

"I thought so."

"And I can't drink. Like—ever again."

"Yeah."

I see Lazy Larry driving down the hill to the main strip, and I know I need to get to work. "Dude. I gotta go. I'll probably see you tomorrow."

James gets into his car and waves. I drive across the parking lot to the store and hide the cigar box under my seat. I feel the urge to drive home and lock it up somewhere safer before anyone else sees it, or in case it's stolen. I panic at the thought of it being in my possession. There is no going back now.

"Anything yet?" I ask Marie.

She nods at the next order and holds up three fingers, which means I've got three minutes.

I go to the back door and out to my car again, and to the box.

I sent the flowers early, so they'd be there when you got home.

I turn to the next napkin page, where the letters vary in size.

But then everything went to shit.

I turn to the third napkin. He's scrawled diagonally on it.

You have to understand, the whole thing was fine until she found out. I wasn't getting hurt.

Something inside my body is making me feel weak and tingly. I pull out the yellow envelope and feel what's inside. Stiff and bulky in the front, and something round in the back. A CD or a DVD. The pervert from when we were eleven appears in my mind's eye. He says, "Pretty blond pigtails."

Marie stands at the door and gives me the signal. It's a quick run to the burbs outside of the old high school. I get a three-dollar tip and a wink from the anchovy-loving old lady. When I get back to the car, instead of driving to the store, I drive up Overlook Road to my house.

Dad is there, in his office late because it's April. I run upstairs with the box hidden in my baggy Pagoda shirt, and I wedge it between my headboard and the wall.

"Everything all right?" he asks as I speed-descend the stairs.

"Just forgot something," I say, and wag my red Pagoda cap in front of him.

There are a hundred of these at the store, but he doesn't question me.

"Be safe!"

"You too," I answer, a little pissed off at how obvious he is. "Don't let the stacks of paper bury you or anything."

The whole way back to the store, I feel Charlie heavy in the air. I say, "Don't worry, man. I'll clear everything up." But he doesn't trust me. He's trying to get me to steer the car back toward my house. He wants me to do it now. He's waited long enough.

When I pull into the parking lot, Lazy Larry is standing there, smoking a cigarette. I don't know why, but I like him. He's Dad's age—around forty—and even though he's lazy and can't mop and hates cardboard paper cuts, he has an air of confidence that Dad doesn't have. He puts the cigarette out and walks in with me.

"James left this for you," Marie says, and hands me a small, folded piece of paper.

Charlie-in-the-air makes me crumple it, put it in my

mouth, chew it, and swallow it while Marie and Larry watch me. I smile at them and go back to the steps and fold boxes.

Larry arrives in the back room thirty seconds later. Marie shouts back, "I'm nearly out of large boxes up here, man!"

"Grab a box," I say. I sound cold, but I don't mean to. I'm not really thinking about what I'm doing. I'm having an out-of-body experience. I'm floating to my bedroom and reading the rest of Charlie's box of McDonald's napkins. He's making me do this. He's like alcohol in my veins, completely dulling my senses except for what he wants me to feel.

Larry says, ". . . do I?"

I stare at him, trying to re-hear what he just said, but I fail. "I'm sorry. My mind was somewhere else."

"I was asking about the stupid hats. Do I really have to wear one?"

I nod.

"Can I wear it this way?" He puts it on backward and folds his arms like a bad rapper.

"Nope."

"Damn."

I say, "We all know you're cool, so who cares, right?"

"I just never thought at my age I'd have to abide by pizza delivery guy dress code."

"Technician," I correct. "It's pizza delivery technician."

He laughs. "Okay. Technician."

I nod but don't answer, because I am now distracted by the thousand Charlies racing toward me from the front of the store. They are as big as a jet plane, and are aiming for my head. They want me to climb on board and buy a ticket to the Mount Pitts police station.

"You okay?" Larry asks, and then he leans in close—right in my ear—and speaks with Charlie's voice.

He says, "Please don't hate me."

A BRIEF WORD FROM THE DEAD KID

So I make him say what I want him to say. He doesn't even know he's doing it, but Vera will understand.

She knows I am her pickle.

I am the pizza box and the light switch.

I am the note from James dissolving in her gastric acid, unread.

One thing about the other side is, when you die, you find out the truth.

If Vera were to die right now, she'd know everything that's in that cigar box I left her. She'd find out Jenny Flick always hated her because she's classy without having to try. She'd see how it all played out—how Jenny fought when I tried to break up with her. How she took my dad's old gas can from the garage and took it to Zimmerman's. How she stole my Zippo lighter, too. She'd see how I drank a bottle of tequila and ate the worm later on to forget and feel better about the whole thing. How John gave me a handful of pills while we drove around in his car, and how I'm not really sure how many I took.

She'd see that her mother loves her but never wanted children, and feels so guilty about it, she's paralyzed. She'd see that her father is just about to face his shit and get on with his life. (He's going to start by asking Hannah at the bank out to dinner.)

On one hand, it's nice on the other side. Secrets don't exist. There's nothing to ignore, and no destiny. On the other hand, the same thing is possible in life, if only we'd start paying attention to the right stuff.

DRIVE CAR, DELIVER PIZZA—
TUESDAY—FOUR TO EIGHT

I walk out the back door and stand in the fading, dusky sunlight. Larry joins me and lights a cigarette. The Charlies can't get ahold of me here like they can when I'm in a small space. I don't want any more drama. I just want to finish my shift, get home, and read the rest of Charlie's note.

The dinner rush begins. Larry takes the town runs. Charlie stays with me all night as I deliver to the nice parts of town. He continues to try and steer the car to Overlook Road, but I keep telling him that I get off work at eight and that he'll have to wait. In protest, he makes me endure an AC/DC song on his favorite heavy-metal station.

It slows down, like only a Tuesday can, and Larry and I are standing around in the back, talking and folding boxes. He tells me that he used to be a computer programmer, but hated it. So he's working here and taking a few courses at the community college while he figures out what to do with his life. He wants to make movies. Says he's written a bunch of scripts. I don't tell him anything personal except that I'm a senior, and that I think he's smart for going to community college.

He folds boxes tonight as if he's been doing it for years.

"What classes are you taking?" I ask.

"The easy ones, for now. Catching up on math. Comp. What about you? You have a favorite class in school?"

I nod and reach for another box. "I love Vocab. It's like spelunking in a cave you've been in your whole life and discovering a thousand new tunnels."

When I stand up, Larry's next to me, whispering Charlie's voice into my ear. "Being dead is like that, too." Then he adds, "Don't open the envelope. You don't want to see what's inside."

When I turn away from Larry and look toward the front of the store, the room is jam-packed with Charlies again. Fat ones. Skinny ones. Tall, short. Over by the bathroom, there's even a black Charlie with an Afro and a 1970s pick stuck in it. There is a Charlie with a gray parrot on his shoulder, and a Charlie in a sad-clown costume, juggling limp puppies. I want to scream at him, "Jesus, Charlie! Will you just wait until I'm done with what I'm doing?" And as frustrated and freaked out as I am, I'm laughing a little. I'm laughing because Charlie is as hysterically impatient in death as he was in real life. I must be truly ready if I'm laughing at this.

Larry folds boxes next to the back door with an unlit Marlboro Red hanging out of his mouth, oblivious to the room full of Charlie molecules. I hear Marie up front, slapping fresh hot pies into boxes and slicing them, and I claim the order, even though it's not my turn.

I know the road and vaguely know the address, so I grab four Cokes from the cooler and get into my car before anyone notices I've taken the wrong run. In the car, I hear the voices of a thousand Charlies, all of them at once. So I say, "Shut up, Charlie! Go away!" but they will not quiet. I think about what my father would do. The Zen master. Mr. Cool. He would relax his muscles. He would concentrate on his diaphragm, breathing. He would transcend. Breathe in. Breathe out. We have a wooden sign in the downstairs powder room that says: CHOP WOOD, CARRY WATER.

I think Zen-like, and whisper, "Drive car, deliver pizza."

My delivery is in a Hispanic neighborhood. I pop in Santana to block out the loud whispers of Charlie. It's a warm night, so the old Caribbean men are sitting on the sidewalks in dinner chairs, breathing. They don't make eye contact. When I get back to the store, I sit there for a second and search for Charlie molecules, but he is gone. Marie is already cashing me out. I go into the bathroom to change, and have a quick look at myself in the mirror. There are no ghosts crowded in here with me, making me scribble things on toilet paper and eat them or trying to steal the air out of my lungs. I breathe on the mirror and fog it up, which proves I am alive—which, in turn, reminds me how lucky I am to be alive.

As I load my shirt into the washer for the night, I daydream about making a sign and hanging it around my neck. I could wear it to school tomorrow. It could read, I MISS CHARLIE KAHN.

As I drive home, I picture other signs—one for everyone

who has a secret. Bill Corso's would say, I CAN'T READ, BUT I CAN THROW A FOOTBALL. Mr. Shunk's would read, I WISH I COULD TOSS YOU ALL ON AN ISLAND BY YOURSELVES. Dad's would read, I HATE MYSELF FOR NO GOOD REASON.

My idea grows.

I imagine signs on every house on Overlook Road. I pass Tim Miller's house at the bottom. PROUD HATERS. Up the hill past Charlie's. WIFE BEATER. Past the Ungers' house. WE BUY SHIT TO MAKE OURSELVES BIGGER THAN YOU. And up to the pagoda, where I'd stick the biggest sign of all. USELESS BEACON OF DELUSIONAL OPTIMISM AND FOLLY.

I park in the lot next to the glowing red beacon and look out over the city, and I feel like I belong here, even though I hate it here. We are one, the pagoda and me. Because when I think about it, I was also built from delusional optimism and folly.

A BRIEF WORD FROM THE PAGODA

Hey—the whole freaking world was built from delusional optimism and folly. What makes you so special? We're all just making it up as we go along. No one really knows what they're doing. Anyone who tells you otherwise is talking out of their butt.

WHAT REALLY HAPPENED TO
CHARLIE KAHN—PART 1

I get home and shower the grease off myself, and before I'm even dressed, I pull Charlie's cigar box from behind the bed and open it. I finger the yellow sealed envelope and still can't bear to think about what's in it. I open the next napkin, which he'd unfolded and printed on, in small block letters.

> VALENTINE'S DAY, JENNY WAS WAITING OUTSIDE JOHN'S HOUSE WHEN I CAME OUT. SHE TOLD ME THAT SHE WANTED TO GO OUT WITH ME BEHIND CORSO'S BACK. I TRIED TO STAY FRIENDS WITH BOTH OF YOU, BUT JENNY HATED YOU. I DON'T KNOW WHY, BUT SHE JUST HATED YOU.

I say to myself, "No! You think?" The next napkin is written in a spiral, in tiny letters. The writing is becoming sloppy.

pictures. I think he did video, too. (Files on CD.) Instead, he told us we should come back for a few, but he wouldn't, so she could sell him anything from her. She told me to introduce her to John so she could sell him some of her stuff, too, but he wouldn't

Okay.

I am completely grossed out.

I look at the clock and wonder what cop at the Mount Pitts police station would be willing to sit down and deal with this. Would they believe my side of the story, nearly nine months later? Would they pay attention because I had something to back it up, or blow it off to avoid the paperwork? Either way, I want Dad with me. I need him to help me do this, because even though earlier today I gave birth to myself, I am still a kid who needs his help.

I read on. The next napkin is written in all block letters again.

WE ONLY MADE ABOUT $100 FOR THEM. IT WAS NEVER ENOUGH FOR JENNY. JOHN TOLD ME THAT HE WASN'T GOING TO DO IT ANYMORE, AND I WANTED TO GET AWAY FROM JENNY, SO I BROKE UP WITH HER. SHE WENT FUCKING CRAZY. SHE SAID SHE'D GET ME ARRESTED FOR WHAT WE DID. SHE SAID SHE'D PUT ME IN JAIL. SHE SAID SHE'D GET CORSO TO KILL ME. THEN SHE SAID

SHE WAS GOING TO BURN DOWN THE STORE BECAUSE SHE
HATES HER STEPDAD FOR MAKING HER WORK THERE. SHE
SAID SHE WAS GOING TO TELL PEOPLE THAT I DID IT.
SO I CAME TO YOU. I NEVER THOUGHT YOU'D ACTUALLY
GO TO ZIMMERMAN'S. I DIDN'T KNOW WHAT TO DO,
VERA. I NEEDED SOMEONE TO KNOW THE TRUTH.

HISTORY I'D RATHER FORGET—
AGE SEVENTEEN—AUGUST (LAST ONE)

I lied to Dad and told him I'd forgotten to go to the office store for school supplies. Because he had to find a coupon from the morning's paper, I was a little late.

It was 7:03 when I arrived. Zimmerman's looked normal from the outside. I drove past first, and then parked between two pickup trucks. I didn't see Charlie's bike anywhere.

The "open/closed" sign on the door read CLOSED, even though they closed at eight on Sundays. The two sheltie pups in the front window seemed agitated. When I opened the door, the smell of gasoline overwhelmed me and I was instantly nervous that the whole place was going to explode any second.

"Hello?" I yelled. "Charlie?"

I took two steps in, but my legs refused to take me any farther. Then I saw Jenny, a small red gasoline canister in hand, ranting behind the glass in the reptile area. She tipped the spout into each cage and poured a trail of gas through the

303

room. Then she saw me and her eyes bulged with the kind of insane evil you see in horror movies.

Right then, as my stomach moved into my throat and the gallons of adrenaline took over, everything went into shock mode. Everything looked different, everything sounded different. The animals even seemed to know what was going on. The birds to my right squawked and pecked on the bars of their cages. I heard the cats in the back hissing and the adoption center dogs barking danger barks. I'm pretty sure a lot of the fish were already floating. I didn't see the usual darting of neon tetras, and the guppy tanks were all dark.

"Get out!" she screamed.

"Where's Charlie?" I yelled.

"Charlie's fucking dead."

"Is he here?" I pictured him tied to a chair or something. The way she stood there, like a character in a Stephen King novel, she was capable of anything.

I'd been in the store for less than a minute so far, and it felt like an eternity. My whole body was shaking and I felt like throwing up. From what I saw, Charlie wasn't there, but that didn't stop me from worrying. (Only for a second did I think maybe he sent me on purpose. Only for a tiny milli-second did I imagine that he wanted me burned alive along with the multitude of helpless animals. Only for an itsy bitsy nanosecond did I suspect that they were working together to frame *me* for the whole thing.)

I was steps from the door and ready to bolt when twelve-year-old Vera kicked in. She reminded me that my mother abandoned me. She showed me pictures in my head of abandoned, charred puppies. She froze my legs.

I said to twelve-year-old Vera, "I can't do anything for them! I don't even have keys!"

Twelve-year-old Vera said, "But you *have* to do something!"

I said, "We have to get out of here!"

She said, "We have to save the animals!" and wouldn't let my legs move.

I said, "Stop being so crazy! Can't you see? I can't do anything to save them!" It was true. I felt horrible about it and it sucked, but I couldn't save them. I just couldn't.

Twelve-year-old Vera sobbed in my head. I tried to mentally hug her. I said, "Sometimes there are no choices, Vera." She answered by making me think of my mother again.

Before I could argue, I heard the backroom door slam shut, loudly, and it snapped me back to reality. Jenny Flick was about to burn the place down—and she didn't care if I was in it or not.

Twelve-year-old Vera finally allowed me the use of my legs, and I pushed myself out the door.

When I got out, I felt dizzy from the fumes. I ran to my car and started it.

Shock warped time. When the clock on the stereo lit up, it said 7:07. It had only been four minutes since I parked, but it felt like an hour. I backed out of the parking space, drove to the farthest corner of the parking lot, and thought about calling 911, but called Charlie instead. The first two times it rang out and went to his voicemail, and I started to panic. (That would be panic inside of panic inside of panic.) The third time, he picked up.

"Dude!" I said. "She's burning it down!"

"What?"

"Zimmerman's!"

"You went?"

"Yeah!" My diaphragm was so jumpy, I had to catch my breath. I reached for a tissue. "Where are you?"

"Hiding." I heard him cover the phone and heard muffled talking.

My concern for him turned into a mix of anger and embarrassment and disappointment and pretty much every bad emotion I could think of. Charlie Kahn had just dragged me into something so awful, I'd gone nearly schizo from it—and he wasn't even in trouble. He was fine. Probably driving around, drinking beer.

"Are you still there?" I asked.

He was silent but for heavy breathing.

"Are you drunk?"

"Not yet."

"Charlie, I—"

"I didn't tell you everything, Vera."

"It doesn't matter. You need to go to the cops before she does."

"Maybe I belong in jail."

"Don't say that." What I meant was: *Oh my God, stop being such a drama queen.*

"No, Vera. Maybe I do. You don't know what I've done."

This just pissed me off. "Fine, Charlie. Do what you want."

"I'll write you a note or something. I'll leave it where only you can find it."

"What?" I said. What I meant was: *Say that again so you*

can hear how stupid you sound. Because that's going too far, isn't it? I mean, there's a line between pathetic and dangerous, right?

"I'm going to leave you something," he repeated—without an ounce of noticing how stupid he sounded.

I said, "Whatever," and hung up.

I looked at the clock. 7:12. It felt like I'd been gone at least five hours already. I looked over at Zimmerman's. So far, no fire. Still time to call 911, but rather than dial those three little numbers, I drove toward the mall exit because I wanted to get away from it all first. When the light turned green, I took a left and drove a minute up the strip, to the car wash. When I got there, I put the car in park and picked up my phone to call, but then I heard the fire station's sirens, followed by fire engines and an ambulance racing down the main strip. Rather than get more involved than I already was, I rummaged through my purse to find a five-dollar bill, fed it to the machine, and drove my car into the auto wash until the buzzer sounded and the red light came on, directing me to stop.

When the car wash started, I thought I'd have a minute to lose myself in the loud darkness of it all. I thought I'd have a minute to work it all out—the right things to do—but I just sat and stared. I thought about those poor animals—were they going to be okay? I thought about Jenny, and wondered was she going to burn up in there, too? What happened to her to make her so crazy? Could Charlie breaking up with her really make her this mad?

As the auto wash soaped and rinsed the car, the thoughts continued. What would happen to Charlie? Would he go to jail? Would he be blamed for Jenny's death? And what about the people in the mall? How many would die? Would he be blamed for that, too? If I told the truth, would anyone believe me? Why was I in this position anyway? How did I, after a lifetime of being safe and reasonable, end up *here*?

When the unit switched off, I drove out into the lot and opened my window again to the sounds of chaos unfolding down at the Pagoda Mall, and I made my choice. Charlie Kahn had screwed me over enough. I would never trust him again, and I would forget this night had ever happened. I would pretend that I was just out buying school supplies. When the story came out and he got carted off to jail for life, I wouldn't even wave. I was done.

The clock read 7:22. Suddenly the biggest thing on my mind was how I'd lied to Dad. I was worried that if I came home with no supplies, he'd think I was sneaking around doing something bad. So I drove to a completely different mall two miles in the opposite direction from the mall that was presently on fire. Ten minutes later, I was in line at Kmart, buying three spiral notebooks, a new calculator, a pack of unsharpened pencils, and a pack of Skittles. I felt people looking at me. I think I smelled like gas.

When I got home, it was past eight and Dad was reading in the den. I went inside and straight upstairs and took a shower. When the hot water hit my hair, I smelled the gas again. I said good night to Dad from the steps and I turned off the upstairs hall light and got into my bed and under the covers. I was still in complete shock. I tasted that weird metallic adrenaline in my mouth and my skin felt cold. I listened to the frogs and the crickets and the cicadas. I blocked out two overwhelming thoughts in my head—twelve-year-old Vera talking about the suffering animals and Charlie saying, "I'm going to leave you something"—and I tried to think about something positive. Senior year. My cool job. My bright future. An hour later, I was thinking about how there was no way I would ever fall asleep . . . when I fell asleep.

After a restless night of helpless-animal dreams, I woke up and went downstairs to find Dad crying on the couch. I'd never seen him cry before, not even when Mom left, so this was a big deal. He told me Charlie was dead. I didn't understand. How did this happen? How could Charlie be dead?

"I didn't get any details yet, Veer. Mrs. Kahn just told me he passed away last night sometime."

I was still so numb from the night before, I found it hard to even fathom the fact of it. Charlie—dead. The worst part was, I couldn't cry. As if I believed all the vowing and promising I'd done the night before never to care about Charlie Kahn again, I just couldn't cry.

And then, Dad told me about the fire at the Pagoda Mall. I acted shocked. He showed me the newspaper article, and I was happy to learn that no one was dead or injured, aside from the animals (though many survived, including the nasty gray parrot and a lot of the adoption center animals, thanks to the sprinkler system and the fire-retaining walls between the pet areas).

As I sat pretending to read the story while Dad watched

me, my mind wandered. Now I knew that Jenny Flick was not dead. But I knew that Charlie was. I just couldn't understand this. Even if I said something right then about everything I knew, the wrong person had died and the wrong person had lived. I couldn't help but feel like I'd been so busy arguing with twelve-year-old Vera about saving the animals that I overlooked that I could have saved human beings. Or— maybe just one human being.

Dad and I sat together for quite some time on the couch. We didn't say anything. A few times, Dad reached out and held my hand. It seemed harder on him then than it was on me, and he told me, "I just can't imagine what it must be like to lose a child. Please, Vera, be careful." We each took a shower and tried to eat breakfast, but neither of us could swallow anything. I called off work for the day, and Dad canceled the only appointment he had, which was for a haircut.

We went over to the Kahns' to offer our sympathy. They didn't really make eye contact, and after ten minutes of saying we were sorry and telling them we were there if they needed us, we went back home. Dad made a big pot of chili for them while I took a walk.

I went to the pagoda first, but I couldn't fly airplanes or even sit on the rocks because it'd been ruined by the Detentionheads. I wanted to walk to the Master Oak, but that was ruined, too, with Bill Corso's big, ugly initials. The only place to go was the tree house, which was worse than either of the others, but something was telling me I had to go, so I did.

I didn't go inside. I just sat on the octagonal deck, with

my legs swinging over the edge. I read the old bumper sticker out loud. "The more I know people, the more I love my dog." I finally cried.

They'd found him on the front lawn. They said he was probably pushed from a car. He'd landed folded into himself, so that when Mr. Kahn came out to go to work at 6:00, he saw a mystery lump in the front yard until he got close enough to see Charlie's shoes. The ambulance didn't put its lights or siren on. Dad and I slept through the whole thing, which was probably for the best. Nobody knew anything for sure yet, but it looked like Charlie might have died from alcohol poisoning or asphyxiating on his own vomit. His blood alcohol level was really high, and it looked like he was involved somehow with the fire at the Pagoda Mall. That's what the Kahns told us. As they said these things, I pretended I wasn't hearing them. My body and brain had gone into shock overdrive, where nothing made much sense. How was this happening? How could it be possible that after all that, Charlie was dead and Jenny Flick was still alive?

The Pagoda Mall closed until Halloween, when they opened a new, improved Zimmerman's Pet Store. Before then, the newspaper ran a few articles about the fire, with details about how the deceased Charlie's Zippo lighter was found at the scene. Stories went around town about how Jenny had broken up with him and he was so angry, he burned down the store to kill her. People said, "Thank God it wasn't the school he burned down," or "That boy was trouble from the start." The Kahns had to go through a series of police interviews and in the end, no one went to jail. But no one knew the truth, either.

The night of the funeral, a pickle talked to me inside my head. It said, "Eat me and you will know the truth." Sure, it was after I took those shots of vodka, but it did talk to me, and I did eat it. I've been waiting ever since.

WHAT REALLY HAPPENED TO
CHARLIE KAHN—PART 2

There are three more napkins. The first one has only four words on it.

> Please don't hate me.

I'm crying now, and there's snot dripping off the tip of my nose. I feel so bad for Charlie. I wish he had told me this stuff. I wish he had told my dad or the guidance counselor or a teacher or something. I wish he had stopped before it went this far.

> I'm going to run away tomorrow. I'm going to get on the bike and drive as far as I can. I'm going to start over. Either that or by the time you get this, I'll be in jail.

"I wish you were in jail, Charlie," I say. I do. I wish he was in jail. I'd visit him tomorrow and bring him a carton of Marlboro Reds. I'd be his best friend again. I'd show him that it's possible to become the opposite of your destiny.

The last napkin I find, unattached to the others, has been crumpled and then straightened out again. It says,

I wish we could go back in time and climb trees together again. I love you, Vera. I always will.

I stare at the yellow envelope and wonder are its contents enough to make a small-town cop reopen a closed case? Will anyone care that a dead kid didn't set that fire? (A dead kid who died choking on his own puke, with a blood alcohol level of .31?) I pull the sheets up to my neck and look around my room. I look out the window at the trees swaying in the night breeze. No one will ever know if Charlie died on purpose or if he was just being reckless. No one will know who saw him last or who kicked him out of their car. I thought, when I found this box, that I'd know more about how he died, but I don't. I'm not sure why I thought it would matter, though. Knowing won't bring him back.

I flip through the napkins with my thumb. There is nothing left to read. So I read *I love you, Vera. I always will* over and over again. Then I put them all back in the cigar box and shove it into my backpack. I see my Vocab notebook and I take the study sheet out and browse the words, and every single one seems fitting. *Fugacious, tourbillion, moiety, repugn, sacrosanct, censure, morass, El Dorado,* and *turpitude.*

None of them matter, though. Because I'm not going to make it to my Vocab class tomorrow. This should make me feel relief, but it doesn't. It makes me scared and nervous and jittery. I'm afraid I won't ever see the thousand Charlies again, and that he'll stop making me turn on heavy-metal radio stations.

As I lie here in the dark, I say, "But if I do this, then I'll lose you."

Clear as day, he says, "You'll never lose me, Vera. I'm the Great Hunter now."

LIVE A LITTLE—WEDNESDAY

Charlie is the almonds in my granola. He is the 2% fat in my milk. Ingesting him is making me stronger.

Dad looks at his watch. "You're late, Veer."

"It's cool. My Vocab quiz isn't until ten."

"I'll write you a note," he says, searching for a spare piece of paper in the earthenware bowl on the breakfast bar.

"What are you doing today?"

"Oh, you know. Exciting stuff. Tax returns and payroll."

"Want to come with me?"

He looks up. "To school?"

"Eventually."

"You're not making sense," he says, and then he notices the tears in my eyes and adds, "You okay?"

"Better than ever. You want to come, or what?" I say that confidently, but really, I'm scared.

He stares at me.

"It's a magical mystery tour, Dad. Live a little."

He smiles and nods. "Okay. I trust you. Why not?"

I drive along the road through Mount Pitts for five minutes with the stereo up, and Dad is trying his best to maintain a laid-back Zen appearance about not knowing where we're going. When we're two blocks away, I say, "I lied to you." He's having too much fun to notice the change in my tone. I pull out the cigar box from my backpack. "We're going to clear Charlie's name this morning. He didn't burn down Zimmerman's. He was messed up in a bunch of other stuff. The proof is in this box."

He's staring at me now as if I just smacked him.

"I need you to help me talk to the police."

"Vera, I—"

"You wish you knew more? Seriously. You don't." I think, *And when you do, you'll wish you didn't.*

Dad says nothing for the next two blocks, but that's because he's leafing through Charlie's stack of napkins and fingering the yellow envelope. He won't feel too bad until I tell him about where it all started. Back on Overlook Road—so long ago, Mom still lived with us. When I tell him, he will be consumed with regret like I am.

We get a guy who knows Dad from community college. What luck. I start with what I should have told the police nine months ago. I tell him everything about what I saw on the night Zimmerman's burned down.

I hand him the cigar box and explain about John the pervert. I tell him about the underwear and the things Charlie wrote about in his note to me. Dad looks so appalled, I feel scared to answer the detective's questions about when it all started, but I figure it's all or nothing.

"Charlie and I were walking one day, when we were eleven. We were right across from my house when he stopped his car and asked us if we wanted to get our pictures taken."

Dad tenses.

"Charlie told me a few years later that was the first time he sold something to him."

The detective asks, "And you know where he lives?"

I tell him.

At the end, the detective makes us sign a few forms and tells us we'll have to come in again for more formal affidavits, but that they'll need some time to prepare a case.

Dad says to me, when we get back into the car, "Vera, I—" He shakes his head as if he doesn't know what to say. "What you just did was really responsible and right," he says.

He can see that I'm crying. He says, "Oh, come on. Don't be sad."

I manage "That was so hard" before I can't say any more. I'm thinking about how regret begets regret begets regret, and about the cycle I've just broken. I thought I'd feel better when I did it. I thought part of me would feel lighter. It doesn't.

"I really loved Charlie, Dad."

"I know," he says, rubbing my back.

"I really wish I could have saved him," I say.

"I know. But it was out of our hands."

"I really wish I could have stopped the whole thing," I say, still unable to erase the image of the barking puppies and the screeching birds and the mewing kittens and the fish, belly-up, floating atop the water. No matter how many police I tell, these images will always be with me.

"Don't be so hard on yourself," he says. "You just did something most people can't do." He holds my chin in his hand and wipes my tears. I take a deep breath.

I say, "Is that why I'm so hungry?"

Ten minutes later, we're in the local diner. It's slow—between breakfast and lunch rushes. Dad orders a sunny-side-up platter with whole wheat toast, and I order scrambled.

"It must have been a hard year for you," Dad says.

"Yeah."

"I wish you would have told me about that creep."

"I know," I say. I look at him. "I just didn't think it was something to bother you with at the time—or Mom. You know how she got when I'd come to her with stuff."

He nods, staring out the window with that look on his face. Either he's still thinking about John the pervert or he's remembering how hard it was to talk to Mom about anything.

"I'm sorry, Vera," he says.

"For what?"

He looks into my eyes. "I wish I could have been a better parent—you know—to fill the void."

"You *did* fill it."

"But I couldn't be your mother."

"Bullshit," I say. "You were a better mother than Mom was. Can't you see that?"

He shakes his head.

"I think you've got it all wrong," I say, eyeing the approaching waitress. "You've always been the one I could count on."

Two plates are placed before us, and we say thank you in unison.

He looks at me and says, "I tried to compensate."

"For what? Mom didn't want to be here, and we all knew it."

He shakes his head again, so I say, "The void was inside *her*. When she left, she took it with her."

He puts his elbows on the table and rests his mouth on his knuckles and looks at me. I know what he wants to say—stuff about being proud of me and how much I've grown up. It probably sounds stupid, but I want to tell him that, too. It's like we were both living inside a lie and now we're free. Isn't it funny how we live inside the lies we believe?

Halfway through the meal, he says, "You knew she wasn't really *there?*"

I nod. Anyone with eyes would have seen she wasn't really there.

He sighs. "I thought there was something I could do, you know?"

I shake my head. There was nothing he could do, and he knows it.

"I just wish it had been different."

I say, "For the record? I liked it just the way it was."

He is emotional through the rest of the meal. He mentions twice more that he's pissed off that I never told him about John the pervert. He apologizes twice for never doing something about Mr. and Mrs. Kahn. A few times, I see him take his napkin from his lap and dab the corners of his eyes. I realize that all he ever wanted was someone to love him. So when we're a few steps out of the diner, I hug him and tell him how much I love him.

Once I pull out of the parking lot and head down the main strip, he says, "We're going home now, right?"

This makes me laugh. Like—maniacal laughing.

He says, "We aren't?"

I put on my shades and smile. "I told you that we were about to live a little, didn't I?"

An hour later, when we're both done packing an overnight bag, I make a sign on a large index card and ask Dad to tape it to my back. It says: EX-STRIPPER'S DAUGHTER.

He wants to make one for himself, but doesn't know what to write on it, so I help him. PARSIMONIOUS. I tape it to his back.

Here's me using *tandem* in a sentence.

We will learn to forgive ourselves in tandem.

EPILOGUE—ROAD TRIP

"I haven't done anything daring since I met your mother," Dad says, slurping a cup of Dunkin' Donuts coffee.

We're on I-95, headed for a beach. James Brown is blaring. Dad's eyebrows look worried.

"Stop worrying about your clients," I say. "They'll live two days without you."

I peek at him from the corner of my eye. He still has his sign taped to his back: PARSIMONIOUS. I still have mine on, too.

We hit the Beltway around Washington, D.C., and roll down the windows. Dad sits forward to put on his sweatshirt. His sign flaps in the wind, then detaches and is sucked out the window.

"Shit," he says.

I see it as symbolic. The label no longer fits. His emotional parsimoniousness just got sucked away by the beautiful blue sky. I lean forward and reach my hand behind my back, then take my sign off, and I toss it out the window, too. I am no longer an ex-stripper's daughter, either. I have gone from invisible Vera Dietz to invincible Vera Dietz.

Five hours later, we're eating seafood at a little shack on a North Carolina beach, looking out to sea, licking tartar sauce from our fingers.

"I'm sorry I didn't listen to you about drinking," I say. I am apologizing to myself as much as I am apologizing to him.

"We all find our own way, Veer. I'm glad you finally figured it out."

"Yeah," I say, and crack open another crab leg.

"I'm sorry about Charlie," he says.

"Me too."

"I'm sorry he got caught up in that mess," he says. "And I'm proud of you."

It's been a long day. I look at the ocean and take a deep breath. I feel like an adult—his equal, and his friend. I feel like we're in this together, and I'm glad for that. I can't think of another person I'd want on my team. He's a good man.

"I'm proud of you, too, Dad."

He looks at me as if he's expecting me to say more, but I don't know what to say. So I ask, "Can I have your pickles?"

ACKNOWLEDGMENTS

I owe thanks. Specifically, to my parents and my sisters. To my friends, who offer endless support, and to my many writing buddies, who keep me sane. Thanks to Lisa McMann for invaluable feedback on this book, and to Robin Brande and Joanne Levy for laughing at my jokes about hot Italian sandwiches.

Thank you to Gary Heidt, who sold this manuscript, and to my brilliant editor, Michelle Frey, and to editor Michele Burke, who helped shape the book into what it is today and who taught me many things along the journey. Also, thanks to Michael Bourret for understanding who Heidi of the Field was the minute I mentioned her.

Thanks to Tim Button, who schooled me in modern-day pizza delivery, and to Jay Carnine, who helped me with the details of fire.

I owe huge thanks to my fans. Every one of you who has written to me, come out to see me at signings, or spread the word, thank you. To the amazing booksellers, librarians, teachers, and bloggers who have supported my work, thank you so much.

And as always, to Topher and the kids. When this job feels like the factory, one look at you inspires me to punch my time card. All my love and gratitude for your daily support and affection.